PRAISE FOR SAMANTHA A. COLE

"There are only a handful of authors that write MM that I will read. I will be adding Samantha A. Cole to this list. Nick and Jake are just perfect for each other, if they would just figure it out. This story is very well written and I just fell in love with the characters!! I really hope at some point, she writes another MM book."

— RHONDA

"Love the two alpha personalities and how one submits! It's a true love story and overcomes some of the best obstacles. You won't be disappointed buying this book!"

— MORGAN

"I am not a huge fan of M/M books and have probably only read about three which includes this one. The reason I will read any M/M book again is because of this author. She made a previously non-favorite genre readable. I love all the Trident guys and the fact that a person's sexual orientation does not affect how they treat one another is something that the rest of the world should try and emulate. Will it ever be my favorite genre, probably not but if Samantha Cole writes another story you can bet I will not hesitate to one-click. I loved her story about Nick and Jake and couldn't wait to find out if they got their HEA but you will need to read this book to find out that answer."

— ROSEMARY M.

"While I love every book in this series, this is by far my favorite!! While Jake can be a jerk, Nick is exactly what he needs!! This book was my first m/m book and it quickly became one of my all-time favorite books!!!"

— AMANDA R.

"The first book in this series was amazing, but Samantha Cole's writing and storytelling has improved with each book, which has resulted in some must read books. I'd definitely recommend this book (and the rest of the series) to fans of BDSM romances - give them a try, you won't regret it. Topping The Alpha receives five fabulous stars."

— JULIE B.

"This one is probably my favorite out of the entire Trident series! While I have never read M/M before, I think Samantha did a great job of keeping the theme within the rest of her series and I love that Jake got his story! Like every relationship, Jake and Nick have their issues but man is it steamy while they work through them!! They have such a great relationship both inside and outside of BDSM! It was another amazing story and I can't wait for the next one!!"

— DUSTY W.

OTHER BOOKS BY SAMANTHA A. COLE

TOPPING THE ALPHA

TRIDENT SECURITY BOOK FOUR

SAMANTHA A. COLE

SUSPENSEFUL SEDUCTION PUBLISHING

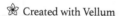 Created with Vellum

WHO'S WHO AND THE HISTORY OF TRIDENT SECURITY AND THE COVENANT

***While not every character is in every book, these are the ones with the most mentions throughout the series. This guide will help keep readers straight about who's who.

Trident Security (TS) is a private investigative and military agency, co-owned by Ian and Devon Sawyer. With governmental and civilian contracts, the company got its start when the brothers and a few of their teammates from SEAL Team Four retired to the private sector. The original six-man team is referred to as the Sexy Six-Pack, as they were dubbed by Kristen Sawyer, née Anders, or the Alpha Team. Trident had since expanded and former members of the military and law enforcement have been added to the staff. The company is located on a guarded compound, which was a former import/export company cover for a drug trafficking operation in Tampa, Florida. Three warehouses on the property were converted into large apartments, the TS offices, gym, and bunk rooms. There is also an obstacle course, a Main Street shooting gallery, a helicopter pad, and more features necessary for training and missions.

In addition to the security business, there is a fourth warehouse that now houses an elite BDSM club, co-owned by Devon, Ian, and their cousin, Mitch Sawyer, who is the manager. A lot of time and money has gone into making The Covenant the most sought after membership in the Tampa/St. Petersburg area and beyond. Members are thoroughly vetted before being granted access to the elegant club.

There are currently over fifty Doms who have been appointed Dungeon Masters (DMs), and they rotate two or three shifts each throughout the month. At least four DMs are on duty at all times at various posts in the pit, playrooms, and the new garden, with an additional one roaming around. Their job is to ensure the safety of all the submissives in the club. They step in if a sub uses their safeword and the Dom in the scene doesn't hear or heed it, and make sure the equipment used in scenes isn't harming the subs.

The Covenant's security team takes care of everything else that isn't scene-related, and provides safety for all members and are essentially the bouncers. The current total membership is just over 350. The fire marshal had approved them for 500 when the warehouse-turned-kink club first opened, but the cousins had intentionally kept that number down to maintain an elite status.

Between Trident Security and The Covenant there's plenty of romance, suspense, and steamy encounters. Come meet the Sexy Six-Pack, their friends, family, and teammates.

The Sexy Six-Pack (Alpha Team) and Their Significant Others

- Ian "Boss-man" Sawyer: Devon and Nick's brother; retired Navy SEAL; co-owner of Trident Security and The Covenant; fiancé/Dom.
- Devon "Devil Dog" Sawyer: Ian and Nick's brother; retired Navy SEAL; co-owner of Trident Security and The Covenant; husband/Dom.
- Ben "Boomer" Michaelson: retired Navy SEAL; explosives and ordnance specialist; son of Rick and Eileen, fiancé/Dom of Katerina (Kat).
- Jake "Reverend" Donovan: retired Navy SEAL; Dom and Whip Master at The Covenant.
- Brody "Egghead" Evans: retired Navy SEAL; computer specialist; Dom.
- Marco "Polo" DeAngelis: retired Navy SEAL; communications specialist and back up helicopter pilot; Dom.
- Nick Sawyer: Ian and Devon's brother; current Navy SEAL.
- Kristen "Ninja-girl" Sawyer: author of romance/suspense novels; wife/submissive of Devon.
- Angelina "Angie/Angel" Sawyer: graphic artist, fiancée/submissive of Ian.
- Katerina "Kat" Michaelson: dog trainer for law enforcement and private agencies; fiancée/submissive of Boomer.

Extended Family, Friends, and Associates of the Sexy Six-Pack

- Mitch Sawyer: Cousin of Ian, Devon, and Nick; co-owner/manager of The Covenant, Dom.

- T. Carter: US spy and assassin; works for covert agency Deimos; Dom.
- Shelby Christiansen: human resource clerk; two-time cancer survivor; submissive.
- Parker Christiansen: owner of New Horizons Construction; Dom.
- Curt Bannerman: retired Navy SEAL; owner of Halo Customs, a motorcycle repair and detail shop.
- Jenn "Baby-girl" Mullins: college student; goddaughter of Ian; "niece" of Devon, Brody, Jake, Boomer, and Marco; father was a Navy SEAL; parents murdered.
- Mike Donovan: owner of the Irish pub, Donovan's; brother of Jake.
- Charlotte "Mistress China" Roth: Parole officer; Domme and Whip Master at The Covenant.
- Travis "Tiny" Daultry: former professional football player; head of security at The Covenant and Trident compound; occasional bodyguard for TS.
- Rick and Eileen Michaelson: Boomer's parents. Rick is a retired Navy SEAL.
- Charles "Chuck" and Marie Sawyer: Ian, Devon, and Nick's parents. Charles is a self-made real estate billionaire. Marie is a plastic surgeon involved with Operation Smile.
- Will Anders: Assistant Curator of the Tampa Museum of Art Kristen Anders's cousin.
- Dr. Roxanne London: pediatrician; Domme/wife (Mistress Roxy) of Kayla.
- Kayla London: social worker; submissive/wife of Roxanne.

- Chase Dixon: retired Army Ranger; owner of Blackhawk Security; associate of TS.
- Doug Henderson: retired Marine; bodyguard.
- Reggie Helm: lawyer for TS and The Covenant; boyfriend/Dom of Colleen.
- Colleen McKinley-Helm: office manager of TS; girlfriend/submissive of Reggie.
- Carl Talbot: college professor; Dom and Whip Master at The Covenant

Trident Support Staff

- Colleen McKinley-Helm: office manager of TS; wife/submissive of Reggie.

Members of Law Enforcement

- Larry Keon: Assistant Director of the FBI.
- Frank Stonewall: Special Agent in Charge of the Tampa FBI.
- Calvin Watts: Leader of the FBI HRT in Tampa.

The K9s of Trident

- Beau: An orphaned Lab/Pit mix, rescued by Ian. Now a trained K9 who has more than earned his spot on the Alpha Team.
- Spanky: A rescued Bullmastiff with a heart of gold, owned by Parker and Shelby.

1

*N*ick Sawyer flipped on the lights and closed the door to his hotel room. Striding across the room, he unbuttoned the jacket of his Navy dress whites and tossed it on the back of a chair near the windows as he kicked off his spit-shined shoes. His brother's fiancée—now wife—had insisted the men in the bridal party wear their formal uniforms, and Nick prayed when his oldest brother, Ian, got married, his future sister-in-law, Angie Beckett, agreed to elope. After years of being in combat gear, T-shirts, sweats, or jeans, dressing up in his monkey suit was irritating as hell—especially in the heat and humidity of Florida, the weekend after Labor Day.

Entering the bathroom, he pulled his white tee over his head and dropped it next to the sink, then took a piss in the toilet. He flushed and washed his hands before heading back out to the main room. It was oh-two-hundred hours and he was still nicely buzzed from an evening of partying. Devon and Kristen had thrown a big shindig for their wedding, but Nick knew most of it, if not all of it, was Kristen's idea. Devon had collared her in a BDSM ceremony at the club he owned with Ian, and would've been happy with a quickie ceremony with one of the Tampa justices of the peace to make it legal. But his brother loved the woman and a man in love would do anything to see his significant other happy.

Seconds after Nick flopped face first onto the king-sized bed, there was a knock at his door, eliciting a growl from his chest. Wishing he could just yell "come in," he sighed and stood again to answer it, figuring it was either Ian or their dad. He turned the knob and pulled, shock punching him in the gut at the sight before him. It wasn't his brother or father. It was Jake. Jake Donovan—his brothers' teammate in the SEALs and now in their operative business, Trident Security. Otherwise known by his nickname from the Navy —Reverend. And, fuck, the man was hot. As uncomfortable as Nick had been in his dress uniform, Jake looked completely at ease in his. And hot. Had he mentioned that already?

"Hey." Was that all he could say to the sexy-as-sin man standing in front of him?

He watched as Jake's emerald-green eyes traveled downward, taking in Nick's bare chest, sculpted abs, open belt buckle, and everything below it. His breath hitched as the man's intense gaze returned to his face, and his cock began to swell at the heat he saw there.

"Mind if I come in?"

Holy shit! Nick knew exactly what Jake was asking. It was what he'd been fantasizing about all night. Him . . . Jake . . . together. *Holy shit!* "Um, yeah."

He took a step to the side and opened the door wider. As Jake brushed past him, Nick inhaled deeply and his cock twitched against the material of his pants. The man smelled incredible—like a forest, fresh from a morning rain, combined with a hint of leather—and he wondered what cologne it was. Letting out a long exhale, he shut the door before turning around and . . .

Fuck! Jake was lying on his side along the bottom of the bed with his head propped up in his hand. Posing like that, he could be modeling for a magazine. He certainly had the body for it, and the only thing marring his beautiful, sculpted face was a small scar next to his left eye, but it only enhanced his good looks. The top two buttons of Jake's white dress coat were undone, revealing the collar of his T-shirt and a few light strands of chest hair. Nick's mouth watered as his legs became weak.

What was it about this man which made him want to drop to his knees and beg? Nick had always been the alpha in every relationship he'd had since he joined the Navy at eighteen, but Jake had him yearning to submit in every way. He knew all about the BDSM club his brothers owned, and Jake was a member of. He'd even been inside a few times and cleared to play, but he never did . . . play, that is. It wasn't as if he hadn't seen any guy he could get interested in, because there had been a few good-looking men who'd caught his eye. What was holding him back were the facts that he didn't quite understand the draw to the lifestyle, and he also hadn't come out to his family yet. And hooking up at The Covenant was not the way he wanted to do it. He knew his parents and brothers would have no problem with him being gay, so why he hadn't come out to them was a question he kept asking himself. But with Jake Donovan in his hotel room with blatant desire in his eyes, Nick didn't give a shit about anything else at the moment.

"I was . . ." He cleared his throat. "I was just getting ready for bed." Shit, that sounded so fucking lame. *Get a grip, Sawyer.*

"Really? Then don't let me stop you. Please continue."

The whiskey-laced voice sent shivers down Nick's spine and he didn't move a muscle. He knew Jake was ordering him to undress, but he was being held in place by his penetrating stare. Those eyes seemed to delve straight into his soul, trying to figure out what made him tick, nonetheless still hiding the man's own secrets behind a shroud. Swallowing hard, Nick crossed his right arm over his chest and grabbed the opposite elbow. It was a defensive, yet unsure stance, and he watched as Jake's pupils widened in unadulterated lust. Nick felt like a sheep being eyed by a hungry wolf and his breathing and pulse rates increased. "I . . . um . . ."

He didn't know what to say. He wanted this man in the worst way and he was sure the feeling was mutual. They'd been avoiding each other all night, but their eyes had met hundreds of times over the last ten hours or so. It had been a few years since they'd seen each other. Since SEAL Team Three was based out of Coronado, California, Nick hadn't had many opportunities to get to Tampa. The few occasions he'd made the trip to the Sunshine State, Jake had been out of town on different assignments each time. Nick had arrived in Florida two days ago and been floored by the hunk when they first saw each other at the bachelor party later that night. He'd always thought the guy was good-looking, but the sudden attraction, which had hit Nick over the head this time, was stronger than anything he'd ever felt before.

Jake was four inches taller than Nick's six-foot-one, and at about two-ten, had around fifteen pounds more muscle— in fact, lean sinewy muscle would be a more accurate description. His medium brown hair was a little longer than Nick remembered and he longed to run his fingers through it to see if it was as silky as it looked. At the party the other night, which was held at Donovan's, a pub owned by Jake's brother, the man had sported a two-day growth of whiskers on his chiseled face. He'd since shaved for the wedding, and Nick wasn't sure which way he preferred, because both were sexy as hell.

He flinched when Jake leapt from the bed and stalked toward him—the wolf had morphed into a panther, but the same hunger was displayed in his eyes. The man hadn't missed the involuntary jerk and an evil grin spread across his handsome face. How long had Nick been standing there staring? Seconds? Minutes? Eons? He retreated until his back hit the wall and he had nowhere else to go—not that he wanted to escape. *Hell, no!*

Jake bit his lower lip, his gaze roaming Nick's face. "Let me help you finish getting ready."

Praying he wouldn't embarrass himself, Nick almost came in his boxer briefs when the man's hand reached for the open belt buckle and pushed it out of the way. An arm crossed his chest and held him prisoner against the wall. All he could do was clench his fists as they hung heavy at his sides while his boiling blood surged through his veins. The rich, smoky scent of Jack Daniel's Single Barrel hit his nose, however, Jake showed no signs of intoxication . . . well, maybe he was a little buzzed, but no more than Nick.

Jake's face moved closer and Nick licked his lips in anticipation. He felt the zipper of his pants being lowered over his throbbing erection and once again he prayed he wouldn't cum prematurely. That hadn't happened since he was fifteen and he sure as hell didn't want it happening now. Not with this man. Puffs of breath caressed his mouth and chin when Jake stopped inches from where Nick wanted him.

"You ready to be topped, little boy? Because I'm going to dominate you and you're going to submit to my every whim."

Nick stiffened and tilted his chin in defiance. "I'm not a boy." He wished he'd also added the fact he wasn't a submissive, but the Dom before him wouldn't have believed him anyway. This man was the only person who'd ever made him feel submissive, made him want and need in ways he'd never known, and he unsuccessfully fought the feeling in his gut.

"Tonight, you are. Tonight, you're *my boy* and I'm going to fuck *my boy* any and every way I want."

Nick never had a chance to respond as Jake's mouth came down hard against his and . . .

"Sir? Excuse me, sir?"

Shaking his head, Nick opened his eyes to see the blonde-haired, first-class stewardess staring at him. He glanced down quick and was relieved to see the book he'd been reading was open on his lap and hiding his painful erection. He looked back up with a sheepish expression. "I'm sorry. What did you say?"

She gave him a thousand-watt smile which he was sure had heterosexual males drooling all over her. It did nothing for him. "We're getting ready to land, sir. Please put your seat and tray-table up."

Nick reached for the lever and sat forward, wincing as his jeans tightened further in the crotch. The memory of that incredible night two months ago faded away, and he wondered what Jake would say when he saw him again. He was on a four week leave and instead of visiting his parents and old friends in Norfolk, Virginia, he'd decided to take a chance and spend the time off in Florida. He hoped he was doing the right thing.

2

---

*H*is frustration mounting, Jake paced back and forth in the baggage claim area. Ian had sent him to the airport to pick up his brother, Nick, and bring him back to the Trident Security compound. He would've refused his boss if he could, but there was no one else available. Ian had to take a last-minute conference call with the Pentagon and Jake couldn't come up with a valid excuse to avoid the errand, so here he was. Pacing . . . and waiting.

Fuck! What the hell was he supposed to say to the guy? Hey, thanks for the romp in the sack two months ago, but it's not going to happen again. You were a great fuck, but that's all it was—a one-night-only fuck. Maybe something a little less crude, however, that was pretty much the gist of it. Maybe the guy wouldn't even mention it. Yeah, that was a fruitless prayer.

He stopped and glanced up at the monitor for the hundredth time since his arrival fifteen minutes ago. American Airlines flight 1780 from San Diego was officially at the gate. It was about fucking time. His stomach clenched tight as his heart rate sped up. Running his fingers through his hair, he began pacing again. Maybe Ian had an out-of-town assignment he could go on for the next four weeks. Just until Junior went home. He almost chuckled at the nickname, knowing the youngest Sawyer brother would hate it, but at twenty-five, nine years Jake's junior, it's what Nick was.

He knew he was being a fucking chicken about seeing the kid again, but that night, as amazing as it had been, had been a mistake. A colossal alcohol-induced mistake. Yeah, he hadn't been drunk, but he did have some buzz-fueled courage that night. And wasn't that a fucked-up thing? When had he ever needed alcohol for courage to hook up with a guy? Only once—the night he'd lost his homosexual virginity at the age of sixteen. He'd lost his "true" virginity a year earlier trying to convince himself he wasn't gay. It hadn't worked. Yes, he'd gotten off with Vanessa Thatcher in the back of his father's Cadillac, since she'd been warm, wet, and enthusiastic. But the whole act had felt forced and left him unsatisfied deep in his gut. Afterward, he'd conclusively admitted to himself that women were never going to do it for him.

Another group of travelers came down the escalator from the gates and Jake scanned their faces. As much as he didn't want to see Nick, he wished the kid would get there soon. The faster he showed up, the faster they could get on their way. Then Jake could drop him off at the Trident compound with Ian and get the hell out of there. Yeah, running was the shitty thing to do, but it was exactly what he'd done a few hours after they'd screwed around. Not wanting anyone to know of their wild tryst, Jake had snuck out of Nick's hotel room and headed home a little past oh-five-hundred, while his satisfied lover slept. Then he found excuses to avoid seeing Nick for the next two days until the kid returned to California.

Jake had no idea what led him to knock on Nick's hotel door that night. Oh, who the fuck was he kidding? He'd ended up there because he'd been thinking with his aching cock. He'd been thinking how hot Nick looked in his dress whites and how much he wanted to top him. He'd been thinking about those broad shoulders, narrow waist, and tight ass. He'd been thinking about the gaze of those baby-blues . . . staring . . . making his skin tingle as they roamed his body from head to toe. He'd wanted to make the swaggering stud submit. And he'd done it . . . holy hell, had he done it. He'd let his inner Dom take over and the results had been better than he'd hoped for.

Yeah, the kid had resisted at first, but it was probably because he'd never been topped by a Dom before. It hadn't taken long for him to surrender though, and as soon as it happened, he'd been rewarded. Jake had taken Nick's belt from his pants, then spun him around until his chest was against the wall. Using the belt, he'd restrained Nick's hands behind his back before grabbing him by the arm and shoving him onto the bed. He'd roughly pulled Nick's pants and briefs out of the way and . . .

"Jake? Hey, what are you doing here?"

Wrenched out of the erotic memory, he blinked and tried to focus on the guy standing in front of him. *Shit.* It was Drew Murdock, a Clearwater cop who he'd dated last fall. They'd broken up after Jake failed to tell him about two attempts on his life when a hit-man had targeted the operatives of Trident Security. Drew had been pissed to find out several days afterward and not from Jake, but from a newspaper article and photo. Jake had told him it was because he hadn't wanted to worry him, but it had been more than that. Drew had been bugging him about introducing each other to their respective families. Although Jake's family and friends knew he was gay, he'd never introduced his mom and Mike to anyone he dated and he'd had no desire for Drew to be the first one. At The Covenant, his teammates knew who he hooked up with there, but Jake never scened in public unless he was asked to whip a submissive for another Dom. And even then, it was a non-sexual scene.

"Oh, hey, what's up? I'm here to pick up my boss's brother. Ian had a meeting he couldn't miss." Drew knew Ian by name, but had never met him. Jake lifted his chin toward the other man's carry-on hanging from his shoulder. "Coming or going?"

"Just got back from Quantico. The job sent me there for a three-day training seminar." He hesitated, looking unsure about what he wanted to say next. "You look good, Jake. I, uh . . . I've been thinking about you lately. Do you think we can get together some night and talk?"

Jake was about to say it probably wasn't a good idea, but he spotted Nick out of the corner of his eye. The kid had evidently overheard some of their conversation and, if his frown was any indication, he was down-right pissed off. Not giving any hint he knew Nick was there, Jake answered, "Yeah, Drew, that sounds good. Give me a call and we'll make plans."

The elated grin on the cop's face almost made Jake wince. He really didn't want to hook up with Drew again, but if going on a date put Nick in his place, then it was worth it.

"Great. I've gotta run. One of the guys from the station is waiting to give me a lift. I'll talk to you soon."

"Sure." After his ex turned and walked out of the

terminal, Jake pretended to scan the crowd again before his gaze fell on Nick and . . . *fuck* . . . he was smoking hot. The kid was in faded jeans and a snug navy-blue T-shirt, and Jake had to mentally strip down his sniper rifle to its individual parts to prevent himself from getting hard. Their eyes met and he could see Nick wanted to ask who Drew was, but Jake didn't give him the chance. "Hey. About time you got here. Ian had a last-minute meeting. What carousel is your luggage on?"

Ten minutes later, Jake led the way to his Chevy Suburban in the short-term parking lot. He popped the trunk for the luggage. Nick had barely said a dozen words to him and he hoped things would stay that way until he dropped the guy off at Trident.

He wasn't so lucky. As soon as he started the SUV, Nick pinned him with an angry stare. "Who the fuck was that?"

Jake let out a heavy sigh and backed the vehicle out of its spot. "An old friend."

"Old *friend* or old *boyfriend*?"

He shifted gears and steered toward the exit. "Not that it's any of your business, but, yeah, Drew and I dated last year."

Nick stared at him with narrowed eyes as an unbearable silence filled the air. *Shit*, this conversation was about to go downhill faster than an avalanche.

"What, Nick? You thought one night made us exclusive? It was a fucking roll in the sack. Nothing more. And it's not going to happen again. I was horny and your ass was available. There were plenty of guys before you and plenty since." Jake almost choked on the lie. There had been no one since that night in the hotel two months ago. Any offers he'd had, either in or out of the club since then, he turned down, because none of them had compared to *his boy*.

Yeah, although he didn't want to, he still thought of Nick as his.

"Fuck you, Jake."

"No, thanks. We already did that and it wasn't anything special." God, he was a fucking prick.

"You son of a . . ." His jaw and fists clenching, Nick turned his head toward the passenger window. "Whatever."

The rest of the ride was made in awkward silence. Not even putting the truck in park, Jake dropped the guy off at Trident, then did a U-turn and drove away without a word. After he hit the highway again, he made a call via the truck's Blue-tooth feature to Charlotte Roth, a.k.a. Mistress China. Jake and she made up two-thirds of the Whip Masters at The Covenant. They, along with Master Carl, were in high demand by the single masochistic submissives at the club, as well as Doms who weren't experienced enough to whip their subs. Over three years ago, when the demand for their services had grown, they'd created a rotating schedule with one Whip Master taking appointments per night, giving the others free time to play and socialize. As it stood now, they were hoping to add another two or three Dom/Dommes to the rotation.

The call connected with a click and a sultry voice greeted him. "Hello?"

"Hey, Charlotte. It's Jake. Can you do me a favor?"

A husky, little laugh came through the vehicle's speakers. "I thought you weren't interested in my favors, sweetheart. You decide to try a little pussy for a change?"

He couldn't help the grin which spread across his face at her teasing. "No. But if I ever do, you'll be the first woman I call. I was hoping you and I could switch tonight and tomorrow night. I have some stuff I need to take care of and would like to get it done tonight." He wasn't going to tell her he was afraid of hurting a submissive because he wouldn't be able to concentrate tonight. His thoughts would revolve around Nick until he was able to purge the guy out of his system.

"Sure thing, sweetheart. I owe you from the swap a few weeks ago anyway."

"Thanks. You're a doll, as always. I might come by around midnight, but if not, I'll talk to you tomorrow."

After hanging up, he headed home while trying to come up with a solution to his dilemma—how to spend the next four weeks avoiding the man he wanted more than he wanted to breathe.

NICK PACED BACK and forth in Devon's office as Trident's canine, Beau, watched him in what appeared to be entertained amusement. The protection-trained, lab/pit mix was lying on the leather couch and his big head swiveled from side to side as he followed the human's aggravated movements. Nick's blood was just now coming down from a full boil. He didn't know what he'd anticipated when he saw Jake again, but what happened in reality hadn't been it. And he definitely hadn't expected to see him hooking up with some guy in the airport. Then the man had been intentionally antagonizing him and it'd worked. If they hadn't been doing sixty-five miles per hour down the highway, he would have taken a swing at him when Jake said their night together had been a meaningless fuck. Instead Nick had gritted his teeth, turned away, and stared at nothing in particular outside his window.

Now, still frustrated, he ran a hand through the jet-black hair all the Sawyer boys had inherited from their father.

While Ian was still on a conference call, their other brother, Devon, was on a mission in Ecuador with the rest of the Trident team. Nick wasn't sure what the assignment was, but he could guess since their secretary, Colleen, told him it was a government contract. Trident had many federal government connections and, since the team consisted of six former Navy SEALs, their expertise was in high demand for black-op missions.

The four-man team was due back in three days, so for now, Jake and Ian were the only ones in the states holding down the fort. And damn it, just thinking of his one-time lover made him hard. When he'd spotted him in the airport, Jake had been wearing a pair of camo-cargo pants and a white wife-beater which had shown off his incredible physique. Nick hadn't missed how men and women alike were checking out the hunk as if he'd just walked off a *Fitness Magazine* photo shoot. His chocolate brown hair had grown a little longer and been pulled back into a ponytail which landed an inch or so past the collar of his shirt. A two or three-day growth covered his jaw and upper lip, and Nick wondered what the rough whiskers would feel like on his bare ass as Jake's tongue rimmed his hole.

Fuck! He quickly adjusted himself when he heard Ian's office door fly open, and finished untucking his T-shirt just as his brother walked into Dev's office.

"Hey, little bro. How was the flight?"

Nick gave Ian a hand-clasp and back-slapping. "Not bad. The only thing better than traveling first class would've been if you sent the company jet to get me."

"Yeah, sorry about that, but it's down in Ecuador with the team. You hungry? I haven't eaten lunch yet."

He grinned. "When have you ever known me to pass up food?"

His brother put his arm around him and squeezed his shoulder before pushing him out the door. "Only the time Devon convinced you hotdogs were made out of real dogs."

"Hey, I was six, and it wasn't just any dogs, it was those wiener ones."

Ian laughed. "You mean dachshunds?"

Rolling his eyes, he led the way to the parking lot. "Whatever. Feed me."

Within fifteen minutes they were sitting at the bar in Donovan's. Jake's brother had taken over the family business after their father died almost five years ago. Mike Donovan was tending bar while Ian's god-daughter, Jennifer Mullins, was waitressing for the lunch crowd. When she had a free moment, she walked up behind Nick and gave him a big bear hug. "Hey, Nicky. We missed you."

While she called Ian and his teammates "uncle," Nick was only five years older than her, so she didn't use the title with him. He knew she'd had a crush on him for a few weeks when she was in junior high, but that'd changed after some kid named Ryan had transferred into her school and caught her eye. He squeezed her hands where they lay clasped on his chest. "Hey Baby-girl. How's my favorite blonde-haired, blue-eyed girl?"

In the mirror behind the bar, he saw her eyes roll. "Yeah, right. I'm sure you have blue-eyed blondes throwing themselves at you left and right."

He chuckled. "I'm not denying it, but none of them can hold a candle to you."

"You're so sweet." Grinning, she ruffled his hair before stepping away and heading toward the kitchen.

"Today's burger looks good." Ian handed him a "Daily Specials" menu. "So, where did Jake run off to? I figured he would've come to lunch with us."

Instead of looking at him, Nick lifted his gaze to the basketball game on the TV above the bottles of booze behind the bar. Who was playing, he had no idea as he shrugged. "Didn't ask. He just dropped me off and said he had things to do." Hell, the fucking bastard hadn't even told him that much.

Mike approached them from the other end of the bar. "Hey, Nick. I forgot you were coming in for a visit. What can I get you?" Not needing to know Ian's order, he slid a bottle of Bud Light in the man's direction and then grabbed another when Nick said he'd have the same. "How long you in for this time? I only got to see you the night of the bachelor party and at the wedding last time."

He took a much-needed swig from the ice-cold bottle and swallowed. *Damn, it tastes good.* "I've got a month's leave before I have to report back for some new equipment training. I'll be here for most of it, but might be heading up to Mom and Dad's for a few days after Thanksgiving. Playing it by ear."

Chuck and Marie Sawyer still lived in the boys' hometown of Charlotte, North Carolina, but had several residences up and down the east coast, and one in San Diego near Nick's condo. Their dad was a self-made, real estate mogul, but did a lot of traveling and charity work with their mom, a plastic surgeon, while the company board ran things during his absence. While the boys had plenty of luxuries most kids their age didn't have while growing up, their parents made sure they worked to earn everything they got. Each one of them had a trust fund in their names which they gained full access to at age thirty, but received a small monthly dividend from the fund to help with bare-bones expenses until then. Anything they wanted beyond that had to come from a paycheck. They'd all been earning their own money since they were old enough to work. And each one of them had gone into the Navy, with the exception of John. The second youngest of four boys, John had plans to enter the military almost nineteen years ago, but it never happened. A closet alcoholic, he'd died at the age of eighteen after several hours of binge drinking.

While Mike took their lunch orders and entered them into the computer behind the bar, the two brothers settled in to watch the game. Nick did his best to force Jake from his mind. He'd deal with him later. And he wasn't letting the bastard run next time.

3

*J*ake strode into The Covenant's luxurious bar area, feeling a little better after spending a few hours working out in his condo complex's gym, instead of the one at the compound. It was smaller with less equipment choices, but there was no worry about Nick walking in to confront him again. An intense cardio session, coupled with some weights, had helped him force a few demons from his mind, as well as a certain boy-toy. After his longer than normal workout, he'd gone back to his unit, grabbed some dinner, and then showered. Dressing in his favorite black leather pants and boots, he'd forgone his usual T-shirt. Instead, he was wearing a button-down leather vest which he knew would draw the gay and bisexual submissives like moths to a flame. He wasn't being egotistical—he just knew the attention his sculpted arms and shoulders got from past experience. And tonight, he planned on using that attention to forget Nick completely.

The club's manager greeted him as he approached the bar. Mitch Sawyer was also the bosses' cousin and part owner of the club. As he shook Jake's hand, his eyebrow raised in curiosity.

Unsure what the problem was, Jake asked, "What?"

Frowning, Mitch shook his head. "Nothing."

"Bullshit. What?"

"Nothing." He shrugged. "It's just been a while since I've seen you in your vest."

Jake glanced down at the sleeveless leather top, and then his eyes narrowed at the other man. "Yeah ..." He waved his hand, gesturing for Mitch to continue. "And?"

"The last time I remember seeing you wear it was after you broke up with the cop last year. Seems to me, it's your 'purging' vest. You know, when you want to get over someone." He paused and tilted his head to the side. "Is that why you traded nights with China? I know you won't use the whip when you've got something distracting you."

Sighing, Jake ran his hand through his hair which was now down from its earlier ponytail. There was one thing he wouldn't lie to Mitch about and this was it. But ... he could stretch the truth a little. "Yeah, I've got some shit on my mind, but it's not because I broke up with anyone. I haven't been seeing anyone lately. It's just work and some other shit, and I didn't want to take a chance with the subs tonight."

Mitch nodded and his voice filled with empathy. "You know, if you ever want to talk ..."

Barking out a short laugh, Jake brought one hand to his eight-pack abs and shook his head in disbelief. "Are you fucking kidding me? Since when did you become Mister Sensitive and offer an ear?"

With a broad grin, Mitch scoffed, "I wasn't offering *my* ear, you dumb fuck. I was going to tell you to call Doc Dunbar for an appointment." Dr. Trudy Dunbar was a one of the psychologists whom The Covenant referred its members to, if needed. While she wasn't in the lifestyle herself, she had done her dissertation on the BDSM society and understood it better than most. She had also become Jake's good friend over the past few years.

"Yeah, well, I don't need the ear or Trudy. Just need to blow off a little steam." He scanned the bar and surrounding areas, not seeing who he was looking for. "Have you seen Tyler tonight?" Tyler Ellis was a bisexual switch Jake hooked up with every so often. The stockbroker and operative had a mutual attraction, but it didn't go beyond the club. Personality-wise, they were too much alike, with the major differences being Jake was a gay Dom and Tyler preferred to submit to men, but top women. When he was stressed out, giving up sexual control to another man was something he benefited from.

"Yeah, and I think he was looking for you, too. I saw him head down into the pit." Mitch clapped him on the shoulder. "I'll catch you later."

Jake headed for the stairs leading down into the pit. In some sex clubs, it would probably be called the dungeon, but The Covenant members had dubbed the recreational area "the pit" when the club had first opened up and the name stuck. The main entrance to the club was on the second floor, which consisted of a lobby, bar, sitting areas overlooking the first floor, and at the far end, a fetish store and the offices. In addition to the pit, there were also locker rooms and private playrooms downstairs.

After having his alcohol consumption/ID card swiped by a security guard—there was a two-drink maximum if a member intended to play—he descended the grand staircase, searching the crowd for Tyler. But . . . *fuck* . . . his eyes found Nick, standing with his brother, Ian's fiancée, Angie, and another couple. The huge room was congested enough—about one hundred and twenty members in attendance—so he was able to pretend he hadn't spotted them on the left side of the room. Veering to his right, he was stopped by several people who either just wanted to say hello or had something more to chat about. He managed to put as many people as he could between Nick and him, but the tingling on his neck said his body was still aware the other man was in the room.

His eyes continued to search the crowd as he talked to a few members and forced himself to concentrate on looking for Tyler and not Nick. *Damn it.* He knew he shouldn't have come tonight. There'd been a good chance Nick would be here, but Jake had planned on making it obvious to the kid that there was no future between them. Nick wouldn't make a scene here because it would mean he'd have to come out of the closet to Ian and everyone else, and he was still refusing to do it. Why, Jake didn't know, but it wasn't his place to out the guy. And that was another reason why a relationship with Nick wouldn't work. Since the night Jake's father had beaten the crap out of him sixteen years ago for being gay, he vowed never again to feign he was straight. It'd been his "fuck you" to his father from then on, and he refused to be in a relationship with anyone who was hiding his sexual orientation.

As he was about to excuse himself from a conversation he was only half listening to, he noticed Tyler walking towards him and his anxiety eased a little. He deepened his voice to let the other man know he was in full Dom mode and wanted to play. "Tyler."

The relief in the switch's eyes was evident before he lowered his gaze to the ground in respect. "Master Jake. I was beginning to think I wouldn't see you tonight. May we please negotiate a scene?"

"This way." Jake gestured with a side nod of his head for Tyler to follow him to an empty table a few feet away. Instead of taking a seat, he leaned an elbow on the pub-height table. Some other Doms may have ordered the switch to his knees, but Jake rarely issued the command in the open recreation area. And public humiliation was one of Tyler's hard limits. For someone who was a Dominant part of the time, it would be humiliating to kneel in front of another Dom unless they were somewhere private. The switch would still be respectful and it's all Jake would require of him until they were alone. "Bad day?"

Tyler nodded. "Very, Sir. The market was all over the fucking place, and I had clients calling all day long, on top of meetings. Damn, if I was into drugs, I'd be doped up and jonesing for more right now."

Rubbing his chin with his finger, Jake regarded the man for a moment. "I won't use a bullwhip tonight, so that's off the list, but any other of your green or yellow limits, I'll consider."

"Restraints. And a flogger and crop can replace the whip, Sir."

"Sex?"

A grin spread over Tyler's face. They'd been playing together off and on for over two years. He knew if Jake asked about sex, the Dom wasn't dating anyone. If he was, the relationship would be exclusive when it came to sex, but he would still be available for certain scenes with a submissive, as long as his significant other didn't make it a hard limit between them. Not all BDSM scenes were sexual in nature. Sometimes a submissive needed an emotional release which could result from a variety of their green or yellow limits.

"If Master Jake is in the mood, I have no complaints."

Jake narrowed his eyes at the snark in the other man's tone of voice. "Keep it up and you *will* have some complaints by the time I'm through with you." He pointed with a thumb over his shoulder. "Go find an available room and I'll be there in a few minutes."

"I already reserved one after I saw you walking down the stairs. Room number five."

Frowning, Jake raised an eyebrow. "Topping from the bottom, boy?"

Tyler knew he'd almost overstepped his boundaries and his gaze immediately dropped to the floor. "No, Sir, not at all. Just optimistic."

"Uh-huh. Let's see how optimistic you are after I refuse to let you cum." They both knew he would eventually get the guy off, but there would be plenty of begging before the Dom allowed it. Jake suppressed a grin when he saw the switch swallow hard.

"Yes, Sir."

"I'll be there in five. Strip and present before I get there."

"Yes, Sir."

As Tyler headed to the private playrooms at the far end of the pit, Jake turned toward the locker rooms. The entrances to the male and female lounges were on either side of the grand staircase. There were also entrances and stairs down into them from behind the second-floor bar. When Jake entered the men's locker room there were only three other people there. A male submissive was on his knees waiting patiently as his Dom talked to another Dominant about something to do with local politics. Jake rolled his eyes as he continued on to the urinals in another room—politics in this venue was never a good mix. He quickly relieved himself and stepped over to the sink. Washing his hands, he glanced up into the mirror and saw the reflection of Nick standing in the doorway, staring at him. And the kid did not look happy. Tough shit, Jake thought.

He shut the water off and grabbed a paper towel from the metal receptacle to dry his hands, his gaze never leaving Nick's. "Something you want to say, Junior?"

"You're such a fucking prick."

Jake snorted and threw the towel into the garbage before turning around and leaning his ass against the sink. He crossed his arms and gave the kid a look which had made lesser men pee their pants. "Tell me something I don't know. What do you want, Nick?"

The kid growled . . . actually growled at him. He kept his voice low to avoid being overheard by the men in the other room. "You know damn well what I fucking want. I want us to get together again. But instead, you're going to chicken out and go play with that jackass I saw you talking to, aren't you?"

Jake took three steps faster than Nick could blink. He yanked him out of the doorway and shoved him up against the wall, his hand around the kid's throat. His voice was deep and menacing. "Listen, you little shit. There are a bunch of reasons why I'm going to fuck someone else tonight. One—I already told you, what we had was a one-night-stand, nothing more. Two—you've never scened with anyone other than me, and don't fucking lie and tell me otherwise. I went easy on you that night and I doubt you can truly submit to me. Three—this isn't your lifestyle. If it was, you would be playing here whenever you visit, but you don't." *Fuck*. He just gave away the fact he'd been doing some discreet research on Nick through members of the club he could count on to keep their mouths shut. He knew the guy had been cleared to play a long time ago and provided his military physicals to stay current. This way, he didn't have to be considered a guest whenever he was in town. But regardless, he'd never once done a public or private scene with anyone at The Covenant. "Four—there is no *us*, so I can play with whomever the fuck I want to. And five—until you decide to come out to your family and the rest of the fucking world, you and I will never be together again, and even then, it's questionable. You got it, *Junior*?"

Jake had to hand it to the kid. He knew Nick wanted to start brawling with him right then and there, but he didn't. Instead, with rage flaring in his baby-blue eyes, he pushed Jake away and stormed out of the locker room without another word. The big bad Dom hung his head. God, he was such a fucking prick.

$\mathcal{N}$ick flopped face down on the guest bed in Devon's apartment, hoping he hadn't woken his sister-in-law when he'd come home all pissed off a few minutes ago. He was staying in their spare bedroom for a few days while his brother was out of the country. The first of the four warehouses in Trident's compound was home to The Covenant. The last one had been converted into large apartments for the Sawyer family. Ian and Angie had the unit on the bottom floor, while Devon and Kristen lived in the one above it. The warehouse was so huge, that even though both apartments were bigger than some houses, there was still plenty of square footage they hadn't used.

When Angie had moved in with Ian a few months ago, Nick's older brothers hired the original contractor, a club member, to create two more apartments behind their own. One belonged to Jenn when she wasn't at the University of Tampa dorms where she was enrolled. She'd come to live with her Uncle Ian after her parents were murdered a few months before she graduated high school. Ian had stayed in Virginia with her until she graduated, then moved her to

Florida and into his three-bedroom apartment. She was old enough now to have her own place, but this way she was still surrounded by family.

An apartment above hers had also been completed and currently sat empty. Ian had shown it to Nick after their lunch and handed him the keys. It was his. Nick was still in shock his brothers had given him his own apartment within the compound. Well, he shouldn't be, since they were a close-knit family, but sometimes he felt the wide age difference between his brothers and him. He was twenty-five with his birthday a little more than two months away, while Devon was thirty-six, and Ian, two years older than that. Their deceased brother, John, had been a year younger than Dev. Nick had been an unexpected, but well-loved surprise for his parents and older siblings.

Tomorrow, the girls—Jenn, Kristen, Angie, and Boomer's girlfriend, Kat Maier—were taking him shopping to fill the place. He tried to let them do it without him, telling them he trusted they would make the place look nice, but they'd insisted he at least pick out the furniture. They wanted him to be comfortable with the couch, chairs, and bed. After that, they would take over and do what they did best—decorate. Thank God, they could do that without him. Ian had told him the only other alternative was allowing their mother to hire the decorator she'd used for his brothers' places several years ago. Her two oldest sons had been single at the time and both apartments had screamed bachelor pads. So out went the mismatched furniture and windows without curtains, and in went classy and chic. Nick thought it was the perfect way to go until Ian had told him about the endless phone calls and meetings he'd had with the decorator over every little thing.

He flipped over to his back and moved around on the

pillow until his head found a comfortable spot. His mind wandered to Jake—the fucking asshole. Why was he longing for a man who had made it quite obvious the feeling wasn't mutual? But the thing was, Nick wasn't too sure it wasn't mutual. Yeah, the guy was saying all the right negative reasons why they shouldn't be together, but Nick had seen Jake's eyes as he'd rattled off his numbered list. There had been heat there. And not angry heat, but an I-want-to-fuck-you heat. The Dom had kept their hips from touching, but Nick was convinced if they had, it would've been hard-on against hard-on. And fuck, the thought made his cock stiffen painfully again.

He was lying there in nothing but his boxer briefs and his hand went to his cotton-covered shaft almost on its own volition. He glanced over at the door, trying to remember if he'd locked it. It was doubtful Kristen would come into his room at oh-one-thirty hours without knocking, but it would be embarrassing for both of them if she did. The silver moon shining through the window blind slats provided just enough light for him to see the lock was engaged and he settled his head back on the pillow.

Pushing the briefs down, he fisted his cock and began to rub it up and down. In his mind, he brought up the memory of his one and only night with Jake Donovan.

"You ready to be topped, little boy? Because I'm going to dominate you and you're going to submit to my every whim."

"I'm not a boy."

"Tonight, you are. Tonight, you're my boy and I'm going to fuck my boy any and every way I want."

He never had a chance to respond. Jake's tongue was in his mouth and he was devouring him. Holy shit, the guy could kiss. Nick tried to kiss him back, but the Dom was in charge and taking what he wanted. A hand went down the open zipper of

Nick's pants and he thrust his hips forward. He was immediately punished for the action when Jake reached down and squeezed his balls until Nick was almost screaming into the man's mouth. The Dom released his aching sac at the same time he ended the kiss.

Nick was panting from both the pain and pleasure coursing through his veins. "What the fuck, Jake?"

He didn't get an answer as his belt came out of his pant loops in one swift yank. Jake spun him around and shoved his chest against the wall. His wrists were grabbed and tied together with the belt at the small of his back and Nick couldn't believe he'd allowed it to happen. He should be resisting, shouldn't he? He wasn't a fucking submissive, was he? Jake seized a handful of his hair and yanked his head back until he gasped. His scalp shrieked, but the pain made his cock weep as drops of pre-cum oozed from the slit.

That deep, baritone voice was at his ear, sending electricity to the hair on the back of his neck. "You don't take any pleasure I don't give you, boy. You do exactly what I tell you and nothing more, or you won't like the consequences. Understand?"

"Y-yeah." Nick was breathing so heavily, the word barely escaped his lips.

"Uh-uh, little boy. The answer is 'yes, Sir.' Let me hear you say it."

"Yes, Sir," he whispered.

Jake growled. "Louder! I know they taught you how to answer properly in the Navy. Now, say it!"

The hand in his hair tightened. He hissed. "Yes, Sir!"

"That's a good boy. Your safeword is 'red.' If you say it, everything stops. I'll go back to my room and we both deal with our own hard-ons." He licked the shell of Nick's ear, which caused a delicious shiver to course through his body. "But I promise you, you'll have a lot more satisfaction if I take care of it for you."

Nick held back a moan of anticipation as Jake propelled him onto the bed and pulled his pants and briefs down off his hips. His rock-hard cock sprung free and he almost cried out in relief. His clothes disappeared and he was now completely naked . . . and vulnerable. He gulped and his eyes fluttered closed, but he kept his body still as a hand closed around his rigid shaft and pumped it a few times.

"What's your safeword, Nicky?"

His eyelids reopened while his ass and thighs clenched, trying not to fuck the hand wrapped around him. "Ah, shit. It's . . . it's red, Sir."

At that last word, Jake gave him an evil grin as he continued to massage Nick's cock, and more pre-cum pearled at the head. "You learn fast, boy. That's good. It means more pleasure and less pain. You have any lube? It'll make it easier for me to prep that hole I plan to fuck."

"B-bathroom." Nick gasped. "Travel bag."

He immediately missed the contact when the hand released him, but Jake was back in a few moments. "Turn over."

Nick struggled to follow the order while his arms were useless behind his back. A hand gripped his bare hip and helped him the rest of the way. He heard Jake remove his own clothes before the bottom of the bed tilted under the man's weight. A hand landed on his right butt cheek with a resounding smack and pain then pleasure shot through him. "Shit!"

"That's a mighty fine ass you have there, Nicky-boy. I can't wait to get inside it."

Cool, slick liquid oozed into his crack and his cheeks were separated.

"Ah fuck!" A finger worked the lube into his hole and another was quickly added. He pulled against the belt restraining him, wanting to clutch the bedsheets or anything but the air his hands were grabbing. He tried not to pump his hips into the bed because if he did, he knew two things would happen—he'd cum and then he'd be punished for it. He had no idea what the punishment might be, but Jake was into BDSM, so the choices were endless.

"Mmmm. Nice and tight. Clench for me, baby. Let me feel what it's going to be like to have my cock deep inside you." Nick did as he was told as he was fucked by the two fingers. "Yeah, just like that. Again."

Adding a third finger, Jake continued to stretch him for another minute or two, and the only sounds in the room were the grunts coming from Nick's throat. It felt so fucking good, but he knew what would feel even better. "Please."

"Hmm, please what? Please, fuck you nice and slow? Please, fuck you hard and fast? Please, leave? Please, what, Nicky-boy?"

He knew he shouldn't answer the way he wanted to, which was hard and fast. If he did, Jake would accuse him of "topping from the bottom." He'd never played in The Covenant, but he knew what the phrase meant from hanging out there. It meant the submissive was trying to tell the Dom what to do, and it was a big no-no in Jake's world.

"Answer me, boy. Please, what?"

The fingers deep in his ass stopped moving and the need to grind his steel hard dick into the bed grew while Jake waited for the answer he demanded. Nick groaned. "Anything . . . a-anything you want. Please, do anything you want . . . Sir."

"Good answer, little boy, good answer."

Nick could hear the smile in Jake's voice as the fingers slid from his ass. Hands grabbed both his hips and pulled him up on his knees with his face in the mattress. The sound of a condom wrapper being opened hit his ears. He knew he would get what he wanted, but it would be at the Dom's pace. Biting his bottom lip, he held back his urge to scream and beg.

Yes, God help him, he wanted it so bad. Do it! Do me! Please!

He felt Jake's cock at his puckered entrance and suddenly . . .

"Ah, fuck!" It was a simultaneous curse and whisper as

streams of cum squirted from Nick's cock as he pumped and squeezed it. The hot semen seared the bare skin of his torso while he growled with the release. Damn, what that man did to him. He'd been jacking off to that memory for the past two months. It was his own personal porn flick in his mind—one he couldn't banish, nor did he want to.

After his breathing and pulse returned to normal, he stood and stumbled into the room's attached bath. Flipping on the light, he shuffled toward the shower and reached in to turn the water on. As he waited for it to warm up, he stared at his reflection in the vanity mirror. He had it bad. Bad for a guy who was going to fight him fucking tooth and nail, but damn it, he was done with the bullshit. If Jake thought a few shitty put-downs were going to chase Nick away, then he better think again. It was time to turn up the heat. He just hoped he didn't get burned in the end.

5

*J*ake woke up with a raging hard-on and Nick's name on his lips. *Fuck!* Why couldn't he keep the kid out of his thoughts and dreams? Last night hadn't turned out as he'd hoped. Yeah, he'd gotten Tyler off, but the only way he'd been able to cum himself, was to close his eyes and imagine he was fucking *his boy*. So much for purging him from his mind.

Purging. Mitch had used the same word with him last night. He hadn't realized what he'd been doing before his friend pointed it out. Every relationship he'd had since he graduated high school had ended the same way. After the "getting to know you" period, which usually lasted anywhere between one to four weeks, as soon as a guy wanted to introduce Jake to his family, he balked and ended the relationship. He'd been out of the closet for years, so that wasn't the problem. It was the family thing which sent him running. Probably because he'd resisted introducing anyone to his own family for so long. It never would've happened while his father was alive and nothing has changed since the old man croaked a few years ago.

Flipping on his back, he covered his eyes with his forearm. To this day, he could still feel his father's fists, then belt, hitting him. The blows landing on his back, chest, stomach, head . . . everywhere. *No son of mine is going to be a God-damned faggot! No fucking way! You hear me!*

Yeah, *Dad*, he thought. Loud and fucking clear.

Well, at least the thoughts of his father and that night so long ago had the right effect on his body. As he scratched the pubic hair above his now soft cock, his phone chimed with the alarm alert. Oh-seven-hundred. He needed to get up and going. Ian had the first two members of Trident's secondary Omega team reporting for duty today. Their new helicopter pilot was also supposed to be starting this week, but due to a death in her immediate family, Ian had told her to take all the time she needed. With most of Alpha, which Boomer had dubbed the original company team, finishing up a reconnaissance mission in Ecuador, Jake was the only other person available to show them the ropes and evaluate their weaknesses for future training.

Throwing the sheets off his naked body, he stood and stretched the kinks out of his muscles before heading into the bathroom. He turned the shower on and as soon as it was lukewarm and not freezing, he stepped under the spray. Putting his hands flat against the wall under the showerhead, he let the water soak his head and body.

He knew the Trident women were taking Nick shopping for furniture this morning, so he might manage to avoid the kid today. That would be day two out of thirty, and he was only batting five hundred so far. *Shit.* Maybe after the team got back on Monday, he'd ask Ian for some time off and take a trip up to the company safe house in North Carolina, which the team also used for down-time. There was a lake he could fish in and plenty of acreage he could hike through. He couldn't stay there the whole month, but maybe a week or two if the case-load was slow. He'd check with Boss-man after he dealt with the newbies.

Thirty minutes later, he strolled out of a deli with a toasted buttered bagel, a container of fresh fruit, and a black coffee. Hopping into his Chevy Suburban, he tossed the food bag on the passenger seat and placed his coffee in the cup holder next to his thigh before turning the ignition key. From its perch attached to one of the air-vents, his cell phone rang and he checked the screen. *Shit!* It was Drew. Jake had too much going on in his head to talk to the guy, so he let it go to voicemail. Maybe if he didn't return the call, Drew would get the hint.

Sighing, he put the truck in drive for the five-point-three-mile trip to Trident's complex, where he waved at the daytime guard who opened the gate, allowing Jake to enter. Passing the first warehouse where The Covenant was located, he pulled up to the second gate and rolled down his window. A computerized scan of his palm print would open this one, letting him into the remaining compound consisting of three more warehouses. The first one on this side of the fence was for the offices of Trident Security, with bunk rooms on the second floor. The rear of the building was a garage for their extra vehicles. The middle structure housed the training facilities. The last building was home to four huge apartments—Ian and Angie's, Devon and Kristen's, Jenn's, and then . . . Nick's. At some point, the kid's two older brothers expected him to join their business ventures and made sure he knew he was welcome. That's why the women were taking Nick shopping today—to fill the empty apartment—and he was sure the SEAL was fucking thrilled to death.

Pulling into a spot at the entrance to the offices, Jake was greeted by an enthusiastic Beau, carrying a drool-covered rubber ball. He took the disgusting offering and threw it hard across the compound to the dog's delight. After repeating the ritual two more times, he ambled into the building with his canine buddy on his heels. It was too early for their secretary, Colleen, to be in, so he checked his message slot at her desk and retrieved a few pink pieces of paper, while the dog laid down in the reception area.

Shuffling through the call-backs, he entered his office and flipped on the light before realizing someone was sitting in his chair. And not just anyone . . . but Nick. *Fuck!* Jake frowned and kicked the door shut with his foot. He wanted to cross his arms and stare down at the kid, but with his coffee, food, and messages in hand, he couldn't pull it off. Sighing loudly, he placed everything on his desk and assumed the stance he wanted. "What're you doing here?"

Nick didn't seem affected by Jake's dominant tone. Instead, he leaned further back in the leather chair and the corners of his mouth ticked up in apparent amusement. "I want to talk without you shoving me up against a wall or bitching at me. I figured this was the ideal place."

Jake raised his eyebrows over narrowed eyes. "You seem sure of that. No one else is here yet, so there's no reason for me not to haul your ass out of my chair and throw you out the door."

"You're right. There's not."

That wasn't the answer Jake had expected. He was even more shocked when Nick got up and gestured for him to take the seat. Stalking around the desk, he tried to get a read on the kid. He was up to something, but Jake wasn't sure what it was. He sat, but before he had a chance to pull himself closer to the desk, Nick lifted a leg and straddled his thighs. *Ah, shit!* A denim covered semi-hard-on was only inches from his face. He knew it wasn't a full-fledged one because he'd seen exactly what Nick looked like at full attention—impressive would be an understatement. The thought caused his own dick to stir. "What are you doing?"

"Stating my intentions," the kid replied smugly as he leaned his tight ass against the desk's beveled edge.

The Dom forced his gaze upward to the other man's handsome, chiseled face. "Your intentions?"

"Yup. My intentions. You rattled off a list of reasons why we won't have a repeat of our one night together. Well, I have a few reasons of my own as to why we should have a repeat. In fact, I think we should have several repeats."

Letting out a snort, Jake glared at him. "This should be enlightening." He clenched his hands into fists to keep them from grabbing the guy's hips and pulling him forward.

"I hope so." Nick crossed his arms. "One—yes, it was a one-night-stand, but fuck, it was the best one of my entire life. You did things to me I never knew I wanted before. Two —you were right, I've never played in the lifestyle before. I never understood what drew people into it, and I think it's because I was looking at it from a dominant standpoint and not a submissive one. I'd never been submissive when it came to sex before you. I still don't know why I submitted that night. All I know is, I want to do it again, Jake. But only for you. Three—if we do this, I don't want you holding back on me. I want to try and take everything you have to offer. You might be right and the lifestyle might not be for me, but I won't know unless I give it a shot. Everyone has to start somewhere, right? Four—again, if we do this, it's exclusive. I don't share. I know you're a Whip Master at the club, and while I've never seen you in action, I have watched China and Carl. I know there doesn't have to be sex involved, and I'm fine with you scene-ing with submissives in that capacity only. But it has to be in public. If it's not, then I have to be in the room with you. I guess you can call that a hard limit for me. That's what it's called, right?"

Jake didn't answer him because his mind was racing as Nick threw every one of his reasons back at him, shredding each as he did. But the kid had only listed four, and that wasn't enough for the Dom. "What about reason number five?"

This was the big one, and Nick swallowed hard. "I'm willing to come out to my family—I've been thinking about it a lot lately—but not yet. I have to take this one step at a time. It'll be too much for me if I tackle everything at once."

Rubbing his bottom lip with his fingers, Jake stared at the beautiful man in front of him. The urge to order him to strip was strong, and he almost did it just to see the sculpted body he'd spent a few hours exploring two months ago. Jake stayed in top physical shape and had always been attracted to men who also took care of their bodies. He preferred hard, muscular flesh over soft, but not too well-built, since steroid-pumping gym buffs did nothing for him. However, bodies that came from hard physical labor and training were a total turn-on. Just like Nick's.

Damn. This wasn't some short term fling he was looking at here. It was something much more, which thrilled and terrified him at the same time. He had to be crazy to think this might work out, but the temptation to try was getting harder to resist. He'd never dated anyone whose family he was close to, much less knew, and Nick may not have met Jake's mother yet, but he'd met Mike on numerous occasions. "I'll give you two weeks."

Jake's stomach sank when Nick's face fell. They hadn't even started and he was already fighting the Dom. *Shit.* He should've known it was too good to be true.

"Two weeks," the kid whispered. He shook his head and brought his voice up to a normal level again. "No. No way."

Pushing his chair back so he could stand, Jake raised his eyebrows as raw disappointment flowed through him. "No? I thought you just said you were willing to come out to your family. I'm giving you two weeks to do it and you're saying 'no'? Then we have nothing more to talk about."

He skirted the desk, and was halfway to the door when Nick's broken voice reached him. "Wait . . . wait a minute." He stopped, but didn't turn back around, afraid of caving and telling him to forget the demand—that it didn't matter. But it did matter—it mattered a lot. "I misunderstood what you meant. I thought you were putting a time limit on us. Two weeks is . . . is okay. I'll do it. I'll talk to Ian, Dev, and my folks. Please, Jake. Don't walk away."

The sheer desperation in the other man's voice had Jake's gut and heart clenching. As he spun around, he heard the sounds of people arriving to start the workday out in the reception area. The new recruits were here as well as Colleen. He strode purposely toward Nick, his intent evident in his stare. Stopping inside the kid's personal space, he grabbed him by the back of the neck, holding him tight. "There's more to this than just tying you up and fucking you senseless. Do you understand that?"

"Yeah. I do."

"Then go over to the club sometime today. Behind the front desk, you'll find submissive protocols as well as a blank limit list. I want you to fill it out and bring it to me tonight."

Nick's eyes widened. "At the club?"

"No, my place. Before anything else happens between us, we're going to sit down and negotiate both of our limits. And then . . ." He couldn't resist his urges anymore. Drawing

Nick closer, Jake kissed him. Hard. Demanding. Dominating.

Nick parted his lips for more, but Jake pulled back again, stopping only a few inches away. "Can't get started here. I've got meetings and I'm not going into them with wood." He smirked. "But be prepared, Junior, because I plan on continuing this . . ." A quick peck was placed on Nick's mouth followed by a lick. "Later. My way."

6

An hour later, Jake watched one of the two new Trident operatives, Tristan McCabe, run his way through the military-style obstacle course the team had set up north of the main compound. It was surrounded by a quarter-mile running track and sat parallel to the new heliport. The chopper would arrive after the new pilot reported to work, and then traveled to California to fly it back. Ian and Devon were currently in negotiations for the property south of their current acreage and had plans for a multi-story hollowed out building which would be used for mission practice runs as well as routine training. The walls could be moved around in order to simulate different setups. An outdoor shooting gallery with pop-up bad guys was also in the future plans. It would work with computerized weapons and targets, so there was no need for live ammo which always ran the risk of accidental injuries—insurance companies tended to frown on that.

Patiently waiting at the starting line of the course was Nick. After they'd left his office earlier, Jake had introduced him to the two new operatives, and Nick had stood by when

Ian joined them, laying out the agenda for the day. The first matter Jake took care of was showing Foster and McCabe the bunk rooms and living quarters above the offices. The second floor housed six bedrooms, four with a set of bunk beds, a desk, and a dresser, as well as an attached bathroom. The other two bedrooms had the exact same setup, but had a queen-size bed instead of the bunks. A kitchen and large recreational area, complete with couches, recliners, sixty-inch HDTV, pool table, and dart board, made the entire floor a comfortable place for the new team members to stay until they found their own housing.

Next Jake gave them a tour of the training building. It sat between the Trident offices and the residential one, and contained a gym, indoor shooting range, training room, and a panic room, in case of an emergency. Upstairs was currently spare space and storage. He informed the two men that Marco would set them up with the standard-issued equipment when he and the others returned from their current mission.

For now, Jake was running the men through their paces, trying to assess their strengths and weaknesses. Nick had volunteered to run the course with them to keep up his own physical fitness routine. He'd managed to convince the women to go shopping without him today, and promised to go to the furniture store with them tomorrow. Jake had a feeling he was trying to find another way out of the excursion.

While McCabe grabbed a thick rope and swung his body over a water trap, Cain Foster stood next to Jake, trying to catch his breath. He'd just completed the course in seven minutes and forty seconds, which was pretty good for his first run-through. The course was a slightly modified version of the Navy SEALs' famous O-course in BUD/s training, which Jake had spent countless hours on during his time in the military.

"What's the course record?" Foster asked between gulps of air.

Jake watched McCabe clear the rope webbing before answering. "Devil Dog's got it. Five minutes, twenty-two seconds."

"Shit. I wasn't even close."

Letting out a quick snort, Jake shook his head. "Don't worry about it. It took Dev two weeks to get that time and he helped design the course. Besides, it's not like you had to do many O-courses like this in the Secret Service. You'll get there . . . then you have to do it with a thirty-pound pack." He hit the button on his stopwatch as McCabe crossed the finish line. "Not bad for an Army grunt. You beat Foster by sixteen seconds. Seven-twenty-four."

The former Delta Force operator cursed as his lungs heaved for oxygen. "Fuck, that sucks."

Jake just grinned. It seemed like that was everyone's reaction to the first time they ran it, but he wasn't worried. According to Foster, he hadn't run an intense obstacle course in years, and McCabe was still gaining the strength back in his left bicep after taking a bullet four months ago. Poor guy got nailed two weeks before his last tour in the Army's Special Ops was complete.

"What time do I have to beat?"

His gaze found Nick standing at the starting line and he willed himself not to have a reaction. The kid was in a pair of grey sweatpants and military green tank, and was in peak physical condition. The day's temperature was in the low eighties, which was normal for the beginning of November, but it was wise to wear sweatpants on the course unless you wanted splinters or rope burns on your thighs. "If you want to impress me, you gotta beat Dev. Five and twenty-two."

"Shit, that's nothing. Big brother is going down." He shrugged his shoulders and swiveled his head, making sure his neck muscles were as loose as the rest of him. Lining up at the start, he grinned at Jake.

Cocky little shit. "Ready? Three. Two. One. Go!"

Nick took off like the devil was on his heels. He vaulted the first short wall then raced across a low balance beam without a moment's hesitation. Jake's gaze bounced between his stopwatch and the kid, his thoughts urging him on. Four minutes into the run, Ian walked up and stood next to his teammate. The boss's eyes were on his younger brother while Jake handed him a clipboard with the other men's times on it. Ian didn't even glance at it. "How's he doing?"

"Faster than a fucking jackrabbit. If he doesn't miss anything, he's going to beat Devil Dog's time by a good fifteen to twenty seconds."

Ian snorted in feigned disgust. "Great. Just what he needs . . . fucking bragging rights."

The four men watched as Nick completed the last few obstacles and lunged across the finish line. He pulled up short, panting hard, and raised an eyebrow for his time.

"Four-fifty-nine." *Damn it*, Jake thought. Was that pride in his voice?

"Hoo-yah!" The smug bastard did a dance which belonged in an NFL end-zone while the other men groaned. Yeah, it was obvious he was going to crow about that record for a long time.

Before he could say something snarky, Jake's phone rang and he grabbed it from its hip holster. *Unknown Caller.* He swiped the screen to connect and brought it to his ear. "Donovan." He was greeted by silence, but when he checked, the call was still connected. "Hello? Anyone there?"

There was crackling across the line and then a whispered voice. "J-Jake?"

He froze and the hair on his neck tingled. "Alyssa? Alyssa, baby, is that you? What's wrong?" All eyes were suddenly on him at the elevated concern in his voice. The men knew something bad was about to go down.

There was a gut-wrenching sob. "J-Jake, t-they killed her. T-they killed my m-mom."

"Shi . . . where are you, Alyssa?" He turned and began to jog toward the office building with the others fast on his heels. "Alyssa? Answer me. Where are you?"

"I . . . I'm hiding in the b-bathroom at the park. I'm s-scared, Jake. You . . . you have to help me. Please, help me!"

She was close to being hysterical and Jake still needed information from her. "I'm going to help you, but first, sweetie, you need to tell me exactly where you are. Remember? They wouldn't tell me where you and your mom went. Give me the town and state you're in."

"Canon City, Colorado. P-please, come get me! Please!"

"I'm coming, sweetheart. Stay on the line with me." Barging into the office, they startled Colleen, but Jake continued past her desk and into the conference room, followed by the others. He grabbed a laptop and slid it across the table to Ian, who was in the process of taking a seat. "Canon City, Colorado. I need a contact there fast. Critical extraction."

Ian brought the computer out of sleep mode and started typing as Jake returned his attention to the scared young girl on the phone, trying to get more information from her. The other three men stood silently around the large conference table waiting for further details as their secretary appeared in the doorway. Without taking his eyes off the computer screen, Ian ordered, "Colleen, call Chase Dixon. Tell him we need to borrow one of his planes, ASAP. Ours is still in South America. We need to go to . . . here it is . . . we're heading to Colorado Springs or as close to Canon City, Colorado as we can get. It'll be a round-trip or to another location. Not sure yet. Take-off within the hour."

"Got it." She disappeared again to make the call to Blackhawk Security.

Ian snatched a landline phone from the table and started dialing, then glanced at Jake. "You're in luck. Archer lives in Colorado Springs, not far from her. Where exactly is she? I'll see if he can intercept and lock her down until you get there."

Jake handed over a piece of paper where he'd written the cell number she'd given him, then interrupted her renewed pleading. "Alyssa, I swear, I'm coming to get you, but I'm sending someone closer to look after you until I get there. His name is Pete Archer and he's a good friend of mine from the Navy. You can trust him. He's going to keep you safe, but I have to know exactly where you are. Do you know the name of the park you're in?"

"Y-yeah. It's the C-Centennial Park, but I forget what street it's on. It-it's about six blocks from our house."

"Centennial Park, okay, good. You're doing great, sweetheart. Now, are you well-hidden? Did they see you? Were you followed?" He needed to get as much from her as he could, in case they lost the connection.

"N-no, no one followed me and I-I don't think . . . I don't think they saw me."

Jake took the note Ian handed back to him with his own scrawl added on. He read it, then raised an eyebrow at his boss. When he mouthed "forty-five minutes," Ian grimaced and nodded. If that was the best they could do, he'd have to take it. "Alyssa, listen to me, sweetheart. Stay where you are. I have to hang up now—"

"No! Don't hang up, Jake! Please don't hang up—"

"Sweetheart, I have to. I have to get to the airport and fly out to get you, but I'm going to have my friend call you right back. Remember? His name is Pete Archer. He's going to call you as soon as I hang up and he's about forty-five minutes away from you. I'm going to text you his picture, so you can recognize him. He's going to stay on the line with you until he finds you. Okay? And he'll keep you safe until I get there in a few hours."

"O-okay, but hurry."

Jake's heart was breaking for the teenager. She'd been through so much already. "I will, Alyssa, I promise. Now, hang up so Pete can call you."

"Okay, hurry."

The call disconnected and his worried eyes met Ian's. "Can you send her a photo of Archer? And put a trace on her phone in case we lose her?"

His boss nodded and began typing again. "Give me a sitrep while I'm doing this. I vaguely remember her case. Runaway, about a year ago, right?"

Running a hand through his hair, Jake paced the length of the room while the others watched in silence. "Yeah. Alyssa Wagner. Her father's a local businessman with political ties to the mayor and governor. He reported her as a sixteen-year-old runaway, claiming she took off after being grounded for missing her curfew a few times. Turns out he was sexually abusing her for years." Muttered curses filled the room. If there were two things the men of Trident hated more than anything, it was rapists and child abusers— Oliver Wagner was both, which made him the scum of the earth. "A few days into the investigation, when I managed to get a chance to talk to the mother alone, she broke down and told me the truth. Carrie was terrified of the asshole. The whole meek, submissive, 'he's going to kill me' thing was going on, so I offered to help her and her daughter get new identities."

Ian knew what he meant by that, but the others weren't aware of Trident's resources yet, so Jake filled them in. "There's a group called 'Friends of Patty.' A few women started it years ago after a friend of theirs was killed by an abusive husband. They now have contacts all over the U.S. and it's run like the old Underground Railroad. Female victims of abuse are given the means to escape and start new lives. And I tell you, this group would give the U.S. Marshals a run for their money. They're that fucking good.

"Anyway, Alyssa's mother knew where her daughter was hiding. She was with an old college friend Carrie hadn't seen in years, but kept in contact with, without the husband knowing. Wagner hated the woman and forbade Carrie to stay in contact, but she did anyway. The friend lived in Georgia. I went up there, got Alyssa, and set them up with Friends of Patty. Same rules as the Marshals—name changes, no contact with anyone from their previous life, etcetera. I gave them my cell number for emergencies only and this was the first I've heard from either of them." He stopped pacing and clasped his hands behind his head in frustration.

"Alyssa says she went to work waitressing at six this morning and forgot something—a baby's gift—she wanted to give one of the other waitresses. About an hour into her shift, she got a break to run a few blocks home and saw a strange car parked across the street. For some reason, it set off her inner alarm and she snuck around to a window at the side of the house. Her mother was dead on the floor, shot in the face, and two guys were tearing the place apart. She's hiding in a nearby park now."

Colleen stuck her head in the doorway. "Mr. Dixon said the plane is no problem. It'll be ready when you get there. And you owe him—again."

Waving his acknowledgement at the efficient secretary, Ian stared at Jake. "All right, what's the plan after you recover her?"

He planted his hands on his hips. "The safe house for now. Can you send Pete a text and tell him to put an anonymous call into 911 after he gets Alyssa? Have the police go to her house, so they can get the ball rolling on an investigation." Ian nodded. "Then we need to figure out if this is a random burglary gone wrong or did her father's people find her. And if they did, then how? Once we know what we're dealing with, we'll go from there."

"Good. Dev called this morning and said they finished early. They'll be back sometime tomorrow. I'll have Egghead start investigating things while he's in the air."

"Egghead?" Foster asked. He'd only met five of the six members of Trident's Alpha team on previous visits and some of them had just been brief introductions.

"Brody Evans is our resident geek. If the information is out there, he's the man who can find it."

The Omega team member nodded. "Okay. Do you want us to go with Donovan? At least until the rest of his team can catch up?"

"I'll go."

Ian and Jake's eyes flashed at Nick in surprise.

"What?" He shrugged his shoulders. "I've got nothing else going on for the next few weeks. And I'm damn good at watching someone's six. Uncle Sam trained me, remember?"

He may be sarcastic and cocky, but he spoke the truth. Nick went through the same BUD/s training as everyone on Trident's Alpha Team and none of them would have any problem with him covering their asses.

The two men stared at each other for a moment before Jake nodded his assent to his boss. Ian glanced back at his brother and then the others. "Okay. Smartass and Cain, you two are with Reverend. McCabe, you'll stay here with me. I know you're good to go, but I'm not sending you on assignment until you get your final medical clearance tomorrow." The man tilted his head in understanding, but it was obvious he wasn't happy about it. "Jake, make sure they're suited up before you leave—vests, headsets, the works—just in case. Nick, you carrying?"

"No. Too much of a hassle on a commercial airline."

"Okay, we have an arsenal for you to choose from. I'm sure you'll find something you like."

The corners of Jake's mouth twitched when Nick grinned. He was going to be like a kid in a candy store when he saw the selection of weapons Trident kept in a walk-in vault. If the situation wasn't serious, Jake would've laughed at the younger man's enthusiasm. "Let's move."

7

The phone call ended and Alyssa prayed with all her might that it would ring again. Tears rolled down her pale cheeks. She was terrified and Jake's voice had been a lifeline to hold onto, but now, the silence was driving her crazy. Hopefully, no one would need to use the park's bathroom at this time of the morning, but there were two other empty stalls so she could stay locked behind the one she was in for now.

Her body wouldn't stop shaking and she wrapped her arms around her torso, trying to hold it together. She trusted Jake with her life because he'd saved her once before. If it hadn't been for him, she never would've had this last year with her mother. Instead, she would still have been living with her mom's friend or someone else. The woman had been nice, but Alyssa had missed her mom. And now her mom was gone. What was she going to do? She had no one else left in the world except her bastard father, and she'd rather be dead then return to him.

Her phone rang, the shrill tone echoing throughout the

brick enclosure. She recognized the number's area code as being from Colorado Springs. "H-hello?"

"Alyssa? My name is Pete Archer. Jake gave me your number. I'm on my way to get you, honey, but it's going to take a while to get there. How much battery time do you have on your phone?"

She pulled the phone away from her ear and checked the screen. "It's almost fully charged."

"Good. Keep checking it, because I don't want to let it run out until I reach you and can get you somewhere safe. Stay on the phone with me and let me know if anyone comes near where you're hiding, okay?"

"O-okay. Please hurry. I'm s-scared."

The man's voice softened. "I know you are, sweetheart. But I swear, Jake and I are going to help you and anyone who wants to hurt you is going to have to go through us first. We're not going to let anything happen to you."

If Mr. Archer was anything like Jake, she knew he would keep his promise. She just hoped he got there before the men who killed her mom found her. "H-Hurry."

THREE HOURS LATER, Jake, Nick, and Cain were soaring through the air at 41,000 feet, somewhere over the Mid-West. The private jet they'd borrowed from Blackhawk Security was similar to Trident's own. There were three rows of first-class-style seats with two seats on either side of the aisle. Behind them was a large sitting area with couches, recliners, tables, and a wide-screen TV. A fully-stocked kitchen and bathroom were located in the rear of the plane.

With a set of noise-cancelation headphones on, Cain was dozing in a first-row seat, while Nick browsed through the TV channels from one of the couches. It was one of those days when there was nothing good on. Jake hung up the jet's phone and stood from his recliner. Nick's head swiveled to face him. "What's up?"

He walked back to the kitchen and grabbed two sodas from the mid-size fridge as he spoke. "Pete has Alyssa hidden at his place. He's positive no one was on her tail. Placed the 911 call and had a buddy he trusts wait up the street for the cops to show up. The problem is—Carrie Wagner wasn't there. From what Pete's friend could find out, the place is trashed, but there's no body. Whoever killed her doesn't want her found."

Nick's eyes narrowed in confusion. He wasn't used to regular civilian crime scenes. In his job, it was rare to take a dead body from where it originally dropped. And usually, he was the one dropping them. The only exception was if it was a member of the United States military killed in combat. Then every attempt was made to bring the fallen home for a proper burial. "Why take the body? I don't get it."

Handing Nick one of the cold Coke cans, Jake remained standing. "Taking the body doesn't surprise me . . . if this is the work of Oliver Wagner or one of his minions, which I'm pretty positive it is. When his wife and daughter took off last year, the story was they disappeared while on a road trip somewhere between Tampa and Albuquerque. That's where his mother-in-law lives, but she and Carrie weren't close anymore. There were the usual pleas for help on TV, search parties, the works, but it slowly drifted away from being front page news. Wagner's lawyer alluded to Carrie running away with a guy she was allegedly having an affair with and that she was mentally unstable. All false accusations."

Nick popped open his can and took a sip. "What about their car? Didn't someone find it?"

"Nope. APBs on their vehicle were moot because I took it to a chop-shop. I knew if Alyssa and Carrie were ever found, he would have them disappear for good. He couldn't risk either of them telling the press he molested his own daughter when he's got political aspirations of his own. Getting rid of Carrie's body would prevent any connection between her alias and real name. Then, as far as the public is concerned, it's just another unsolved mystery—and he garners the sympathy vote. The big question is, if Wagner is behind this, then how the hell did he find them?"

"Damn, there's fucked up people in the world."

Jake snorted. "You're just figuring this out, Nicky-boy?"

After flashing his eyes toward the front of the cabin, he glared at Jake. "Can you knock off the 'boy' shit?"

The Dom straightened to his full height and crossed his arms. It was time to set some ground rules with the kid. Besides, it would give him something else to do other than worrying about Alyssa. "The guy is snoring with headphones on. Trust me, I've flown in jets like this for the past four years. He couldn't hear me up there even if he tried. And you're nine years younger than me, frog. No one would think twice about me calling you 'boy' the way I just said it. I would never embarrass you inside or outside of a D/s setting. Not in front of people you barely know, and especially not in front of a team member. I'm not into public humiliation. Now, in private, it'll be a different story. I'll call you anything I want. I'm a Dom, through and through. And if you want a relationship with me, you *will* be submissive and I'll treat you as such. Take it or leave it. It's the way I am, and the way I'll always be. Understand?"

SHIT! If anyone else said those things to him, Nick would've been pissed off as all hell. They'd get a "fuck you" response and a possible right hook. But with Jake, he wanted to say, "fuck me" instead. The Dom was glowering at him and, without a conscious thought, Nick lowered his eyes to the floor. "Yeah, I got it."

"Not good enough. You were told the proper way to respond to me when we're in D/s mode."

His eyes flickered toward their sleeping teammate again and then to the man standing over him. "I understand, Sir."

Relaxing his stance, Jake gave Nick a leering grin. "Better. You have no idea how much I want to fuck you right now. Have you ever been inducted into the Mile-High Club?"

Heat built in Nick's veins and groin. "No . . . Sir."

"Well, we'll have to rectify that . . . someday." He sat on the couch, close enough where he was in Nick's personal space, yet far enough that Cain wouldn't suspect anything if he woke up. "But for now, we're going to discuss a few rules. You can relax and drop the 'Sir.'"

Nick swallowed hard and tried to keep his body from reacting to the Dom's nearness—a near impossible feat. He knew the lifestyle had a lot of rules, but each relationship was different and so was each couple's rules. What worked for one couple, didn't always work for another. "Okay."

"Rule number one—your orgasms are mine. There will be no jacking off in the shower, or anywhere else, unless I give you permission. If I find out you can't keep your hands off what is now my property, then there'll be consequences." He waited until Nick, eyes wide in disbelief, slowly nodded his assent. "Rule number two is what I just told you. When we're playing, you'll call me 'Sir' or 'Master' and I'll call you anything I want. If something I use bothers you, tell me, and we'll discuss it. I may or may not change my mind depending on your reasoning. Number three—presenting. When I tell you present for me, the position is on your knees, legs spread as far as you can without being uncomfortable. Hands in 'at-ease' position behind your back and head bowed. I'll let you know beforehand whether you need to strip or not."

The rules weren't as bad as Nick had expected. Well, at least the second and third rules weren't, as long as it was all done in private. Rule One? No hand-jobs? *Shit.* He was a healthy, red-blooded, twenty-five-year-old male—jacking off was almost a daily occurrence. Case in point, he'd done it last night in bed, and in the shower again this morning. How the hell was he supposed to stay sane without it? Well, maybe if he was having sex on a regular basis, it would be doable. "Okay. Is that it?"

"Nope, not even close, but it's a start for now. As things come up, we'll add to the list. But don't think you don't have a say in this. If a rule really bothers you—and not just because you don't like it—tell me and we'll talk about it." Jake paused, his gaze on Nick's face. His expression then softened as he asked, "Have you decided how you're going to come out to your folks and brothers?"

Picking at the soda can's pop-top with his fingernail, he shook his head. "No, not yet. I mean . . . I can't see them having a problem with it, especially Ian and Dev, but to actually say the words to them . . . it's hard, you know? How did you come out to your family?"

Leaning forward, Jake rested his elbows on his knees and sighed heavily. Nick instantly knew what the man was going to say wouldn't be pleasant. "I didn't. Somehow my dad found out my senior year of high school and went ballistic. He was a fucking bigot—plain and simple. Gays, blacks, Asians, Jews, etcetera. If you weren't straight, white, Catholic, and a Democrat, you were fair game for his contempt and vile insults."

"What happened?"

Taking a sip of soda, Jake seemed to disappear into the past for a moment. "I was the starting quarterback for my high school. Did you know that?"

"No, I didn't."

"We were undefeated my senior year. All three years I was on varsity, we went to the state championships and we won two out of three of them. My father was always on the sidelines, yelling louder than everyone else. I was the golden boy. I had scouts at almost every game my junior and senior years, and they were all throwing scholarships and incentives at me. I even had a few pro teams checking me out for future drafts. I finally decided on Rutgers and was getting a full ride. The old man was over the fucking moon."

He took a deep, shaking breath and ran a hand through his hair, while Nick fought the urge to touch him the way he wanted to, in comfort and support. "Anyway, after my senior football season was over, I had more free time and started exploring places to meet guys where no one knew me. By that time, I knew girls weren't doing it for me, but there was no way I was coming out. Not to my family or my friends. I was too afraid of their reactions." He paused and, for a moment, Nick thought he might not continue. "I . . . uh . . . I started doing community service at a food pantry during my sophomore year to pad my college applications. It's where I met Max . . . Max Sterling. He started volunteering there just after New Year's my senior year and became my first real boyfriend—you know, not just a one-night-stand or a friend-with-benefits. He also became my first Dom."

Nick's head whipped up, and he stared at Jake in shock. "You-you had a Dom? I mean, you were a submissive?"

A low chuckle emanated from Jake chest. "What? You think Doms just wake up one morning and decide to be one? Think they instantly know *how* to be one?"

Shrugging, he responded, "I never really thought about it." And it was true, he hadn't. And now that he had the idea in his head, he wondered if either of his Dominant brothers had been subs when they'd first started the lifestyle.

"I know what's going on in that mind of yours, Junior, and those are your brothers' stories to tell—if they choose to. But I will tell you this, any Dom worth knowing has been a submissive at some point. They've at least submitted their way through a limit list. If a Dom hasn't had it done to himself, then he shouldn't be doing it to his submissive."

Nick's jaw was now almost on the floor. He shifted in his seat until he was facing Jake. "You've been whipped?"

"Several times. As a submissive and as a Dom, although it's been a while."

A bolt of possessiveness passed through the younger man. He practically growled. "Who?"

Jake's eyes narrowed in confusion. "Who what?"

"Who fucking whipped you?"

Faster than a cobra striking, he grabbed Nick's jaw and held him firm. The younger man tried to pull back, but it was useless. Jake's angry green eyes were fixed on a pair of startled blue ones. "My past Doms and submissives are not up for discussion, if that's where you're going with this. We'll have to be a lot further along in a relationship for that. I only brought up Max because . . . fuck, I don't know why I brought him up. But as for the last two people who whipped my ass, they were Master Carl and Mistress China. It's been a long time since I've been a submissive, but getting whipped every once in a while reminds me of where I've been and how far I've come. Now shove that jealousy back down where it belongs, Nicky-boy."

Shit, he'd fucked up big time. Jake had actually been opening up, but now he was pissed and shutting down again. Abruptly, the Dom stood and jerked a thumb toward the front of the cabin. Cain was stirring in his seat, so it was just as well their conversation was over. But he couldn't let it end this way—he didn't want Jake mad at him. Before their third impromptu teammate could get up to join them, Nick tilted his head up toward Jake and lowered his voice. "I'm sorry. I'm not normally a jealous person. I took that too far."

A TERSE NOD was Jake's only response, but then he realized it wasn't enough. This was going to be hard for the new submissive. He'd always been a non-lifestyle top, and learning to submit, without fighting it, was going to go against a lot of his ingrained emotions and practices. Yeah, Jake was a little pissed at the moment, but he had to set the rules and parameters before he expected them to be followed. "Yeah, you did. But we have other things to worry about at the moment, so we'll shelve this discussion for later."

As Cain stood and stretched, Jake turned and strode into the bathroom, locking the door behind him. He needed a few minutes alone to get his head back on straight. What had he been thinking bringing up Max? After all these years, he still had affectionate feelings for the man who'd led him down a path of new discoveries. And what was it about Nick that made him want to spill his guts and bare his soul all of a sudden? He'd tried to bury his emotions and just state the facts about his background, but it was fucking hard to do. It'd been a long time since he'd talked about his past to anyone, and no one, not even his team or his brother and mother, knew the entire story. Splashing cool water on his face, he stared at his reflection in the bathroom mirror and forced the ghosts of his past back into the far reaches of his mind ... where they belonged.

8

A little after eleven a.m. on the outskirts of Pueblo, Colorado, Slim Daniels reached for another Budweiser from the cooler and handed it to his best friend, Wally Dunn, before taking one for himself. That was the great thing about fishing, it was never too early for a beer. The current of the Arkansas River was a little calmer today than it had been a few days ago when they had taken Dunn's little boat out, so maybe today they would catch a few—not that it mattered. As the saying goes—a bad day of fishing is better than a good day at work.

The fourteen-foot boat bobbed up and down in a soothing rhythm as Slim cast his line toward a deeper part of the river, where the two of them had successful catches before. They'd tied their towline to one of the pylons holding up the small bridge above them. In addition to being a man-made anchor, the overpass gave them shade from the sun. Slim's face was leathery enough from years of working outdoors in his landscaping business.

"Norma's been pissing me off lately," Dunn grumbled. "I

just finished renovating the damn bathroom and now she wants the fucking kitchen redone."

Slim snorted, but didn't answer. Dunn's wife had been pissing him off since the day they met over thirty years ago. Today was nothing new.

Overhead, the occasional car passed by, but the bridge was two stories high, and after a while, Slim was able to tune them out. It had been a good ten minutes since he'd noticed the last one and another vehicle was just now making its way across the river. But instead of passing over them and continuing on, this vehicle stopped. Stupid idiot, Slim thought to himself. The bridge wasn't that long, so the driver could've made it to the other side easily if he needed to pull over. A tug on his fishing line grabbed his attention and he forgot all about whatever was happening above him. Reeling the line in a bit, he felt the weight of the fish as it fought the hook in its mouth. It didn't feel like a keeper, so it would probably get thrown back after he got it aboard the boat.

Beside him, the other man casted upriver a bit. The quiet surrounding them was broken by a loud splash followed by Dunn cursing. "What the fuck?"

Slim looked over his shoulder to where his buddy was staring at something bobbing and floating toward them in the water. "Did some fucking jackass just toss his garbage off the bridge?"

"Close, looks like a rolled-up carpet."

As the large mass got caught up in the current, the speed with which it approached them increased. Dunn used his fishing rod to hook onto the rug, dragging it closer to the boat. It wasn't until it thudded against the hull that they saw long black hair sticking out of one end. Both men stared at it, then glanced at each other in horror. It was obvious today was one of those times that a day of fishing wasn't going to be better than any day at work.

———

THE MOMENT JAKE walked into Pete Archer's two-bedroom condo in Colorado Springs, Alyssa threw herself into his arms and began sobbing hysterically. It was obvious her tears were a continuation of her earlier crying on the phone. Her eyes were red and puffy, and snot was dripping from her nose. Despite her current appearance, she was pretty, in a girl-next-door kind of way.

They were in the foyer and blocking the front door, so he picked her up in his arms and carried her into the living room. Behind him, Cain and Nick entered the first-floor unit before Pete shut the door. While the three men introduced themselves, Jake sat down with Alyssa on his lap and rubbed her back and arms, trying to soothe her. "*Shhh.* I'm so sorry about your mom, but I'm not going to let anything happen to you. *Shhh.* Calm down."

As Jake continued to murmur words of sympathy to the teenager, something inside Nick stirred. He'd never seen this tender, comforting side of Jake, and a part of him melted at that moment. There were still many things he didn't know about the man, but he couldn't wait to find out more. Pushing the wayward thoughts from his head, he turned to Pete. "Anything new since Jake spoke to you?"

Forty-year-old Pete Archer was about an inch taller than Nick, but not as broad. Due to a receding hairline, he kept his head shaved and reminded the younger man of the guy from the Mr. Clean commercials. He shook his bald head and indicated for the other men to take a seat, grabbing a recliner for himself. "No, not really. My buddy stuck around as long as he could without raising suspicions. Like I told Reverend, there was no body and with the place trashed, it'll take some time before they find any evidence, if there is any. Alyssa thinks the two men had gloves on, and my buddy overheard bleach was used to hide the DNA."

Cain spoke as he sat on the room's other recliner, leaving Nick to take the couch with Jake. "So, this wasn't random and it seems the husband found them. But how?"

Cocking his head toward the teenager, Archer replied, "Alyssa has no idea. She said they were careful and followed all the rules that group of women gave them. I dumped her cell phone after I picked her up just in case they manage to get the number and track it. The Canon City cops are looking for her and saying she's a missing person of interest at the moment. I thought of calling my cousin—he's a cop here in Colorado Springs—but he's going to want to know why I'm asking questions about a crime scene in Canon City, so that's out. At least until she's out of the area. Then I can honestly say I have no idea where she is."

While calming Alyssa, Jake had been listening to the men's conversation. Now that her crying and sobbing had quieted some, he eyeballed Pete. "Will you be able to nose around and keep us informed? I want to get her to a safe house ASAP."

"Sure, no problem. But can you fill me in a little more, so I know what I'm looking for?"

Jake helped Alyssa off his lap and turned her toward a hallway. "Go to the bathroom and wash your face, sweetheart. We'll be leaving for the airport in a few minutes."

Nodding, she silently left the room, and then Jake continued. "I'll have Ian email you the file, but put it this way—Alyssa's father has money and connections. He's not afraid to use both to find and kill her. If she tells anyone he's been sexually abusing her since she was twelve, he's ruined, whether the cops believe her or not. And she's too scared to go to them. In the beginning, I tried to gather evidence, but without her testimony, there was little to go on."

Pete glanced over his shoulder and made sure the bathroom door still closed, before lowering his voice. "Are you positive she's telling the truth about the abuse?" When Nick growled, the other man held up his hands. "I'm just asking, man. She wouldn't be the first girl to claim it for some other reason."

Jake waved a hand at Nick, signaling him to calm down. "It's all right. I know where he's coming from. When I first joined Team Four, one of the guys was falsely accused of rape by a seventeen-year-old SEAL bunny. It was hell for him until NCIS located a home surveillance video—two weeks later—that proved he was across town, jogging alone on the beach, when it allegedly happened." Nick knew all about SEAL bunnies—they were status seekers, just like rock-star groupies. Jake turned back to Pete. "And yeah, I'm sure. The group that helped her had her examined by a GYN. She needed to be tested for diseases and shit. The doc said there was signs of long-time abuse, and not just in one area, if you get my drift. The mother also confirmed she was assaulted any time she tried to intervene."

"Fuck!" Pete spit out, yet keeping his voice down. "Do you mind if I go kill the mother-fucker first?"

"Stand in line."

Jake looked at Nick and nodded his agreement. "Nick's right, there's a line and it's growing. But for now, we have to figure out what the hell is going on. I need to know how he found them, and I hope it's not because of a weak link in the Friends of Patty system."

The bathroom door opened and Alyssa walked out on wobbly knees. "Where are we going to go?"

Jake stood and pulled her into his arms again. "We're going to a place where you'll be safe until we can figure things out."

"What about my mom?"

Pulling back so he could see her face, Jake cupped her chin. "There's nothing we can do for your mom right now except take care of her daughter for her. When this is all over and you're safe again, we'll do what we can to find your mom and give her a proper burial."

The young girl nodded and bit her bottom lip to keep from crying again. "I'm all alone now."

Standing, Nick took a step toward her, without getting in her personal space, and gave her a small, reassuring smile. "No, you're not, sweetheart. You have us." He glanced at Jake, saw his nod of approval, and felt the warmth of his gaze. He hadn't said it to please Jake, but knowing it did made him want to keep pleasing the man. Damn, he had it fucking bad.

A HALF HOUR LATER, they were taxiing down the runway in Chase Dixon's plane once again. Jake had brought a wig, hat, sweatpants, and T-shirt that Ian had loaned him from Angie's closet so they could disguise Alyssa until they were safely out of the area. On the way to the airport, Foster ran into a deli and grabbed everyone some subs to eat during the several hour trip to Spartanburg, South Carolina, where the pilot would drop them off. From there, they would drive an hour and a half to Trident's safe house in Maggie Valley, North Carolina. Even though there were closer airports to their final destination, the team always took extra precautions to ensure they weren't being followed or tracked.

When the plane leveled off, everyone unbuckled their seatbelts and settled in. Jake grabbed a blanket and pillow from a closet by the pantry and brought it to where Alyssa was sitting somberly on one of the jet's couches. "Lay down, sweetheart, and try to get some rest. It's a little over three hours before we land and we have a bit of a drive after that."

Alyssa's adrenaline crash had her sound asleep within minutes of getting comfortable. The men took seats on the opposite side of the jet and pulled out their sandwiches. Foster handed Jake and Nick some napkins from the bottom of the bag. "All right, we've got the girl. Now what? I've got to learn to start thinking like an operative, instead of a fed. I think I'm going to like not having all the bureaucratic red tape to deal with."

Jake snorted as he unwrapped the white paper from his roast beef sub. "It does have its advantages, I'll tell you that. I gave Carrie Wagner's cell phone number to Ian, so Egghead can trace her activity, along with Alyssa's. I know she said they followed the rules, but I want to make sure there were no slip-ups. When we get to the safe house, I'm going to call my contact in Friends of Patty and see if she can trace which network contacts were used to get them from Florida to Colorado. But I don't know if it can be done. From what I understand, the first contact passes the 'package'—that's what they call the women—to another contact. After that, the first contact has no further knowledge about where the package goes. Each contact only knows who they got the package from and who they handed it off to. That way only one person knows the final destination, and anyone searching would have to go through a hell of a lot of people to find the package. The contacts randomly pick who they pass off to, so there's nothing routine."

Swallowing a mouthful of food, Nick washed it down with a swig of soda. "What about Wagner himself? There's got to be a way to put him behind bars for this without her testifying. Maybe there are other victims—I doubt she was the only kid he did this to." He glanced at Alyssa to make sure she was sleeping, but lowered his voice just in case. "Did she ever say if there were pictures or videos? Most of the cases like this I've read about, the fucking perverts like to have souvenirs."

Sighing, Jake nodded. "Yeah, there are. Nothing we've been able to find on the internet—I had Brody do a search —but that doesn't mean they aren't out there. The geek was able to get on a bunch of private pedophilia and snuff porn sites without leaving a trace he was there and he wasn't happy about it. I think he took a three-hour shower afterward and then got drunk."

"Don't blame him," Cain mumbled.

"Neither do I. Anyway, the photos and videos Wagner took are somewhere . . . my guess is in a safe at his house. And at this point, I highly doubt we'll be able to get a search warrant."

Finished eating, Nick crumbled up the empty paper which his sub had come in. "Too bad we don't know a cat burglar who knows how to crack a safe." Jake froze with his almost finished sub halfway to his mouth, and Nick stared at him in confusion. "What?"

A shit-eating grin spread across Jake's handsome face. "I like the way you think, Nicky-boy. And I know just the right person to contact. If he can't do it, he'll know someone who can." He stuffed the last of his sandwich into his mouth and brushed the crumbs from his fingers before grabbing the jet's phone. Dialing a number every member of the team had memorized, he relaxed back in his seat. When the call connected, all he heard was the usual short beep sans greeting. "Dude, it's Jake. I'll be landing in Spartanburg in about three hours. Give me a call because I need your super-spy skills. *Ciao.*"

Hanging up, Jake proceeded to fill Cain in on the team's good friend and U.S. black-operative, T. Carter.

9

Oliver Wagner stared at his right-hand man with fury written all over his face. "What do you mean she got away? Those shit-for-brains idiots I hired were supposed to kill both of them, then get rid of the bodies! I can't have either one of them popping up again!"

Shifting his stance, Craig Allen didn't wither under the Tampa businessman's glare. "That's what you get when you don't leave these things to me. But they recovered your wife's phone and found Alyssa's cell number in it. I was able to trace the last few numbers she dialed. The last outgoing call she made was to a number here in Tampa."

"What?" His boss's eyes narrowed. "Who?"

"Belongs to Trident Security."

"What?" Wagner's face got even redder. "Why would she be calling the company I hired to find her last year?"

"My guess is Trident helped with their disappearance. Or someone who works for them."

"Donovan." The businessman pulled a manila file from his desk and flipped through it. "The guy Ian Sawyer assigned to find Alyssa was named Donovan or something. Here it is, Jake Donovan. Start with him."

Allen nodded and turned to walk out the door. Behind him, Wagner added, "And no more fucking screw-ups. Find my little bitch of a daughter . . . and kill her. And anyone else who gets in your way."

AT A QUARTER after nine at night, a few miles from downtown Maggie Valley, Jake steered the Ford Expedition up a winding dirt road leading to the safe house. Trident had a deal with one of the men in charge of the small airport in Spartanburg, South Carolina and were able to keep three vehicles stored in one of the hangers for whenever they were needed. On the way over the border into North Carolina, the foursome had stopped at a Walmart to stock up on food and get some clothes and toiletries for Alyssa. The two-hour nap she had on the plane had done her good, but since waking, she'd only said anything when spoken to, and even then, it was mostly yes or no answers. Jake knew this was going to be very hard for her to get through. Ian's goddaughter, Jenn, was considered a niece to every member of the original Trident team, and she'd come to live at the compound after her parents were murdered about eighteen months ago. Her dad had been their lieutenant on SEAL Team Four, and they'd all watched their "Baby-girl" grow up into the beautiful twenty-year-old she was today. She was still seeing a trauma psychologist who had helped her through the aftermath of the horrific crime. When they made sure Alyssa was safe, Jake would look into getting her a therapist to talk to—she was going to need it between the abuse and the murder of her mother.

He wasn't sure if she'd been seeing one in Colorado, but he'd ask her about it later.

As Jake pulled up to the house, Cain whistled in appreciation. The outside solar-powered lights were glowing, along with a light in the inside foyer. "Damn, this is nicer than any safe house I've ever seen that wasn't catering to someone with at least a half a million-dollar paycheck."

Sitting behind the ex-fed, Nick snorted while Jake just shook his head. The eight bedroom and bath house had been obtained by the Sawyer patriarch a few months after Ian had joined SEAL Team Four in Virginia. One of the older guys had told him to find a safe place he could retreat to, if needed, and bury it under piles of paperwork, so it couldn't be traced to him. Chuck Sawyer had found his sons the perfect place here in Maggie Valley. Between the rock formation the house backed up to, the surrounding forest, bullet-proof windows, and Egghead's security system, the place was as safe as they could get it. Anyone would find it extremely difficult to sneak up on them without some kind of warning. But despite the security measures, the house was warm and inviting, having a ski lodge feel to it.

Jake popped the trunk to grab their shopping bags with Cain as Nick approached the front door and placed his hand on the scanner. It was the same system Trident had at their compound. The youngest Sawyer brother had only been here a few times in recent years, but knew he could use it anytime he wanted. As the others entered behind him, Nick flipped on more lights and gestured to the hallway to the right of the huge living room. "Alyssa, take the room at the end of hall. It's my folks' room when they come here."

She nodded as she eyed him timidly. "Can I take a shower?"

Handing her the bags with her things in them, Jake

gently told her, "Yeah, sweetheart. Each bedroom has its own bath. The water should be hot enough by now. We have a friend who keeps an eye on things for us. My boss called him earlier and had him swing by to turn on the stuff we don't need on while nobody's here. There's a TV in your room, too, if you want some time alone." After watching her trudge silently down the hallway, he turned to the others who were emptying the bags of groceries. "I'm going to run upstairs and arm the rest of the security systems. When you're done with that, Foster, come up to the loft over the living room. I'll show you how to run everything and scan your hand in. I don't think Egghead thought of adding your print to the system up here yet."

The new guy nodded. "Okay. I'll be up in a sec."

Twenty minutes later, the full security system was up and running, Foster's handprint was entered into the computer, and Alyssa was watching television in her room. The men sat in the living room, watching a west coast basketball game on the widescreen TV. Three frozen lasagnas and two loaves of garlic bread they'd picked up at the store were heating in the oven. Jake called Ian to let him know they arrived without incident and to see if there were any updates, which there hadn't been. Until the rest of the team arrived back in Tampa tomorrow, the three of them would stay here with Alyssa. Also tomorrow, Ian was sending Travis "Tiny" Daultry to Maggie Valley, along with one of Chase Dixon's operatives, to keep the teenager safe. Then Jake, Cain, and Nick would return to the compound and figure out how to get Oliver Wagner's ass thrown in jail for life—without Alyssa having to testify, if possible. The girl had been through too much for someone so young.

"Who's Tiny?" Cain asked, settling into a couch across from the one Nick was occupying.

Jake flipped the feet rest up on his recliner. "Friend of mine from my high school football days. We played for rival schools, but before that, we'd been on the same Pee-Wee team. He went to the pros for two seasons before a career-ending leg injury. He's now the head of security at the club and does some bodyguard work for us, too."

"The man's a fucking gorilla," Nick added with a chuckle. "Taller and wider than Jake. Nicest guy in the world, but can squash anyone who decides to take him on."

Jake snorted, but acknowledged Nick had spoken the truth with a nod of his head. At six-foot-eight and about two hundred seventy-five pounds of solid muscle, Tiny was far from the childhood nickname which had stuck. "Yeah. When we spar, I have to use a lot of dirty tricks if I want to last more than a few minutes against him. But the women call him a teddy-bear—he has them eating out of his hands."

After taking a sip of his soda, Cain raised it toward Jake. "So, tell me about the club. I haven't had the pleasure of checking it out yet and was going to take a look around tonight. But apparently plans change fast at Trident."

"It's a great place. Nick's brothers and cousin, Mitch, did a nice job planning the layout. Plenty of open spaces for public scenes and there are twelve private rooms, but they're talking about putting on an addition for some more. Alcohol is limited to two drinks if you're going to play and everything is computerized, thanks to Egghead."

"How's the membership?"

Jake stretched his arms before tucking his hands behind his head. Without looking at Nick, he felt the kid's heated gaze and willed his cock not to react. The two of them were going to have to find a way to work off some of the sexual tension which had increased between them since their conversation this morning. "Last I heard, we were at about three-hundred and fifty members. Some are seasonal, but on most weekends, there will be at least a hundred and thirty members at any given time. Sundays and Wednesdays are the slowest, but you'll still be able to find whatever you're into. Mondays and Tuesdays, it's closed. Every member is completely vetted, and checks are done on a routine basis to weed out any trouble makers."

"A lot of single subbies?"

"There's plenty of unattached subs to play with, with a wide variety of limits."

The door down the hall opened and the subject of the BDSM club was shelved as Alyssa shuffled into the living room. Her short, wet hair had been combed out, and she was wearing her new sweatpants and a hoodie over a T-shirt. Jake flipped the recliner's foot rest back down and sat forward. "You hungry, sweetheart? You didn't eat all day." On the plane, she had declined to eat her sandwich after awakening from her nap.

Shrugging her shoulders, she sat on the opposite end of the couch from Nick. The distance she kept between Nick, Cain, and herself wasn't lost on anybody. Jake was the one man she seemed comfortable with, and that was simply because this was the second time he'd come to her rescue— she was also aware that he was gay. When he first met her, he'd figured telling her would ease her worry about driving back to Florida alone with him.

"I don't know. I guess."

He stood and stepped into the kitchen area. The house had an open floor plan, so the only thing separating the kitchen and living room a large island/breakfast counter. "Dinner's almost ready. In the meantime, Nick, why don't you pull out the Xbox. Alyssa will kick your butt in *Need for Speed*."

Grinning, Nick jumped from the couch and knelt in front of the cabinet under the large flat-screen TV where the gaming console was stored. "Awesome. It's about time there's some competition worthy of my skills."

Alyssa gave him a smile, and Jake saw her shoulders relax a little. There were plenty of other video games in house's collection, but the racing competition was the first one he'd thought of that wasn't full of shooting and blood. She didn't need that less than fourteen hours after her mother was murdered.

It wasn't long before the four of them were laughing at each other's competitiveness. They took turns playing the game and eating the dinner Jake had served up on the large, square coffee table. He was surprised when he glanced at his dive watch and noticed it was close to midnight. Jeez, no wonder he was tired. It felt like days since he'd woken up in his bed and not hours.

From her spot on one couch, Alyssa cheered, while on the other one, Cain groaned in defeat. But the girl's laughter faded quickly as the horror of what she had been through came rushing back to her. Jake could see the pain and guilt in her eyes. "Sweetie, it's okay to laugh. I know you're hurting, but your mom wouldn't want you to stop living and laughing." He stood and pulled her up into a hug. "Why don't you get some sleep, *hmm*? I think we're all pretty tired. And in the morning, we'll figure out what to do next."

She buried her face in his broad chest as her tears made a reappearance. "He's never going to stop looking for me. He'll either kill me or make me—"

"Oh, sweetheart, neither of those things are going to happen. I won't let him within a mile of you. None of us will." Jake was about to say something else, but was interrupted by an alert emanating from the security system. The three men froze for an instant. The distinct sequence of beeping meant someone breached the sensors fifty yards in from the main road on the way up the long winding driveway.

Shit.

10

*G*ently pushing Alyssa away from him, Jake's eyes met Nick's. "Take her downstairs to the panic room. We'll check it out."

Nick nodded, but before anyone could move, Jake's phone, sitting on the coffee table, notified him of a text. A quick glance at the screen had him calming again as he sighed. "Never mind." Giving Alyssa a reassuring smile, he gestured to the hallway leading to her bedroom. "It's okay. It's a good friend of mine, and he's here to help. Why don't you hit the sack and I'll introduce you to him in the morning?"

The girl nodded, but by the way she was biting her bottom lip, it was apparent she was still wary. Nick took several steps toward her room. "Come on. I'll double check the locks on your windows, then you can get a good night's sleep."

"Thanks." Her stance relaxed at the offer to make sure she was safe and secure. She gave Cain and Jake a little wave. "Goodnight."

Jake waved back. "Goodnight, sweetie."

"Goodnight," Cain added.

As she followed Nick down the hall, Jake strode over to the front door. A few moments later, headlights appeared and a non-descript sedan followed. By the time the vehicle parked and the driver emerged, Jake was descending the front steps with Cain at his heels. "The video game was a great idea. She seems more comfortable around Nick and me now. Is this the guy you told us about?"

"Yeah. Mr. Black-Ops himself." Jake raised his voice so Carter could hear him. "Hey, jackass, a phone call would have sufficed."

The thirty-eight-year-old, six-foot-four, physically fit man grinned at him while retrieving a duffel and twelve-pack of beer from the back seat. "What's the matter, pretty-boy? Did I scare the shit out of you setting off the alarm?"

Jake grunted at the teasing. His friendship with the spy spanned many years after the team ran into him on several missions while still in the SEALs. They would do anything for the guy and vice versa. In fact, Carter had saved their asses on several occasions. "Yeah, well, the seventeen-year-old girl whose mother was murdered this morning was a little freaked out about it."

Stopping in his tracks, Carter's face fell. "You shitting me?" When Jake somberly shook his head, the man grimaced. "Fuck, dude, I'm sorry. I was on my way here to crash for a day or two and only checked my messages an hour ago. I just figured we'd talk when I got here." He took four more steps and extended his hand to Cain. "You one of the new guys?"

The former Secret Service agent shook his hand. "Yeah, Cain Foster."

"Carter." He eyed Jake. "Please tell me you're going to feed me while giving me a sit-rep. There was no way I was stopping for fucking drive-thru crap at this hour."

"Yeah, come on in. There's some leftovers."

Forty-five minutes later, Carter was fed and filled in about the situation. Taking a sip of the beer he'd brought in with him, he sat back in his chair at the rustic-style dining table. "Well, safecracking isn't my thing, but I know who we can call. One of my associates. She has several talents and that's one of the ones she excels in."

Nick raised his eyebrow at the older man he'd only met a few times before. "She?"

"Yes, young Sawyer . . . *she.* Jordyn is the best person for the job."

"But will she do it?" Jake queried, knowing it was useless to ask for the female spy's last name. Hell, none of the men at Trident even knew Carter's first name . . . only that it started with a "T."

A smug expression spread across the operative's face and his baby-blue eyes danced in amusement. "Oh, she'll do it. Especially when I tell her I don't think she can."

Jake barked out a laugh, then remembered Alyssa was sleeping and lowered his voice again. "Let me guess, jackass. Either you've tried to get into her pants or you've been there and now she hates your guts."

"Yup, to the latter, although I can't figure out why." He scratched his temple. "The woman's a firecracker in bed and I set her off many, many times the one night we hooked up. You'd think she'd love me for that alone."

"Must be your charming personality she hates then. When can you get a hold of her?"

Draining the last of his beer, Carter stood and brought his empty plate to the kitchen area. "Her system's like mine.

I'll give her a call now and leave a message. Hopefully, she's not in the middle of assassinating anyone and can get back to me pretty quick."

Across the big space, Cain groaned, and the spy glanced over his shoulder at him. "Problem?"

Snorting, Cain shook his head. "I resigned from the Secret Service two weeks ago. Any form of the word 'assassination' still makes me nervous."

"Well, if it helps," Carter replied as he dried off the plate he'd just washed, "Jordyn's on Uncle Sam's side."

"Always good to know. And on that note, gents, I'm hitting the sack. See you in the morning."

A few minutes after Cain went upstairs to the bedroom he was using, Carter grabbed his duffel and did the same, while Nick and Jake made sure the house was secure for the night. Nick usually stayed in one of the rooms upstairs as well, but since they were being cautious with Alyssa's safety, he was sleeping in Ian's downstairs bedroom tonight. Jake was taking the room next to the teenager, but instead of walking down the hallway, he followed Nick into his room and quietly shut the door behind them. Nick's eyes widened in surprise, but Jake cut off any hopeful thoughts he might be having. "I'm not staying . . ." He took a few steps forward, backing the kid up to the wall. Reaching down, the Dom cupped Nick's denim-covered cock and a satisfied leer appeared on his face as he got the reaction he wanted. "Just wanted to remind you, this . . ." He gave the growing crotch a squeeze, causing a low, sexy growl to emanate from Nick's throat. "This is mine and you will keep your hands off it tonight."

"Fuck! Are you serious?" He somehow managed to keep his exasperated voice low. "You come in here, get my fucking dick hard as a rock, and then tell me I can't do anything with it?"

Jake leaned forward and licked the shell of Nick's ear, pleased when a shiver coursed through the man's body. "I'm very serious," he whispered. "This is mine, Junior. Keep your hands off it or there'll be consequences. And believe me, I'll know if you disobeyed me."

He smirked as he backed away and pivoted toward the door. "Sweet dreams." As he exited the room, a chuckle escaped him when Nick's head thudded against the wall in frustration. Jake eased the door shut behind him. Educating his new submissive was going to be so much fun.

WHEN THE MEN came back inside and she heard Jake's calm, rumbling voice, Alyssa completely relaxed again and climbed into her bed. While Nick and Cain were nice, the real reason she trusted them was because Jake did. The company they worked for had been hired by her father last year, but once Jake had discovered why she ran away, he immediately offered to help her and her mom get away from her perverted father. Alyssa had been very leery when her mom called and said some man was coming to pick her up in Georgia, where she was staying with her mother's old college friend. Oliver Wagner had hated Joanna Lynch and forbade his wife to continue their friendship, but the women had gone against him and secretly kept in touch.

When Jake had arrived at Joanna's house, instead of demanding to come inside, he asked if there was a place where they could talk outside, out of view of the street. He then walked around the house and met them on the patio. Knowing what she'd gone through, and the fact he was a huge man, he'd made himself as unthreatening as possible to put her at ease. The three of them talked for a while and he told her all about himself—his time in the Navy as an elite SEAL and the company made up of former teammates that he worked for. He'd even told her that he was gay, which she didn't have a problem with at all. Alyssa had been sixteen at the time, but Jake talked to her like she was an adult who could make up her own mind on whether or not she trusted him.

After returning with her to Tampa, he had kept her in hiding until there was an opportunity to escape with her mother, when Oliver would be gone for hours, giving them a head start. Jake's friend Trudy, a psychologist, was involved in the group Friends of Patty. They had both believed her and promised to do everything they could so Alyssa never had to see her father again. A gynecologist had examined her to make sure she had no sexual diseases as a result of her years of abuse at the hands of her father. And when the right time came, Alyssa and her mother started a six-week journey of zig-zagging across the United States on their way to becoming Allison and Christine Watson.

But now she was back with Jake, hiding again. Her mother was dead and she had no family left in the world other than the one person who wanted her dead . . . or worse.

A loud bark of laughter came from the living room area and she recognized it as Jake's laugh. He didn't do it often, but when he did, it always made her smile. She rolled over, trying to find a comfortable spot. Jake promised to keep her safe, but he couldn't protect her forever. The only way she would feel completely safe was if her bastard father was dead. Until then, she'd always be looking over her shoulder, waiting for the moment when her world went to shit one more time.

———

GROANING, Nick woke up exactly how he'd fallen asleep late last night—on his stomach, hard, and frustrated—the result of some very erotic dreams of Jake. He pumped his hips a few times into the mattress, fighting the urge to reach down and take care of his aching cock. Of course, it was easier said than done. He prayed Jake would allow him some relief soon, otherwise, he'd be walking around with a serious case of blue-balls.

Rolling over, he stared down at the throbbing bulge in his boxer-briefs. "Down boy. There's nothing I can do about you this morning. At least not yet." And yes, he was now a whack-job, talking out loud to his dick, and it was barely twenty-fours since he'd last jacked off. God help him.

Shit! How was he supposed to take a fucking piss like this? He eyed the door to the short hall leading out to the kitchen, and then the one to the attached bath. It would be easy enough to lock the bedroom door and rub one out in the bathroom. He'd just have to be quiet about it. Hell, he was a Navy SEAL—stealth was part of his job. Jake said he'd know, but seriously? How the fuck would he?

Nick's hand inched toward his crotch, almost on its own will. The second his fingers brushed against his hard shaft, he knew he'd made his decision. He needed relief after dreaming of Jake all night, and he needed it now. The Dom would never know.

Kicking the sheet off his lower legs, he leapt off the bed and locked the bedroom door. Before heading to the bathroom, he paused to listen for signs that anyone else was awake yet. It was oh-six-fifteen, but the house was silent. Walking on the balls of his feet, he entered the bathroom and shut the door. Sitting on the back of the john was the toiletry bag he'd tossed there last night. Unzipping it, he quickly found a tube of lubricant. A small amount in his palm would hurry things along.

After dropping his briefs, he put the toilet lid down, then sat on the cold surface. He hesitated a moment, before cursing and wrapping his palm and fingers around his needy cock. Tightening his grip, he let out a sigh as his hand slid up and down the hard flesh. His head fell back on his shoulders and he concentrated on the rhythm of his hand— down, up, over, around, and down again. *Damn, that felt good.*

Nick closed his eyes and, in his imagination, replaced his hand with Jake's. The drag of flesh against flesh was sweet torture. Pre-cum oozed from the slit at the tip of his cock and he added it to the lubrication. With his other hand, he reached down and cupped his balls, rolling them gently. *Do you like that, Junior? Do you want your Master to let you cum?* "Fuck, yes!" he murmured. "Please!"

Seconds of pleasure turned to minutes. Part of him wanted to race for relief, but the other part wanted to savor the sensations. In his mind, he brought up the image of being on his hands and knees as Jake fucked his ass. His fingers gripped his shaft harder as he sped up the pace. Shifting down on the toilet seat, he was able to thrust his hips forward. His breathing and pulse increased as he felt his orgasm build. The muscles in his ripped abs, thighs, and ass tensed as a tingling shot from his lower spine to his groin. A few more pumps of his hand and he'd be there. *Please. Please let me . . .*

"*Now!*"

"Shit!" The curse was barely a whisper as Nick shot streams of hot semen onto his abs. Black dots appeared before his eyes and he gasped for oxygen. When his heart rate slowed to normal, he let out a sigh of relief, but it was short-lived as a dark blanket of guilt overcame him. For the first time in Nick's adult life, he was ashamed of his lack of restraint and jerking off. *Fuck!*

11

*J*ake rolled over and checked his cell for the time. Oh-six-forty-five. Stretching, he reached down and scratched his groin as he willed his morning wood down. Yeah, he could've had a quiet quickie with Nick last night, since Ian's bedroom was on the opposite side of the house from the occupied bedrooms. No one would've heard them, but whether Nick understood it or not, he was now a submissive-in-training. And that meant learning obedience and restraint.

After using the toilet and washing his hands, he threw on a T-shirt, pair of sweats, and his sneakers. With the extra men in the house guarding Alyssa, he could get a morning run in. There were a few paths through the woods that the team had placed distance markers on. Out to the final marker and back was a six-mile run, which was just what he needed to work off some of the sexual tension surging through his body. Ever since yesterday morning when Nick had begged him not to walk away, Jake had longed to do all sorts of dirty, nasty, wonderful things to him, but now was not the time. Alyssa's safety came first.

Opening the bedroom door, he looked to his left and was surprised to see the teenager's bedroom door was ajar. He was about to peek in when he heard her giggle coming from the living room area. What he found there wasn't what he expected. "Since when the heck do you cook?"

Carter lifted his gaze to Jake as Alyssa glanced over her shoulder from her stool at the kitchen island. "I've always been able to cook. I just seldom come across someone worthy of my culinary talents like sweet Alyssa here. And if you're going to be a jerk about it, you can make your own breakfast."

The young girl giggled again, and Jake shook his head in amazement. Not only was the U.S. dark operative cooking pancakes, but it seemed he'd won over the timid teenager in no time.

"I've been entertaining this pretty girl with my vast repertoire of daring and heroic adventures from around the globe."

Jake snorted as he opened the refrigerator and pulled out the container of orange juice. "You sound like Blackbeard the pirate. Don't believe a word he says, Alyssa. He's actually an insurance salesman and lies like a rug."

"An insurance salesman?" She narrowed her eyes at Carter as he flipped three pancakes off the electric griddle sitting on the island and onto a plate for her. "I knew you were conning me," she chastised, then rolled her eyes toward Jake. "He said he was a government spy, like James Bond."

After filling a glass, Jake smirked at his friend who shrugged his shoulders and gave the girl a sad, puppy-dog expression. "Who are you going to believe, me or Jake from State Farm?"

Orange juice burst from Jake's mouth and nose, and,

thankfully, into the sink. The acidity burned his throat and nostrils as he coughed and gasped for the air which didn't want to be drawn into his lungs. Carter's face turned tomato red as he roared with laughter and bent over holding his stomach, until he was almost as breathless as Jake was. Snatching a nearby dishtowel and wiping his face, Jake glared at the other man. "Thanks an effing lot," he croaked, wanting to say so much more to the asshole, but Alyssa's presence had him biting his tongue.

As it was, she was looking at both of them with a mix of confusion and amusement. "All right, fill me in, because I didn't get the joke."

Using the towel to wipe up the juice that hadn't made it into the sink, Jake shook his head. His voice was still hoarse from the liquid abuse. "It's from that insurance commercial, and a very bad joke."

"Hey!" Carter caught the damp towel which had been intentionally thrown at his head. "Any joke that makes the Reverend shoot orange juice out his nose is damn good. Score one for me."

"Reverend?" Alyssa asked around a bite of her pancakes. "Is that like a nickname, Jake, or are you really a priest or something?"

"Ha! No, sweetheart, I'm not a priest. It's my nickname from the Navy." Jake lifted the carton to pour himself another glass of orange juice, but thought better of it and turned to put it back in the fridge. "You don't get to choose it, it's given to you by your team. But I'll take 'Reverend' over some of the crazy names a bunch of my friends got."

He didn't know how, but before he spun back around he knew Nick had entered the room. It wasn't from any sound the kid had made because he walked as furtively as every other trained SEAL. Instead, the air crackled with electricity and made the hair on the back of Jake's neck tingle with awareness. He eyed the newcomer as Carter offered Nick some pancakes. The kid was fresh from a shower and appeared . . . relaxed and tense at the same time. *Hmmm.*

"No, thanks. I was going to go for a run, if no one minds."

Jake watched as Nick looked at everyone and everything but him. His Dom senses went on full alert. A shower before running? *Oh, Junior, you are in so much trouble.* "Not at all. As a matter of fact, I was on my way out for a run myself." He lifted an eyebrow at Carter. "You mind holding down the fort. Cain should be down soon." The spy shrugged his shoulders in the equivalent of "no problem" as he poured more batter on the griddle. "Thanks. I'll call Ian for an update when we get back. Come on, Junior, let's see how you do off the O-course."

Nick didn't look happy about suddenly having a running mate, but he didn't back down. Jake tossed him a bottled water from the fridge, then took one for himself. "Sound the alarm if you need us."

"No worries," Carter acknowledged as the two headed out the door.

Not saying another word, Jake descended the front steps, and then stretched to loosen his muscles. Nick stood a few feet away, doing the same. A few minutes later they were jogging at a warm-up pace down the dirt trail. At the half mile mark, Jake increased his speed and the kid did the same, staying abreast of him. Smiling to himself, the Dom plotted how he was going to punish his submissive for his disobedience. He was positive the kid had jacked off at some point, either late last night or early this morning.

One mile. *Hmm.* A cock cage would be ideal, but even if Jake had one with him, it wasn't practical due to their situation. Checking his watch for their time, he lengthened his stride. Beside him, Nick was already sweating, and he doubted it was from the exertion. It was a cool fall morning in the mountains, and as a trained Navy SEAL, Nick could do this exercise with a fifty-pound pack strapped to him and still wouldn't be breathing heavy yet.

Two miles. They were now clocking a seven-minute-mile pace. Maybe he could make a switch from one of the numerous types of trees in the area and tan the kid's ass. Ah, nope, that wouldn't work either. Jake didn't have any arnica gel with him for the temporary welts he wanted to leave on Nick's ass. And he couldn't have him in obvious pain when they returned to the house—beside the fact they hadn't discussed hard limits yet, so a switch was out.

Two-point-five miles. That put them past the solar powered cameras Brody had set up as part of the house's security system. No chance of anyone seeing them now unless it was some idiot out hunting, and on this section of the mountain that was very rare. Jake slowed his pace until he stopped altogether next to a large boulder on the right side of the path. Having gone a little further, Nick turned around and jogged back to him. "What's wrong? Got a cramp?"

Leaning against the cool rock, Jake crossed his arms and stared at Nick's face, letting him see the disappointment in his eyes. He dropped his voice, making it stern and threatening. "Something you want to tell me?"

"What?" Nick licked his lips in a sure sign of nervousness.

Jake's eyes narrowed further. "Don't lie to me, Nicky-boy. You'll just be digging yourself a deeper hole than the one you're already in. Now, tell me . . . did you do something you were ordered not to do?"

"Shit," he spat out, then ran a hand down his face. Jake

stood there, waiting him out, as he paced back and forth, clearly fighting an internal battle. After a few moments, he halted and threw his hands up into the air. "I'm sorry, all right? I woke up as hard as that fucking rock you're leaning against and couldn't help myself. I jacked off this morning. Is that what you fucking want to hear? I fucking jacked off . . . and it fucking sucked."

Surprised, Jake raised an eyebrow. He hadn't expected that last part and got the impression Nick was just as stunned by his revelation. "Present for me."

His hands gesturing outward, Nick sounded incredulous. "What? Right here?"

"Yes, subbie, right here, right now." The threat of further punishment was in his growling tone, and he knew the kid was aware of it. Jake waited in silence. After a count of three, Nick inhaled deeply and let it out as he sank to his knees on a blanket of pine needles and multi-colored autumn leaves. His eyes were downcast with his head bowed and knees shoulder-width apart. Jake was about to correct him, but Nick seemed to suddenly remember what was missing from the Dom's instructions on presenting and placed his hands in an "at-ease" position at the small of his back. *Shit!* For someone who had never presented himself to a Dom before, he'd done a pretty good job of getting it right. Jake's cock hardened painfully at the sight of Nick's gorgeous body in submission.

Pushing off the rock, he stepped toward his sub, who didn't move a muscle. He walked around, checking the posture, before stopping behind him and running his fingers through the jet-black strands of Nick's hair. "You do that very well, Nicky-boy. It almost makes me wish I didn't have to punish you."

12

A shiver shot through Nick's veins and muscles, and he leaned into Jake's touch. Why? What was it about this man that made him want to beg for forgiveness? How was he supposed to be what Jake wanted, when he hadn't a clue as to what *he* even wanted? This was all so fucking new and weird to him. Yeah, he'd observed a lot of D/s couples at The Covenant, but there was so much to the lifestyle that he didn't understand. He clearly hadn't thought this whole thing through when he agreed to give it a try. Part of him wanted to stand and tell Jake to forget it—this wasn't for him—but it was the other part which wanted to please the man that had him staying on his knees, waiting for the next command.

Behind him, Jake's voice rumbled low and sexy. "You do that very well, Nicky-boy. It almost makes me wish I didn't have to punish you."

The praise made Nick's breath catch in his chest, but it was the unknown punishment which had his heart beating faster . . . and his cock lengthening. "What . . ." He swallowed the lump in his throat. "What's my punishment . . . Sir?"

Jake circled around and stopped right in front of Nick, his feet inches from the knees on the ground. The hand in Nick's hair clenched, pulling the strands until he had no choice but to lift his chin up. His eyes met Jake's green ones which shimmered like emeralds.

"Due to our current situation, I haven't made a decision about that yet. But don't worry, I'll think of something. For now . . ." He pulled on the string of his sweatpants. "You owe me. You're going to suck my cock and swallow every drop I give you."

His mouth suddenly watering again, Nick's gaze dropped to the stunning erection that appeared before him. All thoughts of uncertainty and punishments fled from his mind. Jake widened his stance and gripped his cock, tilting it toward Nick's mouth. Pre-cum pearled at the slit and glistened from the sunlight seeping through the trees. His hands were still behind his back, and somehow, he knew he should leave them there for now. Parting his lips, he leaned forward and took Jake into his mouth, swirling his tongue around the thick girth.

"Ahh, fuck, Junior. Your mouth is sweet fucking heaven. Suck me."

He suctioned his lips around the shaft, and sucked in deep, drawing a growl from Jake's throat. *Fuck!* How could he have forgotten how delicious this man was? Memories of the one and only other time he'd given Jake a blowjob came rushing back to him. It'd been in the shower at the hotel, and he'd loved every minute of it. He also remembered what he'd done which made the Dom moan in pure bliss. Taking the cock to the back of his mouth and breathing through his nose, he swallowed hard, closing his throat around the tip.

"Fuck, yeah! Mmmm, fucking do that again, Junior. Damn, right like that. You can use your hands now. Make me want to lose control, baby."

Nick brought his hands to the front and wrapped one around Jake's dick while cupping his balls with the other. Gently, he rolled and tugged on them before using his middle finger to stroke the sensitive tissue between them and Jake's asshole. All the while, his head bobbed up and down as Jake fucked his mouth. The soothing sounds of nature surrounded them—birds chatting, animals scurrying, and leaves rustling. But Nick only focused on the sounds stemming from his lover—gasps of pleasure, sexy growls, and tortured moans. The hand in his hair tightened, lighting up the nerves in his scalp.

The Dom threw his head back. "Damn, baby, I could fuck your mouth all fucking day and never get tired of it."

Pumping his hips, Jake drove his cock to the back of Nick's throat, over and over. Nick licked and sucked the steel-hard shaft, encouraged by the words of praise. His middle finger inched closer to Jake's anus with each stroke, and he felt the man's body tense in anticipation of his impending orgasm. Pressing on the tight rim and sucking hard at the same time got him what he wanted—his lover's roar of ecstasy as jets of hot, salty cum shot into Nick's mouth and throat. He swallowed rapidly several times, not wanting to spill a single drop, just as Jake had ordered. He may have screwed up and disappointed him earlier, but he was damn well going to try and redeem himself.

The grip on Nick's hair eased as Jake's hips slowed and his cock softened. Nick released him and sat back on his haunches. Licking his lips, he lifted his gaze to Jake's face and the satisfaction he saw there was more than he could've asked for. Jake reached for the waistband of his sweats and stumbled back a few steps to lean against the rock again. "Damn, I forgot how talented that mouth of yours is." Securing the strings of his sweatpants again, his eyes dropped to Nick's prominent hard-on. "You won't be getting any relief from me, Junior, and you better not think of taking care of that on your own again. I meant what I said—that's my property and *I'll* decide when my property gets to cum. And just because you gave me one fucking awesome blowjob, doesn't mean I've forgotten about your punishment."

"I know. And I'm really sorry, Jake." He gestured with his hand to the two of them. "This is going to take some getting used to."

Jake cocked his head and studied him a moment. "If you don't want this to continue, tell me now, Nick. I won't be pissed, but I will be if you're saying yes just so we can fuck while you're here. The lifestyle is important to me. I need that control. And any relationship I have, the power exchange has to be a part of it. So, tell me now. Is this a game to you? Or are you willing to submit to my control over the sexual part of our relationship?"

"Why?" Nick hadn't meant for the question to come out, but there it was. Jake's gaze narrowed, and he rushed to explain his question. "I mean, I don't know what the fuck I'm doing, but I'm not playing a game. And I want to know . . . why is this so important to you? There has to be a reason."

Seconds passed as the two men studied each other. Nick saw the pain in Jake's eyes and wished he understood why it was there. He suddenly realized he didn't know a lot about his lover's past. He knew the basics—his mother was alive, his father was dead, and his only sibling had taken over the family pub, while Jake had gone into the Navy, eventually becoming a SEAL. But other than all that, and the fact that he was a Dom, Nick knew very little else about him. He watched Jake's expression become shuttered, and knew he wasn't going to get any answers to his question . . . at least not now.

Jake pushed off the rock and extended his hand. Accepting it, Nick let the man haul him to his feet. "You're not going to answer me, are you?"

Stepping back on the trail, Jake shook his head. "Some other time, Nick. Some other time."

Letting out a disappointed sigh, Nick stared at Jake's back as the man, literally and figuratively, ran away.

IT WAS a few minutes before noon when Jake stood on the porch, arms crossed, as a dark SUV parked next to Carter's vehicle. Earlier, he'd finished his six-mile run alone and was still trying to convince himself that was what he'd wanted. Nick hadn't followed him, instead, taking a different route. By the time the kid had returned to the house, Jake had been emerging from his shower. It was obvious to him that both of them were trying to act as normal as possible, but as far as he could tell, no one else noticed the tension in the house. He didn't know about Nick, but for him, it was difficult to pretend there was nothing wrong. He was going to fuck this up, just like every other relationship he'd had over the years. Great sex—check. Exert dominance—check. Open heart and fall in love—never going to happen. But this time, the thought of his lover walking away was something which made him fill with regret.

Fuck! He should've known better. One of the biggest mistakes of his life was going to Nick's hotel room that night.

He needed to end this before things went to shit. Nick would one day retire from the Navy and come work with his brothers. Jake didn't want anything coming between his team and him—especially the bosses' brother. Dev and Ian would kick his ass—not about getting involved with Nick, but for fucking it up and screwing with the dynamics of the team. Trust was a major part of that. If you couldn't trust your teammate in everyday shit, how were you supposed to trust him when it truly mattered? If it came down to Nick or him, Jake knew he would be the one who had to man up and offer to leave Trident. *Damn.* Instead of finding reasons to work things out with the kid, all he was doing was adding to the list of why he shouldn't. And yet part of him couldn't do it—he couldn't end it. *He was so fucked.*

The front doors of the SUV swung open and two men climbed out. One was Tiny, a huge, bald, black man and, according to the ladies, a big mush. The other guy was one of Chase Dixon's operatives, Doug Henderson. It was good to see him back to work after he'd taken a bullet to the chest six months earlier while guarding Jenn Mullins. She'd been kidnapped by dirty DEA agents who were after Ian's fiancée. They wanted to use Angie as a trap for her best friend, an undercover agent, who'd been killed during the women's rescue, along with the other two agents. Henderson's partner that day also hadn't been lucky, dying instantly from a gunshot wound to the head.

After retrieving several bags of Chinese food—Tiny's favorite—from the backseat, the pair approached Jake who met them at the bottom of the stairs. "Hey. How was the trip?"

Tiny gave him a fist bump. "A little late taking off due to a passing storm, but the Blackhawk pilot was able to make up the time in the air. He was going to catch some Z's after refueling. You'll find him by hanger four." Jake wasn't surprised that they hadn't flown up in the Trident jet, since Ian had told him it had landed in Tampa this morning with the rest of the team. Their pilot would need some rest after the flight from South America.

"Thanks." He turned toward the other man and shook his hand. "D.H., nice to have you back. Everything in working order?" Henderson had been cleared for light duty recently and since there was less than one percent chance of anyone finding Alyssa all the way up here, Jake was okay with the former Marine sharpshooter being on guard duty.

The guy grunted and rubbed his chest where the bullet had entered him. "Yeah. Still trying to get back up to my fighting weight, but at least I can blow up balloons for my nieces and nephews again. A collapsed lung and almost bleeding to death sucks."

"I'll take your word for it. Come on inside and I'll introduce you to Alyssa. She's a sweet kid, but wary around men . . . with good reason."

Ascending the steps behind him, Tiny growled. "Yeah. Ian gave us the basics. When you finally put the squeeze on her perverted sperm donor, let me know. It's been a while since I rearranged someone's face and made him choke on his balls."

"Stand in line, my friend. Stand in line."

Jake led them inside to where the other three men and Alyssa were sitting at the dining table, playing Texas Hold 'Em. And judging by the amount of chips in front of them, the teenager and Carter were winning.

"Jack high straight, little lady," Nick taunted, laying down his hand. "Beat that."

Alyssa frowned, but even as he approached, Jake could tell she didn't mean it. Winking at Carter, her grin reappeared as she flipped her cards over. "Full house! Queens over twos. Sorry, *little man*, but you lose."

The guys all laughed except for Nick, who slapped his forehead and stared at the better hand while letting out a string of PG-13 curses. "Dang! A full house? Are you frigging kidding me? Who the heck dealt that hand?"

Tossing his own losing hand on the table, Carter smirked. "Uh, that would be you, ass-hat."

"Hey, watch the language in front of the lady, dirtbag."

While stacking her newly won chips, Alyssa rolled her eyes. "Please . . . I'm seventeen. I've heard a lot worse than that."

Jake placed his hands on her shoulders and she tilted her head back to look at him. "That may be, sweetheart, but it's still not polite to curse like that in front of a lady."

"He's right, honey," Carter acknowledged. "Please, forgive me for being rude. There are times I forget I wasn't raised in a barn." Placing his wide-spread hand on his chest, he gave her that puppy-dog look again—the one that had women, old and young, absolving his sins.

She shrugged her shoulders at the spy's admission of guilt. "It's okay. Apology accepted." She glanced back up at Jake, worry and sadness filling her eyes once more. "You're leaving now, aren't you?"

"Yeah, sweetheart, but we're going to eat first. That food smells too good to pass up." He wanted to give her a little time to feel comfortable with the newcomers before he left. Carter would be around for a few more hours as well before heading out to whatever mission Uncle Sam was sending him on next. "Then Nick, Cain, and I are going to find a way to make sure you never have to worry about your father again. In the meantime, I want you to meet my friends, Travis Daultry, otherwise known as Tiny, and Doug Henderson. They're going to keep you safe here."

Warily, she eyed the two men standing behind Nick's chair.

Knowing his size was intimidating, Tiny gave her a single nod of his head and one of his signature smiles. "Hello, Miss Alyssa. Don't think I'll let you beat me at poker like these pansies. I don't take any prisoners."

Jake leaned down and whispered in her ear. "When he rubs his nose, he's bluffing."

A giggle escaped her as Tiny's eyes narrowed at his friend, but his scoff sounded more teasing than harsh. "What'd you tell her, Donovan? You know I can whoop your butt, just like when we were kids."

Smiling, he held up his hands in surrender. "Just telling her to take it easy on you, big guy."

Laughing and joking, the poker players cleared the table and started to spread out the containers of food while Jake and Tiny retrieved paper plates, utensils, napkins, and drinks for everyone. Before sitting at the table, Tiny pulled a phone out of his pocket and handed it to Alyssa. "This is so you can call Jake if you need to talk to him. I already texted the number to him, so he has it, and his number is programmed in for you, as well as Trident Security's main number. Keep it with you at all times, because it also has a tracking device in it, in case we get separated for some reason."

That'd been another thing Jake had thought would help her feel more comfortable while he was gone. He wanted her to know she could call him anytime she didn't feel safe. He'd discovered last night during their video game rally that she'd been seeing a rape counselor with positive results for the past year. As long as a man didn't remind her of her bastard father, she was able to relax, unless he was a "creep-a-zoid," as she put it. And out of all the guards he could've picked to watch over her, he knew Tiny's personality would win her over very quickly, with Henderson being a close second. Both men were marshmallows when it came to women, yet relentless Rottweilers if any of those women were threatened.

Jake was halfway through his second helping of beef lo mien when his cell rang and Pete Archer's name appeared across the screen. Rising from the table, he headed out to the porch, answering the call as he went. "Hey, Pete. Any updates?"

"Yeah. Just heard a local news report. Apparently, a woman's body, wrapped in a rug, was thrown off a backroad overpass into the Arkansas River near Pueblo yesterday. Whoever dumped her hadn't counted on the two guys fishing under the bridge. They hooked the rug and called the sheriff when they noticed the body inside. No ID yet and they haven't released a description, but unconfirmed reports say she'd been shot in the face."

Jake sat down on the top step of the porch and sighed. "So, it's most likely Carrie. Well, we knew she was dead, so this doesn't come as a surprise to us, but I'd love to see Wagner's face when the cops knock on his door to tell him his allegedly deceased wife was alive. And now dead again."

"So, would I. Anyway, I'll keep my ears open and let you know if I hear anything new."

The door behind Jake opened and soft footfalls followed. Glancing over his shoulder, he saw it was Nick. "Thanks, Pete."

"No problem, Reverend. Give Alyssa my love and stay safe."

"Will do. Talk to you later." Standing, Jake disconnected

the call and faced Nick who was sporting a neutral expression . . . one that bothered Jake, but he wouldn't admit it. "Sounds like they found the mother's body, but no positive ID yet. I don't want to tell Alyssa until we have it though."

Nick shoved his hands into the front pockets of his jeans. "Okay. That makes sense. So, what's next?"

"We figure out how to take down Wagner once and for all, without needing her to testify, if possible."

Nodding, the kid agreed. "Let's do it."

13

Frustrated, Jake hung up his cell phone for the third time since they'd hit the road an hour ago. The first call was to Trudy, his contact at Friends of Patty, who told him that, unfortunately, there was little chance of figuring out which contacts Alyssa and her mother had encountered on their journey to a new life. It was set up that way to safeguard against weak links. They were not supposed to tell anyone who they handed the package off to, even if it was another member of the organization who was asking. But the whole point became unnecessary, anyway, during his second call, which had been from Brody.

The geek had checked out a possible lead, which occurred to Jake while on the second half of his run earlier, after he'd pushed Nick from his mind. While Brody hadn't been able to trace any calls Carrie Wagner had made on her throwaway cell phone, he'd been able to check the incoming calls to her friend's landline phone in Georgia. And sure enough there'd been a call to the friend originating from a Canon City, Colorado cell tower. When Jake suggested they pay the woman a visit, Brody had given him the bad news. She'd been found stabbed to death in her home after she didn't show up for work three days ago. Someone must have been monitoring her calls, and when Carrie, for some unknown stupid reason, had contacted her, it'd sealed the fate of both women. Thankfully, Alyssa's fate hadn't been the same, and Jake was determined to keep it that way. The Trident team would protect her with their own lives.

The final call, which he'd just disconnected from, had been from Carter. The spy had heard from his associate, Jordyn, and Jake's interest was piqued when his friend's earlier sunny attitude toward the woman had soured. The only reason Jake could think of was, even though the female operative had agreed to help them after hearing Alyssa's story, the rest of the conversation hadn't gone the way his friend had hoped it would. Carter had given Jake's cell number to Jordyn because she apparently didn't want to talk to her one-time lover again. Jake would give his left nut to know what was going on between those two since Carter was a man who had women falling at his feet 24/7—submissive or not.

"So, is she going to do it?" Driving the SUV back to Spartanburg, South Carolina, where their plane was waiting, Nick glanced at Jake. *Talk about a soured attitude.* Jake would have to wait until they were alone again to try and smooth things over with the kid. In the back seat, Cain leaned forward to listen in on the conversation.

"Yeah, but it'll take her a day or two to get to Tampa. No clue where she's coming from. Carter called Brody to have him send her the floor plans and alarm info on Wagner's house. She'll call me when the job is done."

Cain grinned. "When she does, give her my number. A combination firecracker, cat-burglar, and assassin is a woman I never would've considered while in the Secret Service, but, damn, does she sound hot.

Snorting, Jake shook his head in amusement. "Dude, I'm not questioning your sexual expertise, but if Master Carter can't handle her, I doubt anyone can. There isn't one female submissive at the club who doesn't sigh when they say his name."

"Maybe, but I'd be more than willing to give it a fucking shot if she fits the image I have in mind. I'm picturing about five-foot-five, a size four or six, long dark hair she keeps in a ponytail most of the time, and exotic-looking eyes. Add in the fact she's probably trained in martial arts and almost every weapon out there and, yeah, I'm fucking interested."

Jake chuckled, knowing the new guy was going to fit in quite well with both Trident and The Covenant. As far as he knew, two more of the six Omega Team operatives were Doms and the new female chopper pilot was a switch, meaning she was a top or bottom depending on her mood or current relationship. The others had no issues with working in the vicinity of the club, nor had any problem with going inside if needed. And whether they were members or not, they still had to sign the non-disclosure oath everyone else did. It'd been part of the interview process and psychological exams the team candidates had gone through. Ian and Devon rightfully refused to hire anyone who could possibly endanger the club's membership with exposure. If at any time during the interview, background check, and testing process, a candidate showed any form of bigotry or closed-mindedness toward the lifestyle, gays, or the opposite sex in general, their file was tossed into the garbage can. Jake knew at least two candidates had been disqualified for those reasons.

He eyed Cain. "If the opportunity comes up, I'll point her in your direction. After that you're on your own."

"Sounds good to me. So, what happens when we get back to Tampa? How are we going after Alyssa's sperm donor?"

Sighing, Jake grabbed his water from the center console and took a sip. "For now, you're heading back to the compound for more training." He chuckled at the other man's muttered curse. "Sorry, dude, but Ian is a stickler for training. Don't worry though, if we need backup for anything, you're in. Anyway, I'm going to check in with some of my informants. It's been a while since I went looking for any info on Wagner. Then we wait until this Jordyn retrieves the photos and videos. Hopefully, by that point we have a plan to bring the bastard down. I'm hoping Jordyn can find something else in the safe that we can get him on, instead of having Alyssa testify. She doesn't want to do it and I understand her reluctance."

"So do I. But I would love to tell everyone on his future cell block what a fucking pervert he is. You know how much most inmates hate child molesters."

Nick and Jake both agreed. Molesters were the scum of the earth even to other criminals. None of them would be surprised if Wagner was shafted after being beaten and raped himself, letting the bastard know what if felt like to be helpless at another person's hands. Jake was determined to make that a possibility by putting the bastard away for what he'd done to the sweet teenager. The sooner the better.

"We've got a tail."

Nick glanced into the passenger side-view mirror and

spotted the dark SUV Jake was referring to. "Two people in front, can't see anyone in the rear. When did they latch on to us?"

Snorting, Jake changed lanes without giving the men following them any indication they'd been spotted. "As soon as we left the compound. Idiots couldn't have been more obvious if they fucking tried."

After dropping Cain off, and giving Ian and Dev updates, Nick was surprised when Jake invited him along to find one of his informants. After the incident in the woods earlier, he was afraid Jake would shut him down for good. There was so much he needed to learn about the man and his lifestyle, but if Jake wasn't forthcoming with information, who the hell could Nick ask?

"You still carrying?"

He glanced at Jake. "Yeah, why?"

A smirk came over the man's face as he flipped on the left turn signal. "Because once I find a more secluded place, I think we'll have a chat with these boys. Sound like fun?"

"As long as I don't have to tell my lieutenant, then count me in." Yeah, the Navy frowned on their SEALs getting in trouble on U.S. soil. But this was important to Jake, therefore, it was important to Nick. "Let's do it."

Hitting the Bluetooth feature on his steering wheel, Jake instructed the female voice prompt to dial a number. When the call connected, he laid out his plan.

Seven minutes and many turns later, Jake found a rundown area, void of witnesses. Accelerating quickly to get their tail's attention, he made his way across an empty parking lot, heading to the rear of an abandoned strip mall. As expected, the SUV sped up as well. After circling around to the back of the building, Jake turned the wheel hard while slamming on the brakes, sending his truck into a hundred and eighty-degree spin, before stopping it and throwing the gear shift into park. Nick and Jake leapt from the vehicle, weapons drawn, using their doors for cover, as the SUV rounded the corner and came to a screeching halt. Before the driver could put it in reverse, Brody's Ford F-150 boxed the vehicle in. The geek and Marco exited, also with guns drawn, and approached the driver and passenger doors, keeping a fair distance to the sides in case Jake and Nick needed to open fire.

When Brody was almost parallel with the driver, he raised his voice to be heard through the closed windows. "Show your hands!"

After a moment's hesitation and a dirty look, the driver held up his hands with the passenger following suit. With his gun still pointed at the driver's head, Brody gave his next commands. "Moving nice and slow, roll down all the windows." Once they were down, the team was assured there was no one else in the vehicle. "Open the doors slowly. Get out and lay down on the ground. Any sudden movements and I'll pump you full of lead." Okay, a little dramatic, but Nick knew it was not a false statement.

With Jake's eye on the passenger, Nick kept the driver in his weapon's sights, praying the guy didn't do something stupid. The last thing they needed was a repeat of a nineteenth century gunfight. This wasn't the Wild West in Tombstone, Arizona—it was modern day Tampa, Florida. And the law was less forgiving around here.

Both doors opened and the men exited, hands in full view, as they dropped to the ground. "You're making a big mistake," the driver growled at Brody, who smirked as he rounded to the man's feet.

"See, that's where you're wrong, ass-hat. Your mistake

was getting out of fucking bed this morning. Hands behind your head and lock your fingers together."

Nick approached the driver, keeping his weapon's muzzle level with the guy's head. On the other side, Jake was doing the same with the passenger. When they were close enough to their targets that they couldn't miss if things went to shit, their other two teammates re-holstered their weapons. Kneeling next to the driver's hips, Brody reached up and slapped a handcuff around one wrist, bringing the guy's right arm around to the small of his back. The left arm followed and the other cuff was closed with a *snick*. Nick couldn't see what Marco had taken off the other guy, but a gloved Egghead pocketed the S&W 9mm semi-automatic, Kahr .380 pistol, and switchblade he removed from the driver's body as he patted him down. These goons had some serious hardware on them. Once both men were secure and relieved of their weapons, as well as their cell phones, Jake and Nick holstered their own handguns.

On the passenger side of the SUV, Jake growled at his suspect, "All right, asshole, what did Wagner hire you to do?"

"I don't know what you're talking about."

The man's bravado and false ignorance earned him a boot to the ribs from Marco, and Nick smirked when he heard the satisfying *crack* and grunt from several feet away.

Jake eyed Brody over the hood of the vehicle. "Is your guy any smarter than this idiot?"

"*Hmm.* Let me see." The grin spreading across the geek's face told Nick he lived for moments like this. It was a guy thing, as well as a SEAL thing—a chance to kick the ass of someone who deserved it was always welcome. Leaning down, Brody grabbed a handful of hair, ignoring the driver's yelp of pain. "Are you smarter than your buddy, fucktard? You want to tell us why you were tailing my friends here?"

"Fuck you!"

"I was hoping you would say that." Nick winced, then chuckled when Brody shoved the guy's face back into the pavement, breaking his nose. The driver screamed in agony. "Damn, that had to hurt. Sorry, Jake. This asshole isn't any smarter. It's your guy's turn to try and grow some balls and brains."

Whatever Marco did to his thug on the other side of the SUV elicited a screech worthy of a girl meeting her teen idol, followed by begging . . . lots and lots of begging. "Please! Oh, fuck, stop! All right! I'll tell you what you want to know, just . . . just get him off me! Please!"

Jake nodded toward his teammate and the screaming dropped several octaves to groans. "Start talking."

The passenger's words were raspy and pain-filled. "W-Wagner and Allen want the girl. We were s-supposed to follow you, hoping you would lead us to her. T-that's all we were told to do and I don't know why they want her."

Snarling, Jake bent at the waist. "I know why, asshole. Wagner's a fucking pervert who's been raping his daughter since she was twelve years old. He's also on my fuckers-I-want-to-destroy list, before I cut off his dick, shove half of it up his ass and the other half down his fucking throat. Now, unless you want to be added to that list, I suggest you turn down any other fucking jobs he offers you and forget we ever had this talk. Understand?"

There was a long pause, then a screech again. "All right! All right! I understand!"

Brody kicked the driver none to softly in the ribs. "What about you, fucktard? You understand?"

"Fuck! Yeah, I get it."

Ten minutes later, after un-cuffing the men, forcing them to strip to their birthday suits, and duct taping them together face-to-face, Marco and Brody stuffed them into the rear of the SUV. Meanwhile, Jake made a call to one of Trident's contacts in the Tampa P.D. to come and release the two assholes in about fifteen minutes or so, long after the teammates were gone. The weapons that'd been confiscated, along with the drugs Nick had found in the glove-compartment, were left for the police to take care of, but Brody kept both of their cell phones to be reviewed later for other contacts. After a quick check to make sure they were leaving no evidence of their own presence, the four operatives took off in their vehicles, heading in opposite directions.

14

*C*licking his seatbelt back on, Nick glanced at Jake. "Back to finding your snitch?"

"Yeah. It's what . . ." He checked the dashboard clock. "Almost eighteen hundred. He should be getting out of work in a few minutes, so hopefully we can catch him." Silence filled the air, making the tension between them grow. If Jake didn't do something, it was going to be a major distraction at a time when they both needed their heads on straight. "Nick . . . I'm sorry I blew you off earlier."

The kid smirked and snorted. "Funny . . . I thought I was the one who blew you."

He couldn't help the amused grin which spread across his face. "That you did, Junior. And very well, I might add." He paused before getting serious again and letting out a weary sigh. "I hate to sound cliché, but you're not the problem. It's me. I've got shit buried so far down inside me that I don't know if I'll ever be rid of it. I've never spoken to anyone about it, either—not the team, a boyfriend, a submissive, a shrink, or a priest, so don't take offense."

"You know, they say confession is good for the soul, or are you just going to suffer in a lonely silence for the rest of your life?"

Good question. Was he? "I don't know. I honestly don't. But with all this shit with Wagner going on, I can't focus on my problems. Neither one of us can afford to be distracted. I just . . . can you let it go for now?"

Mulling over the request, Nick hesitated a moment, then cocked his head to the side in reluctant agreement. "Yeah. I can. But after this crap with Alyssa is over, I'm going to want answers, Jake. I may not know a lot about the lifestyle, but I do know communication is a major part of it. Throwing your words from this morning back at you—is this just a game to you? Am I a convenient fling who'll be tossed aside after I head back to California?"

Pulling into a gas station, Jake parked and turned off the engine. "You're right. Communication is a big part of it. And the only games I play are ones that are mutually agreed upon." He opened his door and climbed out with Nick doing the same on the passenger side. And while both dropped the subject for now, it didn't go unnoticed to either of them that he hadn't answered the second question.

A few minutes later, sitting in the diner across the street from the gas station where Jake's snitch worked, Nick tried to appear relaxed and as non-threatening as possible. While the nineteen-year-old kid was comfortable with Jake, he was still wary with the stranger at their table. Not wanting to make things any worse, Nick remained silent and let Jake do his thing.

From what Jake had told him, Todd Wheeler was a kid who had fallen through the cracks of the system when his single mother died at the hand of an abusive boyfriend.

Wheeler had been sixteen at the time and placed in several foster homes, each one worse than the last. After the third one, the kid ran away, hit the streets and turned to drugs to ease his emotional pain. About a year ago, Jake had come across him one night outside the YMCA where he'd been playing basketball with some guys. The kid had been looking for cars to break into for money or anything he could sell. Luckily for Wheeler, Jake had been the one to catch him and not one of the cops he'd been with.

Something about the lost, strung-out, skinny kid had gotten to him. Instead of turning him in, Jake took him to his brother's pub and fed him. It had taken a few weeks for Wheeler to realize Jake was one of the good guys and wasn't looking for anything in return. The kid started providing his benefactor street information in exchange for cash or food. After a while, when Wheeler took Jake up on his offer to help him get off the streets, the Dom had been relieved. He found the kid a job, a studio apartment, a drug counselor, and got him enrolled in a class to obtain his GED. Aside from one brief, remorseful setback with the drugs a few months ago, the kid seemed to be on his way to a better life.

The waitress placed a greasy bacon cheeseburger and fries down in front of Todd and walked away. After spotting a cockroach when they first sat down, Nick passed on eating anything there. It seemed as if Jake had spotted the same insect or wasn't hungry, because he'd declined to order as well. While the kid began to dig into his dinner, Jake got to the point of their meeting. "Do you know who Oliver Wagner is?"

Swallowing a huge bite of his burger which Nick expected him to choke on, Todd nodded. "Owns a bunch of laundromats, one of those dollar stores, a landscaping business, and a few other stores and shit around the city. Some of them a little shady, but he's got political contacts, so he gets away with it. Treats his employees like crap, too."

"I'm aware of all that. What I need to know is, does he have a new right-hand man? Someone to do his dirty work? The guy he was using last year is serving time for drug possession and I don't know who the replacement is."

Through another mouthful of food, this one smaller than the first one, Todd answered, "Yeah. Some dude named something Allen. Greg or Craig or something like that."

When Jake's eyes narrowed at the name, Nick spoke for the first time. "You know him?"

"Not sure," he answered. "The name sounds familiar, but I can't place it. I'll see what Brody can dig up on the guy." Sliding out of the booth, Jake pulled out some money to cover Todd's dinner plus a tip and left it on the table. "Ask around. See if you can find out anything that has to do with his wife and daughter—a hit may have been ordered."

While Nick stood as well, Todd looked up in surprise, the burger paused inches from his open mouth. "The ones who disappeared without a trace last year?"

"Yeah. Call me if you hear anything, and stay out of trouble."

"Where's the fun in that?"

With a soft smack to Todd's head for his smart mouth, Jake told the kid to watch his back, and then exited the diner with Nick on his heels.

It wasn't long before Jake pulled into the parking lot of his condo. He'd mentioned he had some phone calls to make to Tiny and Brody, then planned on throwing together something for Nick and him to eat. Halfway into a parking space, he braked suddenly. "Shit. Forgot. I was supposed to go food shopping the other day. I've got nothing in the house to eat."

Nick shrugged. "I can go grab us a pizza while you make the phone calls. That is, if you don't mind me taking your truck."

Leaving the Suburban idling, he climbed out of the driver's seat. "There's a place a few blocks up that way," he pointed to the road heading east, "called Mama Rosa's. I'll eat anything on a pie but anchovies. That's Boomer's thing and it grosses the rest of us out."

Nick climbed over the console and frowned as Jake pulled out his wallet. "I got it. Dinner's on me."

Jake seemed about to argue, but then relented. "Thanks. It's condo 112 on the ground floor, just past the stairwell."

Driving away, he was glad Jake hadn't insisted on paying. While he was willing to submit to the Dom in their sexual relationship, he wanted Jake to treat him as an equal outside of the bedroom. He didn't think he could agree to have it any other way between them. *One step at a time, Nicky-boy*

The dinner run took a little longer than expected due to Mama Rosa's being overrun by a bunch of teenagers celebrating their high school soccer team's win against their biggest rival. Parking Jake's truck, Nick shut off the engine, then grabbed the pizza and beer from the passenger seat. It was almost eight p.m. Maybe, if there weren't any new leads they needed to check out, they could spend a quiet evening vegging on the couch together and talking . . . among other things. Striding through the parking lot, he kept his head on swivel. It wasn't that he was expecting trouble, but the need to inspect his surroundings had been ingrained into his psyche from years in the military and combat. As he rounded the corner of the stairwell, he noticed a man about to knock on a condo door. The number on the door was 112 —Jake's unit.

"Can I help you?"

The man turned and Nick came face-to-face with the asshole—Drew, wasn't it? —who'd been trying to set up a date with Jake in the airport. He wasn't bad-looking, with his fit physique, blond hair, and brown eyes, but Nick was having a hard time being this close to one of Jake's former lovers—especially one with an arrogant look on his face. His skin bristled with jealousy and annoyance as the guy arched an eyebrow and regarded him with noticeable distain.

"No, I don't think you can. I'm here to see someone, not that it's any of your business."

If Nick hadn't hated the guy from the moment he saw Jake talking to him a few days ago, then he did now. He stepped just inside the asshole's personal space, with the only thing stopping him being the pizza he was balancing in one hand. "Well, since you're obviously here to see Jake, then, yeah, it is my business. He already has plans for tonight, tomorrow, and every other day in the future, so why don't *you* take a fucking hike."

Instead of taking the advice, Drew crossed his arms and glared back at Nick, who was thrilled, since he was dying for a reason to beat the shit out of the guy. While they were the same height, Nick was broader in the shoulders and chest, and about five years younger. Top it all off with his training and he could take the jackass down in a heartbeat.

"Listen, kid. I don't know who the fuck you are and I really don't care. Jake and I have had a thing going for a long time. You're obviously just a worthless fling he had while we worked a few things out. And since I'm back, you can take the fucking hike."

To punctuate his statement, Drew knocked the pizza to

the ground, and that's all the encouragement Nick needed. He dropped the twelve-pack of cans from his left hand and, at the same time, swung his right fist at the asshole's jaw, hearing a satisfying *crack* as he connected. Drew stumbled back a few steps, but didn't fall. Instead, he bent at the waist and charged, catching Nick in the gut. *Damn, this is going to be fun!*

15

After checking the time, Jake felt a wave of concern hit him. Nick had been gone for a while and should've been back by now. The pizza place was only three blocks away. Normally, he wouldn't be worried, but with Wagner's goons out there, he wasn't taking any chances. Dialing Nick's cell, Jake mentally cursed when it went to voicemail. "Hey, Junior, hope you're on your way back. I'm starving."

Disconnecting the call, he texted Ian with a quick update on the Alyssa situation. Brody wasn't going to have any information for him until tomorrow and all was well up at the safe house. Well, except Tiny was down thirty dollars and Henderson was down twenty—the teenager was kicking their asses in poker.

Glancing again at the clock on his cable box, his apprehension grew. Shoving his phone into his back pocket and clipping his holstered gun to his lower back, he grabbed his keys and headed for the door. He opened it and froze. Someone, most likely Nick, had dropped a pizza and twelve-pack of beer on the ground. Panic assailed Jake, but he swiftly zeroed in on the sounds of a struggle. Dashing around the corner, he came to an abrupt stop and mentally swore.

While Nick had the advantage, Drew was holding his own as the two beat the crap out of each other. Jake winced as Nick caught the other man on the chin, sending him flying backward. *Fuck!* They'd kill each other if he didn't intervene.

Channeling his inner Dom, he barked, "Enough!" and both men froze. They were panting heavily, and it was evident neither one wanted to stop. Nick took a threatening step forward, and Drew sneered, egging the kid on.

Jake knew it wasn't going to take much for them to start up again. "Don't fucking do it, Nick. Get your ass inside."

Halting in his tracks, Nick's glower stayed pinned on his rival. "Not until this fucking asshole leaves."

Drew clearly didn't know when to quit. "Afraid of the competition, you little prick?"

Great. Just what Jake needed right now—two jealous submissives in a pissing match, trying to mark their territory. Rolling his eyes, he stepped between them and pushed Nick back a few steps. "Knock it off, both of you. Nick, get inside. I'm going to have a quick chat with Drew."

"Jake . . ."

"Now, Nick." The deep, ominous rumble left no room for discussion.

The kid glared at him, but, thankfully, heeded his order, giving Drew the finger as he turned around and stormed back to the condo. The Dom turned to his ex, who was wiping the blood flowing from a nose which hopefully wasn't broken. "What are you doing here, Drew?"

"Well, forgive me, Jake, but I thought I was supposed to call you and set up a date to talk. When you didn't return my calls, I decided to swing by. Didn't realize you were baby-sitting."

Jake growled at the sarcasm. "He's only four years younger than you. And next time you decide to egg a guy on, you might want to make sure he's not a SEAL."

"I don't give a fuck what he is . . . he's an asshole getting between you and me."

Crossing his arms, he frowned at the other man. "There is no you and me, Drew. What we had was over a year ago. I shouldn't have agreed to a date with you the other day. Honestly, I saw Nick approaching us and was trying to discourage him from getting too attached."

Drew scoffed as he turned to leave. "Well, I can see how that fucking worked out for you. When you get around to dumping lover-boy, give me a call. If you're lucky, I might be available, but I doubt it."

Jake stared at the other man limping toward the parking lot, thankful Drew was leaving. He would call him in a few days, after the guy had cooled off, and let him know in no uncertain terms they were through for good. But for now, he had his submissive to take care of. Turning the corner of the building, he spotted the beer and now-upside-down pizza still on the ground. Sighing, he picked them up and then re-entered his condo, kicking the door shut with his foot. "Nick?"

He wasn't in the living room or kitchen. Dropping their dinner on the dining table, Jake went in search of him. He strode into his bedroom and found Nick in the attached bath, cleaning the blood off his face and hands. From what Jake could tell, it was mostly the blood splatter from Drew's nose. Nick had removed his sneakers and torn T-shirt, standing there in only his faded jeans. Jake's mouth watered as he eyed the perfect, nude torso. Leaning against the doorjamb, he crossed his arms and kept his voice stern. "Feel better, now that you've kicked someone's ass?"

"Yeah, I do. Especially since it wasn't just anyone's ass, but that dickhead's. And by the way, he started it."

Jake rolled his eyes. "What are you, in kindergarten? I don't give a fuck who started it, I'm just glad neither one of you got hurt more than this." He gestured toward Nick's bruised chin, ribs and bloody hands. "I really don't think Drew wanted to explain to his police chief that he got into a fight with his ex-boyfriend's new boyfriend."

Reaching for a hand towel, Nick paused. "He's a fucking cop?"

"Yeah, he is, not that it matters. He doesn't want the drama of his private life to invade his professional one, so he won't make a stink over this."

A silence fell over them as the younger man dried his hands, face, and sculpted chest. Jake's eyes followed the towel's progress until Nick tossed it on the counter and took several steps forward, stopping inches away from his lover. The Dom raised his eyebrow, but made no other movements. Using one finger, Nick seductively traced the left bicep bulging from beneath Jake's T-shirt. "So, I have a new title now, other than submissive, boy, or Junior, huh?" When Jake narrowed his eyes in confusion, Nick added, "New boyfriend?"

"Caught that, did you?" he murmured, his voice becoming huskier as his desire grew.

"Yeah, I did . . . Sir."

Jake's lust flared as his cock hardened with that one word. The kid wanted to play, huh? Well, that could be arranged. Dinner could wait. "Strip the rest of your clothes off and present next to the bed. I'll be right back."

Not pausing for an answer, he turned around and

walked out to the foyer where one of his toy bags sat in the closet. Knowing it was completely stocked with whatever he needed, he didn't bother to look inside as he carried it back to the bedroom. Tossing it on the king-size bed, he beheld the sight before him. *Holy shit!* Tan, muscular, and naked, the kid was fucking gorgeous. *And he's all yours, to do with as you please.*

Nick was on his wide-spread knees, hands in the at-ease position, and head bowed. Stepping forward, Jake placed a hand on Nick's head and growled when he leaned into the touch. "Fuck, baby, you don't know how much you fucking please me. But I'm going to show you."

Without lifting his head, Nick answered, "Thank you, Sir."

Smirking at the "damn, I'm good" tone in his sub's voice, Jake pivoted toward the bed and dragged his toy bag closer. "But first, Nicky-boy, you have some punishments owed to you."

Nick's breath hitched, but he didn't say a word—snarky or not. Trying not to let out a chuckle, Jake bit his tongue while pulling out what he needed. While on the flight home earlier, he'd run a few possible punishments through his mind. The one he'd settled on was partly inspired by something Mistress China had told him about how she'd disciplined her last submissive. He lined up a blindfold, lube, new ass plug, wrist cuffs, and a nine-tail flogger where his sub would see them in a minute. While he still had to sit down with Nick and go over his limits, he didn't think any of this would be something the kid couldn't handle. But just to be sure . . ." What's your safeword, Junior?"

"Red, Sir."

"Good. Use it if you need to. If you're unsure of

something, use the word 'yellow' and I'll slow things down, so we can discuss your fears."

Still with his eyes downcast, Nick snorted. "Not sure if you remember, but I'm a U.S. Navy SEAL. Hoo-yah. I doubt there's much you can legally do that will scare me."

"Next rule, Nicky-boy, is back-talk will just make your punishments longer. But feel free to keep racking up the minutes. Now, stand and kneel on the bed with your head down and that sweet ass in the air."

Nick's ankle joints cracked as he straightened, but he did as he was told without complaint or sass, even after eyeing the toys on the bed. Once he was in position, Jake opened the new package and applied a generous amount of lube to the butt plug. Before tossing the tube aside, he gave a quick squirt of the cool gel between his sub's ass checks.

"Fuck, that's cold!"

"Don't worry, babe. It's going to get hotter in a few minutes." What the kid didn't know was the ginger lube would soon create a burning sensation, lighting his ass on fire, and making him wish for the coldness. Pulling Nick's ass cheeks apart, Jake rubbed the plug over the puckered hole a few times before pushing inward. "Relax. I'm much bigger than this plug and you took me just fine."

He eased it past Nick's sphincter and then dragged it in and out a few times, fucking his moaning sub. It wouldn't be long before the kid started feeling the first part of his punishment. When the initial curse was spat out, he knew it'd begun.

"Fuck, Jake! What the fuck is that? It fucking burns! Shit!"

Jake grinned. "That, Junior, is ginger lube. And don't worry. It only *feels* like your ass is on fire. It'll be gone in a few hours."

"Hours? Fucking-A!" Nick shoved the comforter in his mouth and bit down on it, muttering his curses into the bed.

Pushing the plug all the way back in, he left it there. "While I'm washing my hands, stand up, but don't lose the plug or I'll extend your already long punishment." When Nick mumbled something under his breath, Jake placed a hard slap on his bare ass cheek. "What was that, subbie?"

"Shit! Nothing, Sir."

"Didn't think so. Make your way out to the living room and wait for me."

Jake took his time in the bathroom, knowing he would be laughing his ass off at Nick trying to shuffle out to the living room without losing the plug that he probably wanted to rip out right now. After removing his socks and sneakers, he changed into a pair of sweats, leaving his T-shirt on. Might as well be comfortable, even if his sub wasn't. Grabbing the blindfold, leather wrist cuffs, and flogger, he strolled out to the living room. Nick was standing next to the sofa, with his ass, fists, and jaw clenched. This time Jake couldn't hold back his chuckle. "The ginger lube sucks, doesn't it? By the way, clenching your ass makes the burning worse . . . oh, wait . . . you have to do that, so you don't lose the plug."

Growling, Nick glared at him. "It's nothing I can't handle." When Jake raised an eyebrow at him, he added, "Sir."

Pushing the coffee table out of the way, he pointed to a spot in front of the sofa. "Present here, facing the couch." When his order was followed, he stepped behind Nick and quickly attached the cuffs to his wrists, making sure they weren't hindering his circulation. A clasp hooked the two together, one on top of the other, so his hands would be completely restrained, yet leaving his ass cheeks vulnerable.

Next came the blindfold. "Hope you're not scared of the dark."

Nick just snorted, but then frowned when Jake turned on the TV with the remote. Ignoring him, the Dom walked into the kitchen, taking the pizza and beer with him. The twelve-pack, minus one, went into the fridge, and then he took a moment to rescue the cheese and pepperoni from the top of the pizza box before throwing two slices on a plate. Carrying his dinner back into the living room he took a seat on the couch, setting the beer on the end table with a coaster.

Lifting his bare foot between Nick's widespread knees to his semi-erect cock and balls, he caressed them gently while explaining, "Here's how this is going to work, Nicky-boy. I'm going to get comfortable, watch a bit of the hockey game, have my dinner, and drink a beer, while you stay right like that. Whenever I'm in the mood, I'll give you some attention ... which you may or may not like. Under no circumstances are you allowed to cum or lose that plug. If you do, then we'll start all over. Any questions, subbie?"

16

*N*ick groaned when Jake's toes curled around his now erect cock, the thick callouses rubbing against smooth, hard flesh was making his legs quiver. He desperately wanted to pump his hips forward, but knew from their first night together it would only result in adding to his punishment. "For how long?"

"Until I think you've learned your lesson about disobeying me and letting your jealousy rule your mind. And until you remember to use the appropriate title of 'Sir' when we're in D/s mode. You're a little lax on that rule."

Shit. He'd already learned the lesson . . . but the jealousy thing, yeah, that might take a while. He wasn't used to that emotion. The last thing should be easy enough—he'd been using the title for years in the Navy. "Yes, Sir."

With his eyes covered, Nick's other senses increased tenfold. He could smell the pizza as well as Jake's unique scent —both making his mouth water. The hockey game was playing out behind him, but he tuned out the announcer and the roar of the crowd. Jake's foot continued to fondle his cock and balls, making Nick harder by the second. But it was the burning sensation deep in his ass which he couldn't ignore. Every time he tried to relax, he felt the butt plug shift and he refused to lose it. Jake wanted to push his limits and stamina . . . well, Nick was up for the challenge . . . in more ways than one.

He could hear the faint sounds of Jake chewing his pizza and occasionally taking a sip of beer to wash it down. The foot left his groin and he wondered what was coming next. He waited . . . and waited. Knowing what Jake was doing— mind-fucking him—didn't make things any easier, even though it was a technique he'd been subjected to many times over the years while training with the SEALs. Inhaling deeply, he concentrated on relaxing every part of his body . . . with the exception of his ass, of course.

Without warning, something slapped softly against his right thigh. It took a second to realize it was the supple leather strands of the flogger he'd seen on the bed earlier. Moments later another strike landed on his left thigh. They didn't hurt—far from it. Instead, the knotted strands felt like a caress—his lover's caress—and Nick's heart-rate and breathing increased with arousal. His cock hardened the point of pain, and a low moan escaped him.

"Like that, Nicky-boy?"

"Yes, Sir."

"Well, don't get too comfortable. After all, this is a punishment."

Nick wasn't expecting the next strike to land between his thighs. "Fuck!" Gritting his teeth, he growled, but remained still. It wasn't long before the brief pain in his balls, morphed to something more . . . something he couldn't explain . . . something he wanted more of. He heard Jake stand, and sensed the Dom moving past him. The flogger landed, softly again, on his right shoulder, followed by the left one. He noticed Jake was being careful not to hit any of the bruises from his tussle with the ex-dickhead. Stroking his body, the leather strands began to dance up and down his back, but as soon as his shoulders relaxed, a hard strike lit up his ass cheeks. *Fuck!*

"Ask me for another, Nicky. Beg your Master for another across your ass."

Swallowing hard, Nick ground out, "Please, may I have another, Sir?"

Another strike landed, harder than the first.

"Again, Junior."

"Please, Sir, may I have another?"

The routine continued several more times, Nick actually lost count, until his ass was on fire as much as his asshole was. A thump behind him told him Jake had dropped the flogger and Nick tried to concentrate on his breathing instead of what might happen next. He had to be crazy . . . he'd just gotten his ass whipped and all he wanted was to beg for more . . . to beg Jake to let him cum because he was harder now than he'd ever been in his life. His ears strained to hear what Jake was doing, and when he heard the leather of the couch creak, he knew the other man had sat back down. Yet again, Nick waited . . . and waited.

This time the lull was longer, each second of unbearable silence grating on his nerves. His head hung forward between his shoulders. His cock throbbed with need. His lungs heaved for oxygen. And his heart swelled with . . . love? *Fuck!* How the hell had that happened so fast? He thought he'd fallen in love a couple of times over the years, but he now knew those times hadn't been the real thing—not even close. This was the first time he thought his heart would break and never recover if the feelings weren't mutual. It was the only time his lover's pleasure and approval meant more than his own. If this wasn't the real thing, it was pretty damn close to it and only a matter of time before he fell hopelessly and irrevocably in love with Jake Donovan.

Endless minutes and two commercial breaks from the game had passed until a hand closed around Nick's sensitive cock, and he bit his bottom to keep from begging for release. He was positive Jake would only delay it further. The rough skin of a working man's hand dragged against his hard flesh, and he felt pre-cum ooze from the slit. *Beg. Beg. Beg. Don't beg. Fight it.*

"Do you want to cum, Nicky?"

Yes! Oh, please, fucking yes! "Only if that's what you want, Sir."

Jake's laughter was a sexy low rumble. "You learn fast. Damn, your cock is so fucking beautiful. Makes me want to lick and suck it. Would you like that, Nicky-boy? Do you want me to suck you even though I won't let you cum?"

"Fuck!"

The hand stopped its mesmerizing ministrations. "I'm not sure if that was a yes or a no." The leather squeaked again, seconds before Jake's wet tongue rasped up Nick's length, causing him to groan loudly while his abs and thighs trembled in anticipation of more. "Is that what you want, baby?"

Teetering on the brink of insanity, he couldn't take it anymore. His need for what Jake offered was overriding every thought and want in his body. "Yes," he gasped. "Fucking, yes. Please, Sir. Lick me. Suck me. Do whatever you fucking want to me."

"If you insist."

Jake's mouth closed around Nick's shaft and he almost wept at the sensations assailing him. Moist heat surrounded him and his head fell back. This was the first time Jake had blown him and it was better than anything he could've imagined. Silky hair tickled Nick's chest as the stubble on Jake's chin rasped against his lower abdomen. The Dom's tongue swirled. His cheeks hollowed as he sucked hard. Teeth dragged along the length, just enough to send shivers throughout Nick's body. *Don't cum. Don't cum. Don't cum. Please let me cum!*

Growls and heavy breaths burst from Nick's mouth and nose. Involuntarily, he yanked on the restraints holding his hands in place to no avail. He tensed as one of Jake's hands cupped and rolled his balls, while the other hand snaked around to tap on the plug still sitting in his ass. A tingling took up residence in his lower spine and his balls drew up tight. "*Arrrgggghhhhhh*! F-Fuck! Please, Sir. I . . . I can't hold back . . . I need . . . Oh, fucking-A, Jake. Please!"

With a pop and one last swipe of his tongue, Jake released the cock from his mouth. "Not yet, Junior. You have to get me off first. Then I'll let you cum." Panting hard, Nick barely heard Jake move back to the couch and push down his sweatpants. "Crawl forward, babe. Bend over and suck my cock. The faster you make me cum, the faster you'll get your own relief."

Jake's hand guided Nick's mouth down onto his cock. Hard velvet met his tongue, and with earnest, he sucked and licked every long inch of it. Jake's moans and murmurs of encouragement spurred him on. Taking the tip to the back of his throat, he swallowed hard, earning him a gasp of pleasure from his Dom's lips. He did it again . . . and again . . . and it wasn't long before the hand in his hair tightened its grip, lighting up the nerves of his scalp and sending shivers down his spine."

"Yeah, baby. That's it. Faster. I'm almost there. Swallow it . . . all of it."

A loud roar filled the room. Cum shot into Nick's mouth, and he greedily swallowed every salty drop until there was nothing left. After licking Jake clean, he sat back on his haunches and did the same to his lips.

"You do that very well, Nicky-boy. Very well." Jake's breathing was heavy and his words were hoarse.

The blindfold was removed from Nick's eyes and he blinked until his vision cleared. Jake tucked himself back into his sweatpants before standing and circling around him. He made quick work of the leather restraints and then pulled the plug from Nick's ass, causing him to groan. Unfortunately, the burning sensation was still there.

Jake's hands went to Nick's shoulders and he massaged them for a minute. "How's that feel?"

"Great, but I think I'd rather your hands were somewhere else."

An evil chuckle reverberated from Jake's throat. "Well, Nicky-boy. That's not going to happen." He came back around and sat on the couch again as Nick's eyes narrowed. "You see, this is the last of your punishment. I never said *I* was going to get you off. You'll have to take care of that yourself. Right here and now. While I watch."

What? Jake had to be kidding him. But one look at the man's expression and Nick knew it was no joke. *Fucking fine.* He was so fucking hard and ready, he didn't care how he got off at this moment, just that he did. He was already on the edge and it wouldn't take much to fall. Grasping his cock, he tightened his fist and pumped furiously, never taking his eyes off Jake's, which flared with heat—heat that shot straight to Nick's groin. *Harder. Faster. Almost there. Going to explode.* Smirking, Jake slowly and purposely licked his lips and . . . *fuck* . . . that was all Nick needed to see to send him into orbit. He shot his load into his hand and on his chiseled abs. The hot cum searing his skin as he bellowed and cursed at the relief coursing through his body. Sexual release had never lasted so long and felt so fucking good. Gasping for air, he brought his gaze back to Jake's, and it was where he saw amusement . . . and respect?

"You did good, Nick. You took your first punishment better than any new sub I've known. Most would have begged long before you did." Jake held out his hand and Nick grasped it with his non-sticky one, letting the Dom pull him to his feet. "Lay down while I get a towel to clean you up. Then I'll get your dinner ready. We can relax on the couch together and watch the rest of the game."

Nick flopped on the sofa in an exhausted heap, looking forward to cuddling with Jake. His Master. His love. *Shit*, he hoped the feeling was mutual someday soon.

NICK ROLLED OVER, reaching for Jake, and found nothing but cool sheets and an empty pillow. Lifting his head, he heard movement coming from the bathroom seconds before the shower turned on. The digital clock sitting on the dresser read oh-six-hundred and he rubbed the sleep from his eyes. As much as he wanted to roll back over and catch a few more winks, the chance to shower with his lover was something he wanted more.

While spooning behind Nick on the couch last night after the game had changed over to the late news, Jake had shoved Nick's boxer-briefs down off his hips. It was the only clothing he'd been permitted to put back on—not that he minded. After retrieving a tube of lubricant and a condom from the end table drawer, the Dom had quickly prepped Nick's asshole and entered him without changing their position, still dressed in his sweatpants and T-shirt. While the prep had been fast, the fucking hadn't been. Instead, it'd been slow and sensual, and hotter than anything Nick had ever experienced with any lover. All Nick had been allowed to do was reach back and wrap his arms around Jake's neck. However, Jake's hands had been everywhere while he nuzzled Nick's ears, neck, and shoulders with his lips and tongue. As he slowly thrust his hard shaft in and out of the tight passage, Jake had explored every reachable inch of Nick's body before pinching and pulling on his nipples. He then used the same rhythm of his pelvis to pump Nick's throbbing cock with his hand. They'd come within seconds of each other, groaning with their individual satisfied releases. After recovering, Jake had wordlessly stood, taken Nick's hand and led him to the bathroom, where they'd cleaned up before falling asleep in bed, wrapped in each other's arms.

Flipping the covers off, Nick pushed his bare ass off the bed and stumbled toward the bathroom while stepping over his discarded clothes from the night before. The door wasn't completely shut, so only a small shove widened the opening. Grinning, he strode into the steam-filled room and saw Jake stepping into the shower stall with his back facing the younger man. Disbelief and anger flooded Nick as he stared in shock. *What the ... ?*

It took him a second to recover and find his voice. "What the fuck, Jake?" The man spun his naked body around. It probably wasn't a move to confront Nick, but more likely to hide the scarring up and down his back. His beautiful lover was damaged in more ways than one, but it wasn't only the physical scars that bothered Nick—it was the emotional ones as well. The ones he found in those haunted green eyes. How had he not seen this before? *Because he's been hiding it from you, asshole . . . among other things.* Now, it made sense why Jake had slept in his T-shirt and briefs last night. And when they'd showered in the hotel two months ago, Jake had distracted him when Nick had wanted to soap him all over. Somehow, he'd never seen Jake's bare back until now. He stepped toward him, trying to get another look at the marred flesh. "Is that from a fucking whip?"

Jake sighed heavily and rotated his upper body, denying Nick a repeat showing. But he wouldn't let up, grabbing Jake's arm trying to turn him around, until the Dom shoved him away—not hard, but enough to say he meant business. "No, it's not. And I don't want to get into it."

"Uh-uh. Not fucking happening. You're not fucking pushing me away again. You want my submission?" He pointed to himself with his thumb. "Well, what about what I want, Jake? What about what I fucking *need*?"

His jaw clenching, the Dom narrowed his eyes and crossed his arms, standing there in all his naked, and angry, glory. But Nick wasn't backing down . . . not this fucking time.

"I get it . . . I get that I want your dominance . . . and that I enjoy it more than anything I've ever fucking known." He couldn't hide the desperation in his voice. "But I want more, Jake. For the first time in my life, I fucking *need* more." He reached up and tapped the other man's temple with his finger, not entirely surprised when he didn't even flinch. "I need what's in here . . ." His hand dropped to the hard, muscular flesh covering Jake's heart. "And what's in here. Why can't you give that to me? Huh? Why is it so God-damn fucking difficult for you to open up and trust me with whatever you're hiding?"

For a long moment, the only sound was the flow of water from the showerhead as it pelted the tile floor of the stall. Nick didn't think he was going to get an answer to his questions . . . again. But then in a huff, Jake did an about-face and spit his words out in disgust. "Fine! You want to fucking stare at them? To know what they're from? It's from my fucking father's belt. My senior year of high school. Somehow, he found out and decided to beat the faggot out of me. End of the fucking story . . ." The venom in his voice turned to pained exasperation, as his head hung forward. "Let it go, Junior . . . I did a long time ago."

Nick gaped at the remains of deep wounds inflicted years before on the otherwise perfectly sculpted back. How could a man do this to his son? There were almost a dozen of them, where the belt's buckle had gouged into the flesh, leaving curved white scars in its wake. His voice dropped to a hoarse whisper, barely loud enough to be heard over the shower. "No, you didn't, Jake. If you had . . . you wouldn't be hiding your scars . . . you wouldn't be refusing to talk about it . . . and you wouldn't be pushing me away." Disappointed more than anything, he turned around and stormed out of the room.

17

*W*hile he was seething on the inside, Oliver Wagner's outward demeanor had the appropriate amount of shock, disbelief, and overall grief. The two detectives from Colorado and one from Tampa had just informed him that his missing wife, who had been presumed dead, had in fact been alive up until two days ago. According to them, she'd been murdered, wrapped in a rug, and tossed into a river where she was discovered by two fucking fishermen. *Damn it to hell.* If Craig Allen didn't kill those two fucking idiots Oliver hired, he would do it himself. They were supposed to make sure the body could never be found or identified. And not only had the jackasses not followed orders, but the police had been able to ID Carrie by her fingerprints within hours after she was discovered floating down the river.

"I know this is shocking news, Mr. Wagner, but we need to ask you some questions about your wife and daughter." The taller guy from Colorado, Detective Paul Shu, seemed to be running the show as he sat in one of the guest chairs in front of the desk, one leg crossed over the other, with a flip-pad and pen in hand. The others eyed every inch of Oliver's home office from their standing posts on opposite sides of the room. He recognized the Tampa cop from last year—the guy had been in on the initial search for his bitch of a wife and cunt daughter.

"Certainly, Detective. Clearly, I want this mystery solved as much as you do. I just don't know how much help I can be. I haven't seen either of them in a year." *Good. Keep the astonishment and confusion in your voice, but be cooperative. Get ready to tear up if needed.*

"I've read the missing person report you filed on Carrie and Alyssa, as well as the file on Tampa P.D.'s investigation, but I'd like to start at the beginning and hear it again from you. Sometimes a person remembers things the longer they've been removed from the situation. Tell me what you can recall from the day your daughter disappeared. I understand she went missing eighteen days before your wife did."

Oliver cleared his throat. "Yes. Yes, she did. Alyssa had always been a wild child. Adventurous, pushing the limits, trying new things without thinking of the consequences."

"Such as?"

Feign embarrassment. "Well, I hate to admit it, Detective, but my daughter was in with a bad crowd. My wife and I found her to be in possession of marijuana when she was fourteen, cigarettes when she was thirteen. There were several times she came home reeking of alcohol. She was hanging out with older boys and, well, I don't have any proof, but I'm sure she was . . . you know . . ." He cleared his throat again. "Anyway, I had Carrie take her to the doctor for birth control. If she was going to be reckless, I didn't want my wife and I to end up raising an illegitimate grandchild, because Alyssa wouldn't have been responsible enough to raise a child properly."

Shu nodded his head in agreement. "I don't blame you. How else did you and your wife respond to her behavior?"

Lean back in chair. Look weary. "We tried everything we could—grounded her, forbade her to see those worthless friends of hers, revoked privileges, and anything else we could think of. She just fought us tooth and nail. I think she was fourteen the first time she ran away."

From his post by the window, the other Colorado detective stepped forward and took the seat next to his partner, yet remaining quiet. Oliver waited while Shu checked his notes before speaking again. "Yes. That's what the Tampa report said. Fourteen. You said that was the first time . . . how many times were there?"

"Honestly, Detective, I lost count. Most of the time I had a private investigator I use for business reasons go find her and bring her back. The Tampa Police have better things to do than look for a rebellious teenager."

Shu consulted his notes again. "I'm sorry. I must have missed that in the report. What's the private investigator's name?"

Opening the top desk drawer, Oliver pulled out the PI's business card and reached across to hand it to the man. He wasn't worried about them contacting the guy, since he wasn't privy to anything that could get Oliver in trouble. "Feel free to contact him, although it's been months since he's had anything to report. Unfortunately, he didn't find anything beyond what the police did." At least that part was true.

Nodding, Shu jotted down the information, then set the card back on the desk. "Can you tell me about the night

Alyssa disappeared? Was there an argument? Who noticed her missing and at what time?"

"I was at a political function for the mayor that night, and before I left, I'd grounded Alyssa for skipping school." He didn't add the bitch had skipped school because of the bruises he'd given her. Served her right for trying to refuse him. "When I returned home at about eleven that night, I stuck my head into her room to make sure she hadn't snuck out. She wasn't there and a bunch of her things were missing. Clothes, laptop, stuff like that, but her cell phone was still locked in my office where I'd put it before I left. Carrie was in bed sleeping—she'd had a migraine earlier, which is why she didn't go out with me. When I woke her up, she had no idea our daughter had left. I didn't report her missing to the police right away, because like I said, this wasn't the first time she'd tried to run away. I contacted my PI the next afternoon after my wife called to say Alyssa hadn't been to school, nor did any of her so-called friends report seeing or hearing from her. The day after that was when we filed the official police report and, as you know, there's been no sign of her since."

Shu jotted down a few more notes. "As far as we can tell, Alyssa and your wife were living together in Canon City, Colorado for the past ten months. No one has seen Alyssa since she left her job the day your wife was murdered."

Point them in the wrong direction. "I hate to say it, but with how she's changed over these past few years, I wouldn't be surprised if she had something to do with Carrie's death. When Alyssa didn't get her way, she could get violent— throwing things and such. She wouldn't do it when I was around, but her mother was easily intimidated and Alyssa would take advantage of that. Is she a suspect in Carrie's death?"

"At the moment, she is only wanted so we can interview her. We also don't know if she met with foul play herself. Now, tell me about your wife. How was your relationship with her? Any marital problems?"

Shaking his head, Oliver tried to look insulted at what the man was insinuating. "Absolutely not. Carrie and I were happily married for nineteen years. Yes, we had arguments, but what couple doesn't?"

"Your wife was very accident prone, wasn't she?"

Oliver was startled. It was the first time the other Colorado detective—Ross Hubbard—had said a word. A brief hint of worry flashed in Oliver's gut, but he squashed it. These men had nothing on him and his whiny bitch of a wife was no longer in a position to accuse him of anything. Besides, he only hit her when she deserved it. "What does that have to do with anything, Detective?"

The man shrugged with an air of nonchalance. "I'm just saying she seemed to be quite clumsy and sometimes needed a trip to the hospital or her doctor for injuries she received. If I recall, there were several times when she accidentally fell, one time she accidentally got her hand caught in a car door, and another time when she accidentally walked into a cabinet door. That's just a few of the reported incidents the Tampa Police Department had in her missing person's file."

Clenching his jaw, Oliver tried to look innocently insulted, instead of how he really felt, which was pissed off. He didn't know any of those reports were in the TPD file—hell, he didn't even know they existed. The bitch must have sought medical help more times than he was aware of. What else was in the files that he didn't know about? He also didn't like how the smug bastard had intentionally emphasized the word "accidentally" three times in his little speech. "I'm not sure I like what you're implying, Detective."

"I wasn't implying anything, Mr. Wagner. Just stating it seems your wife was . . . clumsy."

"Yes, Carrie was. The medication she took for her migraines could make her a little dizzy and out-of-sorts." He was proud of himself for coming up with that answer so quickly. Medications always had side effects like that, and he knew for a fact his wife was sometimes dizzy on her migraine meds. But they didn't know she only got them once every few months.

Shu steered the conversation back to his original line of questioning. "What happened the day your wife disappeared, Mr. Wagner?"

"I honestly don't know, Detective." At least that was true. "I went to work that morning and she was getting ready to do some laundry. I think she also had plans to have her nails or hair done—or something like that. When I returned from work at six o'clock that evening, her car was gone. There was a note that said her mother wasn't feeling well and she needed to drive to New Mexico. I called her mother and she knew nothing about it, so I suspected foul play and contacted the police. There were a few of her things missing, but nothing important. Just some clothes and toiletries. The police didn't find any trace of her phone or credit cards being used after the day before she went missing and there was nothing unusual in their usage before that. I checked the transactions and calls myself. Her car was never found either." *Look sad. Grief should start replacing your shock.* "I honestly don't know what happened to my wife and daughter, Detective. Apparently, my wife had issues she didn't share with me. After she was gone a few days, I started thinking she must have been having an affair and ran off with the guy. While I'm not surprised my daughter ran away, I can't think of any other reason why my wife would have intentionally disappeared. Now, I've answered your questions, and I have a few of my own for you."

Arching an eyebrow, Shu closed his notepad and placed it with his pen into his jacket pocket. "Certainly, Mr. Wagner. What would you like to know?"

"For starters, if it wasn't Alyssa, then who killed my wife? What are you doing to find them? Clearly, I didn't do it, since I haven't left Tampa in several months. And what are you doing to locate my daughter? I want her home and safe again."

The detectives stood and Wagner didn't like the look in Shu's eyes. It was as if the man could see right through him. "We're doing everything we can to answer those very questions, Sir. But at the moment it's still an active investigation. As soon as we arrest a suspect, you'll be the first to know."

"I MUST SAY, I'm not exactly surprised to see you, Jake." Dr. Trudy Dunbar tapped her frameless glasses further up on her nose. "I've been waiting for you to come talk with me about your past, but after knowing you for three years, I had almost given up."

Jake grunted as he stared out her office window which overlooked the Riverwalk in downtown Tampa. The landscaped waterfront walkway was a popular area for residents and tourists alike, and was currently bustling with its usual activity. "Let me guess. You've known I was a tortured soul because what I thought I could hide from everyone is as plain as the nose on my fucking face."

By the time Jake had emerged from the shower, long after the hot water ran out, Nick was gone. Not that he expected anything different, since he'd done everything but kick the kid out of the condo. In the past, Jake hadn't cared when a relationship ended. He just brushed himself off and moved on. But with Nick, Jake felt like his heart had been ripped from his chest. And the thing that sucked was it was all his fault.

While he'd been moping around the condo, his gaze had fallen on the framed pencil sketch Ian's fiancée, Angie, had drawn of his face several months ago. At the time, Jake had been startled to see what he looked like through the artist's eyes—sad. That three-letter-word, while very common and lacking in intensity, basically summed up his life. Yeah, he loved his job and his friends, but something was missing. Sometime in the very recent past, things had changed and he found himself wanting more.

Angie had said she wanted to sketch him again when he found the love of his life and was truly happy. And he still remembered telling her, while he didn't think it would happen, if he did fall in love with someone, he'd hoped the guy was a male version of her. His exact words had been ". . . kick-ass and tender, all wrapped up in one beautiful package. And not afraid of his kinky side." And what had he done this morning? Just when he'd found the one person who fit the bill, he'd pushed him away.

Frustrated, he'd left his condo and driven aimlessly for a while before ending up in the parking lot of the building which housed Trudy's office. In addition to being one of the psychologists The Covenant referred their members to, if needed, Trudy was also his contact in Friends of Patty. She'd been the one to help him make Alyssa and her mother disappear. He'd gotten to know her better when a friend of hers had been dating his brother, Mike, a couple of years ago. While the romantic relationship hadn't lasted, Jake and Trudy's budding friendship had. But this was the first time he'd ever sought her help about his own life.

Eyeing him curiously, Trudy confessed, "I don't know about everyone, but to me, it's been obvious for a long time. So, tell me, what is it about this relationship with Nick that's different than your past relationships?"

Jake shrugged. "If I knew that, I wouldn't be standing in your office, interrupting your lunch hour—which again, I apologize for."

Toasting him with her can of Diet Coke, she smiled. "As long as you don't mind me eating my salad while we talk, it's no problem." She cocked her head. "Tell me about your father. I know things weren't good between you two before he died."

His shoulders tensed—a reaction he knew the good doctor hadn't missed. "What's there to tell? He was an arrogant bigot and a first-class homophobe. End of story." It seemed he'd been saying that a lot lately . . . maybe he should just admit that it really wasn't the end of the story.

"What happened when you came out to him?"

Jake didn't answer for a few moments. Pushing off the window frame, he wandered around the office, looking everywhere at once, but not seeing anything at all. "I didn't come out. At least not to my family. Somehow, dear old dad found out his son was a faggot and tried to beat it out of him. Three months later, I graduated high school and enlisted in the Navy the same day. We spoke maybe a dozen words to each other until he croaked a few years ago."

"What else happened?"

"Nothing." The word instantaneously burst from his mouth . . . no thought needed . . . or wanted.

Trudy sighed, placing her elbows on her desk and giving him a look which said she was calling him out on his bullshit. "I've dealt with many difficult patients over the years, but I have to say, you're in the top three of the most stubborn. I know there's more to it, Jake. You know it, too. And until you admit it and deal with it, then you're never going to get past it. Is that what you want? Or do you want what your friends seem to be finding for themselves lately? The one person who makes your life complete."

Hell, yeah, he wanted what his friends had found . . . the question was, did he deserve it?

18

*M*entally rolling his eyes, Nick took the last seat at the restaurant table after Kat, Kristen, and their friend, Kayla London, had claimed their own. He'd spent the past two and a half hours with them in a furniture store, picking out everything he needed to fill his apartment. Kristen and Angie had previously purchased the smaller things, such as kitchen, bedroom, and bath accessories, without him—thankfully. They'd kept the color schemes neutral and masculine for him, but insisted he pick out the furniture, wanting him to be comfortable with the choices. Who knew there were so many fucking options when it came to furniture—style, type of wood, and upholstery. Back in California, his bed didn't have a headboard and the only furniture he had was simple and functional. When the torturous, selection process was over at last and he'd signed the receipt and scheduled the delivery of the pieces for the six-room apartment, he'd been grateful for their help.

As a big thank you, he'd invited them all to lunch at a Red Robin in the same parking lot as the store. But he was now regretting the decision as the conversation turned to The Covenant. The Trident women were all submissives at the club, as well as Kayla, who was a member with her wife/Domme, Roxy. At least the foursome had a table in the back with no one nearby who could overhear their sometimes racy discussion.

"Hi, can I get you something to drink?"

Nick turned his gaze to the pretty brunette waitress handing him a menu. It was obvious to everyone he was the only one at the table she was interested in serving . . . or servicing, if her flirty grin was any indication. Not encouraging her, he eyed the others. "Ladies? Beer, wine, soda?"

The girls exchanged looks, then laughed as Kristen tossed her car keys at him. "Since we just made you designated driver, dear brother-in-law, it's margaritas all around."

Oh, boy. Shaking his head in amusement, he glanced back up at the waitress. "Looks like a pitcher of margaritas for my ladies, and I'll have a Bud Light, since I have the feeling I'll need one." He would switch to soda or water after the one, otherwise, he'd probably have to call Ian or Devon to come get them all.

While the waitress went to get their orders, Nick opened his menu and scanned the choices. Unfortunately, his mind went where it'd been wandering off to ever since he'd left Jake's condo this morning. After getting dressed and grabbing his duffel, he'd stormed out and hailed a cab back to the compound. Knowing the girls had already put things away in his apartment, he'd gone there to take a shower and change. But Kristen had seen him arrive and cornered him about the shopping, inviting the others along to help. Angie wasn't able to join them, having flown to New York last night for a long weekend which included a baby shower for someone. Jenn hadn't been able to come either since she was working. Figuring it would take his mind off Jake, Nick had reluctantly agreed to the shopping trip. The man's refusal to open up was getting to him and he had no idea what to do about it. If he was smart, he'd say screw it and go visit his folks for a few days. But that was the last thing he wanted to do when things were so messed up at the moment between Jake and him.

"Nick?"

He lifted his head to see the three women were staring at him. Apparently, he'd zoned out for a few minutes. "I'm sorry, what?"

Kristen laughed. "We were wondering if you wanted to meet one of Kayla's co-workers. Felicia just moved to the area and is really nice. And she's vanilla, so we thought she would be perfect for you. I mean, since you're not exactly into the lifestyle."

A lightning bolt moment struck Nick and he bit his lip before quickly finalizing his decision. "Actually, I was wondering if I could talk to you all about something, but it has to stay between us." He pointed at Kristen. "Especially you. I don't want my brothers to know about this conversation. At least not yet."

The women all glanced at each other in confusion, before turning back to him. Sitting to his right, Kristen placed her hand on his arm. "The best I can do, Nick, is to promise not to tell Devon as long as he doesn't ask me a direct question about whatever it is. I won't lie to him. I get enough spankings from him and don't need to earn any more than necessary."

His eyes moved to Kat who took a sip of the margarita the waitress had just handed her. "Benny gave me a get-out-of-a-spanking card because he had to break our plans for a night out last week for an assignment, so I'm in."

Kayla toasted him with her own sweet drink. "I get off on being punished, so your secret is safe with me, too." Behind her, the waitress's eyes had grown wide and wary, however, she didn't say a word about their comments. "But I think this means we better order our food, because I don't think one pitcher of these babies is going to be enough."

Shaking his head at them again, he grinned. It was nice to have them to talk to, since anyone else would probably look at him as if he were nuts. After the waitress wrote down their lunch order and practically ran away, he guzzled half his beer for courage, then leaned forward on his elbows. "Shit . . . um, sorry, didn't mean to curse. I just realized, I don't know where to start."

From his left, Kat softly spoke. "How about at the beginning?"

"Right." He inhaled deeply and then let it out in a rush. "For starters, I'm gay."

Silence fell over the table for a moment, then Kayla chuckled while the others grinned. "Well, damn. Didn't see that coming, but welcome to my end of the rainbow, Nick."

Kristen opened her mouth, closed it, and then opened it again. "Okay, so that explains a few things, like why I've never heard you talk about dating any women. But then again, I never heard you talk about any guys. And obviously there's a guy who you want to talk about. Anyone we know?" She paused and then her eyes widened. "Oh. My. God! It's someone from the club!"

A blush spread over Nick's cheeks as the other girls squealed. Kayla raised her hand in the air like a student in a classroom. "Oh, I know, I know. Is it Matthew? He recently broke up with the Dom he was seeing."

"*Ah*, no, it's not." His face warmed even more. It was evident they thought he was interested in a submissive. "Uh, damn . . . um, well . . . you see . . . it's . . . uh . . ."

"Oh, just spit it out, Nick."

"Jake."

He shifted uncomfortably in his chair as the women stared at him with eyes and mouths wide open before turning their gazes to each other and then back to him again. "Damn, didn't see that coming, either." Kayla extended her half empty glass to Kat. "Fill me up, girlfriend, because we're going to be here a while."

BLINKING at the sunlight streaming through the high windows of his new apartment, Nick stretched the muscle kinks from his body while lying on the floor of the bedroom. Last night, he'd grabbed the pillows the girls had placed in his closet, along with a blanket, and made an impromptu bed. As a SEAL, he'd slept in far worse conditions, so even without a mattress, it felt like he'd spent the night at the local Hilton. But he would've rather have spent it in Jake's bed.

While part of him had wanted to track the man down yesterday after his lunch with the girls, they'd convinced him to give Jake a little space. Hopefully, the Dom would miss him and want to work things out. So, instead, Nick had gotten a little drunk with the ladies, and Ian had not been thrilled when he had to come with Boomer to drive them all home. After crashing in his oldest brother's guest room for a few hours and sobering up, he'd borrowed one of Trident's spare pickup trucks and done some fun shopping, which could only include a visit to Best Buy. An hour and a half later, he'd walked out with two huge, flat-screen TVs, a stereo system, desktop computer for his office, and the necessary accessories for all of them.

He'd spent the evening hooking everything up, then searching the web for anything he could find on BDSM. While he had done some basic reading on the subject a few times after that first night with Jake two months ago, he'd been denying he was a submissive, so he hadn't really concentrated on the information. During his talk with the women earlier in the day, he'd realized there was a lot more to the lifestyle than what he'd observed at the club. Sometime around one a.m., he'd shut down the computer with a new appreciation for the life Jake, his brothers, and their teammates had found.

His research also cemented what he'd come to realize by now—he was a sexual submissive. If someone had told him that three months ago, he would have laughed his ass off. But it had taken someone as mentally and physically strong as himself to make him realize that, and also to top him. Emotional strength was needed as well, but Jake clearly had some things he needed to work out before he got to that point. However, Nick was willing to wait because he believed the man was worth it. Now he just had to convince Jake of that fact.

JORDYN ALVAREZ THREADED her way through the throngs of travelers at Tampa International Airport. To the people around her she appeared to be just a weary businesswoman returning from or heading to another meeting in another city. She doubted anyone would believe she was a former jewel thief turned U.S. government spy and assassin. But that was the whole point. She could blend into any situation with ease and no one would be the wiser.

She'd come so close to not returning that bastard's phone call. Most women in this messed-up world may think T. Carter was God's gift to the female gender, but she wasn't one of them. At least that's what her brain and heart said . . . her body seemed to disagree whenever he was within fifty feet of her. And that sexy, baritone voice of his tended to vibrate in her pussy no matter how much she hated it.

The son-of-a-bitch had known how to press her buttons and get her to help his friends. He'd played the female-teenage-abuse-victim card and she hadn't been able to refuse. Child molesters and abusers were the cockroaches of the earth in her book—and Oliver Wagner was now on the first page of said book.

With her carry-on bag on her shoulder and not needing to retrieve any luggage from the baggage claim carousel, she headed to the rental car area to find a nice, non-descript vehicle. While she loved fast cars, they tended to be attention-getters, and in her profession, it was the last thing she needed. Maybe after this unsanctioned gig was done, she'd take some time off and do something fun—like beat the living daylights out of Carter. But it would mean she'd have to get close to him and that was something she refused to do ever again.

Twenty minutes later, she was exiting the airport, en-route to Wagner's residence to do a drive-by and reconnaissance. Carter's buddy, some guy named Brody, had emailed her dummy account with the floor plans and alarm information. The only data she still needed was a definite time when the pervert wasn't going to be home. If worse came to worse, she could do it in the middle of the night, and pray the guy was a heavy sleeper. She'd done that numerous times, and while it was riskier, it ramped up the thrill and her adrenaline—stuff she lived for.

If anyone from her long-gone youth had told her back then she'd one day be working for a covert United States government agency as a secret agent, she would've told them they were crazy. Growing up in South America, the daughter of a wealthy businessman and a former Miss Argentina, she'd rubbed elbows with the upper echelons of society. But no one knew what was going on behind closed doors until her world came crashing down around her. Orphaned at fourteen and having her inheritance stolen by greedy relatives had changed her life forever.

Jordyn shoved the unwanted memories, which popped up every so often, from her mind as she steered the vehicle down the street where the target lived. Time to get her head back into the game and figure out how to help another young teenage girl whose life had been turned upside down.

19

*J*ake stood at the back of the crowd outside the courthouse where Oliver Wagner was giving a press conference concerning the death of his wife. The Trident operative had woken up to the news report of Carrie Wagner's homicide and heard the bastard was going to issue a statement at 11:00 this morning, so he added it to his agenda for the day. The businessman's lawyer and his friend, the mayor, were in attendance, as well as a few others. Noticeably absent was the Chief of Police, making Jake wonder if the man had wised up to the fact his supporter was a wife abuser and involved in a murder conspiracy.

What surprised Jake, though, was that he recognized a man standing off to the side of the reporters, staying out of range of the cameras. If he wasn't mistaken, the man was Craig Allman from the Alcohol, Tobacco & Firearms Bureau. Jake had met the undercover agent about two years ago during a joint operation between the feds and Trident. But that was in Puerto Rico, so what was the guy doing here? A light bulb went off in

Jake's mind. Craig Allman ... Craig Allen? Could they be the same person? Could the feds have planted one of their own in Wagner's lair? And why? What was the businessman involved in which had brought him to the attention of the ATF?

Quickly shooting off a group text to Ian, Devon, and Brody, Jake refocused his attention to the podium. A lot of the reporters were questioning why Carrie Wagner was living under an assumed name, was Alyssa with her before the murder, and where his daughter was now. Aside from a brief statement, probably written by a P.R. specialist, Wagner hadn't said a word, leaving the talking to his attorney. And that windbag was putting the usual spin on things—Oliver was a grieving husband and father, who had no idea why his wife ran away. He also added enough speculation that Carrie had taken off with another man and turned Alyssa against her father for no sane reason. A mental breakdown was also alluded to—anything to shift the suspicion off where it belonged.

Wishing he could take the man down now, but knowing he had to wait for Jordyn to break into Wagner's home safe, Jake put mental restraints on his desire for justice. The woman had texted him a few minutes ago, letting him know she was in Tampa and scouting out the residence. He didn't expect to hear from her again until she had what he needed. Adjusting his stance, he stared at Wagner with venom. *Your time will come, you son-of-a-bitch.*

The lawyer wrapped things up and ignored the rest of the shouted questions. He hurried Wagner to a waiting vehicle and after the two jumped in, the driver accelerated, leaving the press behind. Glancing around, Jake noticed Allman had also slipped away. Hopefully, by the time Jake got back to the office, Boss-man or Egghead had some information for him about what the hell the undercover fed was doing in Tampa.

Striding back to where he'd parked his truck, he pulled out his cell again. He wasn't really surprised Nick hadn't contacted him, but he was kind of hoping he would. *Why should he, you asshole? Even if you weren't the top, it's still your responsibility to fix what you screwed up.* Opening the door of his vehicle, he climbed into the driver's seat and made a decision. After he took care of a few things at the office, he'd track Nick down and apologize for being a jackass. Maybe if he groveled enough, he could salvage what might be the best thing that had ever happened to him.

When he entered the Trident offices, twenty minutes later, he was surprised yet happy to see Nick standing at the reception desk, talking to Colleen. At the sound of the front door opening, the younger man turned his gaze toward Jake and gave him a small smile. "Hey. You got a minute?"

Trying not to alert the secretary that there was a problem between the two men, Jake nodded. "Sure. But first, we've got to talk to Egghead. Something's going on with Oliver Wagner and I hope Brody's got some info for me."

Following him into the computer geek's war-room, Nick pulled over a straight-back chair, turned it around, and straddled it, while Jake remained standing. Brody held up a finger without looking up from his massive computer set-up —the team often teased him that he could probably launch a NASA rocket into space from this room. "Give me a sec to cover my tracks in the system I just hacked into."

Jake snorted. "I don't even want to know what system. When it comes to you and your hacking, I want plausible deniability."

Shaking his head, Nick chuckled while the geek finished

typing and hit the "Enter" button on his keyboard. Spinning around in his swivel chair, Brody crossed his arms and stared at Jake. "As you've already figured out, Allman is undercover."

Nick's eyes narrowed in confusion. "Who's Allman?"

Leaning back against the wall, Jake hooked his thumbs on the belt loops of his jeans. "Craig Allman is ATF. We met him on a joint op last year in Puerto Rico. I spotted him at the press conference Wagner held this morning with his lawyer. They were announcing Carrie's death and trying to cover up any suspicion that he may've had something to do with it."

"Yeah, I saw the 'Breaking News' alert before I walked over here."

Nodding, Jake continued. "When I spotted Allman at the edge of the crowd, the name clicked, and I was wondering if he was the Craig Allen that Todd was talking about, so I asked Egghead to check it out."

"Didn't take long to confirm it either," Brody informed them. "As a matter of fact, I went through channels first and called one of our contacts. He just got back to me a few minutes ago. Allman wants to meet with you."

An eyebrow went up. "Really? When?"

The geek shrugged. "Don't know. I passed on your cell number. He'll call you when he can set something up without drawing any suspicion from Wagner."

"Okay. So, which is it? Alcohol, tobacco, or guns?"

Performing a drum roll with his hands against his thighs in dramatic fashion, Egghead announced, "Ding, ding, ding, ding, ding . . . and the winner is . . . illegal weapons. Fully automatic AK-47s to be exact. Apparently, Wagner has gotten himself involved with an old friend of ours from Colombia."

Jake paled a little. "Aw, fuck. Don't tell me. Wagner's involved with Emmanuel Diaz?"

"Yup. Remember Carter telling us Emmanuel was busy trying to rebuild after Ernesto's death?"

Glancing between the two other men, Nick interrupted, "Wait a minute. Isn't Ernesto Diaz the big-time drug lord from a few years ago? And the reason you guys had targets on your back last year?"

Several years ago, in addition to drugs, the Diaz cartel had quite a few lucrative side businesses which included white-slavery and arms dealing. Several members of the Trident team and a few other retired SEALs had ended up being targets of an assassin after a U.S. senator realized they'd been on a mission years ago involving Ernesto. He was a distant cousin of the now-deceased drug czar, whom SEAL Team Four had a hand in killing, and was worried the team would make the connection when he ran for President. Three former Team Four members and a civilian had been killed before Trident figured out who wanted them all dead. Two of the victims were Jenn Mullins's parents, and while Nick wasn't privy to any of the classified information, he did know the basics.

Both of other men nodded, but it was Jake who spoke. "Yeah. Looks like we're going to cross paths with his little brother who took over the business. He's been trying to bring the empire back to where it was when Ernesto was running it."

"Shit."

"Exactly," Brody acknowledged. "From what I was told, something big is about to go down, but I couldn't get any details."

Jake straightened. "So, this is the feds chance to catch them both red-handed. Does Ian know?"

"Not yet. He's on a conference call with the Pentagon again. I'd love to know what that's all about. Any ideas?"

"Not a clue." With everything else going on, Jake couldn't care less about whatever Ian was up to. "So, now we have to wait for Jordyn to hit his safe and Allman to fill us in. Let me know if you hear anything else."

"You got it."

Moments later, Nick followed Jake into his office and shut the door behind them. "Shit's getting deeper, isn't it?"

Jake snorted as he leaned against his desk. "That's putting it mildly, but, yeah, things are getting worse by the minute. Hopefully, the only casualty in all this will be Wagner. I have to wait until I hear from Allman before we do anything else, though. I don't want to fuck up a federal investigation, especially when this might be our chance to send the bastard to prison without Alyssa's situation being made public. The last thing I want is for her to have to testify."

He paused. Regret was eating at his gut, and he needed to clear the air between him and Nick . . . again. Rubbing his hand down his face, he took the bull by the horns. "Look. I'm sorry about yesterday morning. I was an ass."

Smirking, Nick took a step closer, crossed his arms and repeated the words Jake had said seconds earlier. "That's putting it mildly. But tell me, are things going to get worse between us or better? I understand this is all new, but, Jake, I need you to talk to me. I'll let it go for now, but when all this with Alyssa is over, you better be able to come clean. I feel like I'm fighting your ghosts, but I can't fight what I can't see."

Well, fuck, when he put it that way, Jake felt even shittier. "You're right. And I'm going to do my best to straighten things out in my head, because that's the first step. But for now, will you forgive me . . . again?"

Nick took another step forward and Jake pushed himself off the edge of the desk. Lust flared in the Dom's eyes and groin when his submissive grinned seductively at him. Nick lifted his hand and brushed his fingertips along Jake's jaw, sending pinpricks of electricity through his skin. "I don't know what it is about you, but I can't stay away. Yeah, I forgive you." With his other hand, he reached into his back pocket and took out a folded piece of paper and held it out for Jake to take. "Here's my completed limit list. I also got a copy of the submissives' protocols."

Holy shit! Jake was stunned. It was not what he was expecting, but, damn, did it turn him on. Taking the paper, he tossed it on his desk, his gaze never leaving Nick's face. He stepped forward and slowly backed his sub up against the wall. "Fuck, Junior. If you only knew what you do to me."

"Show me, Sir."

20

*J*ake pinned him to the wall and crushed their mouths together. Nick hardened in an instant. Their tongues dueled while their bodies rubbed against each other—chest to chest, hips to hips, hard-on to hard-on. Nick moaned, wishing they were in either of their apartments and not where someone could walk in on them. He wanted nothing more than to strip and let the Dom do whatever he wanted. Jake's hands slid from where they'd been holding Nick's head, down his torso, and clutched his hips. Breaking their lip-lock, he kissed and nibbled his way across Nick's jaw to his ear, where he whispered, "I'll tell you what you do to me. You make me beyond horny. I've never wanted anyone the way I want you —not only physically, but in every fucking way. You drive me fucking insane with need."

"Not as insane as you make me, Sir. Please, let me touch you." It had taken everything in him to leave his hands on Jake's shoulders, waiting for a command or acquiescence to touch him elsewhere, now that they were in D/s mode. It was one of the things he'd read about last night—when playing, always ask or wait for permission, otherwise he may be punished. And that was not something he wanted now. Jake pulled his head back so they could see each other, and Nick almost fell to his knees from the heat in his Master's eyes.

Opening his mouth to respond, Jake was interrupted when the door flew open and Ian marched in. The two men jumped apart, but not fast enough. His eyes flashing wide, Ian paused for a moment before striding over to the desk. "Fuck! Seriously?" he spat out.

His blood boiling, Nick glared at his brother as Ian turned to walk back out of the room, holding a file he'd retrieved from Jake's desk. "Fuck you, Ian! You don't have a problem with Jake being gay, but when it comes to your own fucking brother, all of a sudden, it's an issue! You're a fucking hypocrite, you know that?"

"Nick..."

He ignored the warning in Jake's voice as Ian pivoted slowly. But in an instant, the eldest Sawyer brother was across the room, twisting Nick's shirt in his fist and propelling him up against the same wall he'd been pinned to moments earlier. Only this time, the hands holding him were the result of anger. Ian's blue eyes glowered as Nick tried to shove him back, but his sibling was immovable. Short of taking a swing at him, there was no way to gain an advantage. Despite being out of the SEALs for over four years, Ian was still in fighting shape.

"You fucking little shit. Are you fucking kidding me? Close the door, Jake."

Instead of following the growled order, Jake placed his hand on his boss's flexed bicep. His voice was the only calm one at the moment. "Boss-man, let him go."

"Close. The. Fucking. Door." Ian's jaw was clenched with

barely contained fury. "As much as I want to beat some sense into his thick fucking skull, I won't. But it's time my little brother had a come-to-Jesus-moment."

Jake hesitated a moment as the brothers stared daggers at each other, then walked across the room to shut the door. He leaned against it and crossed his arms, ready to play referee if needed. Refusing to release Nick, Ian got in his face and growled. "Listen, you little shit. The reason I reacted that way has nothing to do with you being gay. I left my fucking apartment this morning to find Dev and Kristen making out on the fucking stairs. Then I get here and Boomer is all lovey-fucking-dovey with Kat on the phone, to the point I wanted to fucking gag. *Then* I walk in here and you two are fucking going at it. My fiancée is up in fucking New York for her friend's fucking baby shower, and apparently, everyone around here is getting fucking laid but me. That's what my fucking problem is, ass-hat."

What the hell? Nick gaped at his brother in undisguised astonishment.

Ian gave him one last push before letting go of his shirt and backing up. The ire subsided from his voice. "Yeah, I wasn't thrilled to walk in on this, but it's no different to the reaction I had when I walked in on Mom and Dad last year."

"What? You walked in on them . . . like what, making out?"

"More like having sex." Across the room, Jake let out a bark of laughter as a queasy look came over Ian's face. "I'm pretty sure they've done the dirty deed before, since they had four kids, but I wasn't expecting that. I was near Charlotte for business and decided to stop in to surprise them. Yeah, well, we all had a surprise. I've been trying to scrub the image of them going at it in Dad's recliner from my brain ever since. Thanks for making me bring it up again." Nick felt the blood drain from his face and his brother's eyes narrowed. "What's wrong?"

"I sat in that recliner last Christmas for hours." He was as nauseous as his brother looked while Jake roared with laughter.

"And I avoided it like the fucking plague." Ian let out a deep breath and leaned against the desk. "Seriously, Nick. Jake's one of my best friends, and Toby Walsh has been my best friend since third grade. You think that would be the case if I was a fucking homophobe?"

"Toby's gay? How come I didn't know that?" Nick took a few steps and flopped into one of the two client chairs in front of the desk. This was so not the way he expected this to go. Hell, he didn't know what he had expected. Since Jake no longer had to referee, he left his post and took the other seat next to him, but remained quiet.

Ian shrugged. "I don't know. Probably because he moved to New York City before you went into junior high school, and you only saw him a few times after that. He's been in a relationship with a Broadway actor for about nine years now. Kelly's a nice guy."

"Jeez. I think I remember you mentioning Kelly before, but I thought he was a woman." Nick felt like an ass. Talk about jumping to conclusions without all the facts. "How long have you known?"

"That Kelly's not a woman or that Toby is gay?"

He rolled his eyes. "No, you jackass. Me. How long have you known I'm gay?"

"Since you were fifteen or sixteen." Nick's jaw dropped in utter disbelief. *Ian had known for ten years?* "I was home on leave for Thanksgiving weekend and Dev wasn't. Mom told me to invite Toby, and one night, we took you out for dinner to that sports bar Dev likes. Toby was the one who noticed you checking out the same guys he was and mentioned it to me later on. He knew what it was like to not have the support of family when he came out and didn't want you to go through it, so he let me know. I've been waiting for you to come out ever since, ass-hat. And I'm hurt you thought you had to hide who you truly are all these years. I'm a fucking Dom and own a BDSM club. I probably know more gay people than you do. Did you really think I would judge you negatively?"

Embarrassed, he couldn't look his older brother in the eye, instead keeping his gaze on the floor. "No, I didn't. I don't know why I didn't tell you . . . or Mom, Dad, or Dev, either. I was just . . . I honestly don't know." He ran a hand through his hair in frustration. "Do they know?"

Ian nodded. "Yeah, they do. I told Dev back then, but Mom and Dad asked me about four years ago when I thought you would come out. When I asked how they knew, Mom just smiled and said it was a parent thing."

Groaning, Nick stood and paced the room. "Great . . . just fucking great. So, whenever Mom asked if I was dating someone, she meant a guy and not a girl. And here I was, inventing chick names for my fictional girlfriends. She knew I was lying the whole fucking time."

Stepping into his path, Ian took hold of Nick's shoulders. "Don't worry about it. They understand how hard it can be for some gay people to come out. But now you know you don't have to lie to anyone anymore. We love you, ass-hat—gay or straight—doesn't fucking matter to us. As long as you're not fucking any farm animals, we're good." He smirked. "Well, one other thing does matter. I don't want to see your junk any more than I want to see Dev's or Dad's, all right?"

Nick snorted. "Yeah, I get it. And the feeling is mutual."

His smile dropping, Ian became serious once more. "I have to ask, though. Are you sure about this? The lifestyle isn't a game and I trust Jake as a Dom, a teammate, and a brother, one hundred and ten percent. That being said, I want you to be sure this is what you really want."

"I'll be honest," he admitted. "If you asked me that two months ago, I would have said no. But now, in my gut, I know I have to give this a shot. I'll regret it if I don't. And no matter what happens, it will stay between Jake and me. I won't be some sissy-teenager demanding you fire him or not to talk to him because we broke up. I promise. I'm going into this as an adult with an open mind."

Pulling him into a hug, Ian slapped him on the back before releasing him. "Glad to hear it. Now, if you'll excuse me, I'm going to try and get my Angel on the line for some phone sex. She can't come home fast enough for me."

"TMI, big brother," he called out as Ian hurried out of the office, shutting the door behind him. Eyeing Jake, Nick leaned against the desk and crossed his arms. "You knew, didn't you? That's why you gave me a time limit to come out to them. You knew my family knew I was gay, and you didn't tell me. Why?"

Jake stood and shrugged his shoulders. "You weren't ready to hear it. This was something you needed to do on your own. Coming out is a very personal thing. In my case, I didn't have a choice, but in your case, your family knew about you for a long time and it didn't matter to them. You just needed to come to terms with it." Jake hooked his fingers into the waistband of Nick's jeans and pulled him forward. "Now, where were we?"

21

*N*ick swallowed hard before opening the door to the lobby of the club. Tonight would be different then all the other times he'd been here. Tonight, he'd be here as a submissive. Jake's submissive. Part of him was excited for what they'd planned to do later, but he was nervous about how the people he knew here were going to react to him being a sub. He dreaded the snide comments he was sure someone would make and knew he'd be tempted to deck the speaker. Jake had tried to reassure him everything would be fine and no one would insult him, but he still had butterflies in his stomach. Heck, he still hadn't seen Devon, and while he now knew his brother was aware of his homosexuality, he was nervous about the announcement.

The security guard standing in Tiny's normal spot at the double doors separating the lobby from the club wasn't someone Nick recognized, so he flashed his club card as he walked past. The red-shirted guard pulled open one of the doors for him, allowing him to enter. Pivoting to the left, he quickly spotted Jake standing at the bar and the butterflies took full flight. The Dom was gorgeous, dressed in his black leather pants and boots. The grey T-shirt he wore hugged his entire torso. Nick's gaze traveled over every mesa and valley of muscle as his mouth watered.

Jake was talking to Mistress China, but Nick knew the moment he'd noticed him walking toward them. Eyes which had been haunting him for over two months locked onto his own. Heat and lust had their green color morphing from jade to dark emerald.

When the Domme noticed she'd lost Jake's attention, she glanced over her shoulder and smiled. "Hello, Nick."

"Mistress China. You look beautiful as always." The petite woman was wearing her usual head-to-toe black. Nick assumed the comfortable-looking tank-top, jeans and two-inch-heeled boots meant she was the club's Whip Mistress tonight.

He noticed her eyeing him and Jake, before her grin widened. "Well, it's about damn time."

Both men stared at her, but it was Jake who spoke. "What's about time?"

She used one finger to point back and forth at them in a rapid motion. "You two." Nick's mouth dropped and she placed a hand on his shoulder while giggling. "Don't look so surprised. I've been watching you since you first started gracing us with your rare visits. I knew the first night we met what gender your cock preferred." Jake chuckled, but she ignored him. "I don't know if you noticed, but I never call you Master Nick like the submissives and other Doms do. I figured out that you weren't a lifestyle top, and you would never let just any guy dominate you. I was hoping you'd hook up with Jake because he needs a strong, intelligent sub, but he never seemed to be around when you were."

Nick was flustered. Had his submissiveness been that

obvious? He didn't think so. The Domme turned her attention to Jake. "You know, Master Jake, I have an idea."

He crossed his arms and smirked. "This should be good ... or bad, knowing you."

Mistress China frowned, but it was evident she wasn't insulted. "If you don't want my advice then that's your problem, because I'm going to give it to you anyway. I think Nick would make a great switch."

Nick's eyes widened in shock. What the hell was she talking about? A switch flip-flopped from being a Dom to a submissive, and there was no way Jake would go for that. Right? But the look Jake was giving him said he was considering the crazy idea. "I ... I don't think ..."

"Easy, Junior." Jakes voice had dropped to a lower bass and it sent a shiver through Nick's body. "I think I know exactly what Mistress China is suggesting. Out here in the public area, you can be an assumed Dom. You carry yourself that way anyway and the subs seem to think you are one. You've never played, so no one thinks differently. But behind closed doors, you will submit to me. We've already established that neither one of us is into public humiliation, and I prefer to play in private. I think it's the perfect solution for you to be comfortable when your brothers and the rest of the team are here. You won't have to follow submissive protocols in the presence of other Doms, either. I'm not saying we'll be hiding the fact that we're together, and there may come a time ... an agreed upon time ... when the switch thing may get thrown out. But for now, until you become more accustomed to the lifestyle, I think it's a great idea. We just have to float it by your brothers and Mitch."

At that moment, Nick knew it had happened. He was positive now. He'd fallen desperately and completely in love with Jake Donovan. The man knew his fears and concerns without even asking about them. And then, with a little help from Mistress China, he'd found, and agreed to, a solution for those insecurities.

"Float what by us?"

All three turned to see Ian and Dev had approached along with Kristen, who greeted them with the respect shown to every Dominant in the house. She said hello to Jake, Nick, and China using the title of Master and Mistress in front of their names. Nick had to hold back a grin at the knowing wink he'd received from her.

Instead of answering Dev's question, Jake nodded at Nick. The new submissive took a deep breath, and realized this was going to be a lot easier since his conversation with their older brother that afternoon. "Dev, I had a talk with Ian earlier, and . . . well, I came out to him. I'm gay."

Devon raised an eyebrow as if waiting for him to say something more. It was obvious Ian hadn't told him about what had happened earlier, because his gaze flashed back and forth between his brothers. "And?" When Nick didn't say anything, Devon added, "No shit. I've known for years. So has Ian. It's about bloody time you came out, but don't expect a fucking medal."

Kristen let out little gasp, then put her hands on her hips and gave her Master the evil eye. "You knew?"

"Of course. We've known since he was a teenager." Devon glared at his submissive. "But, Pet, why do I get the feeling that's what you're surprised about and not that my little brother finally came out of the closet? You know I don't like you keeping secrets from me."

Her gaze fell to the floor and she bit her bottom lip. Nick felt sorry for her and intervened. "She only found out yesterday and it was because I wanted advice. I made Kat, Kayla, and her promise not to say anything to any of you, unless you asked a direct question about it. They were going to tell you the truth if they had to."

Devon crossed his arms and frowned at Kristen. "Is that true, Pet?"

"Yes, Master, it is. We promised Master Nick we wouldn't say anything, but told him we wouldn't lie if you asked us about it."

The older brothers glanced at each other. "Technically, she didn't lie," Ian said with mild reluctance.

Nick didn't want any of the women to be in trouble with their Doms, so he intervened once more. "Dev, I'd appreciate it if you didn't punish her for keeping my secret. It was mine to tell, not theirs."

Rolling his eyes, Ian snorted. "The kid's got a point. And he also has something else to tell you, Dev, and I get the feeling your subbie knows about this, too."

His eyes flashing from Ian to Kristen to Nick, Devon held out his hands in exasperation. "Okay, what am I missing?"

When Nick faltered a moment, Jake put his arm around his shoulders and took over. "Nick's a submissive. My submissive."

If Devon's jaw dropped any lower, it would've been at his knees. Nick felt uncomfortable as it took a few moments for his brother to recover from the shock. Dev scratched his head while gathering his thoughts. "Holy . . . um, wow. Didn't see that coming."

Beside him, Kristen giggled. "Those were Kayla's exact words, Master."

Frowning and crossing his arms again, Dev glanced from Nick to his teammate, the man he considered to be another brother. "Jake, I've got no problem with the two of you hooking up for a fling, but Nick's never expressed interest in the lifestyle. I'm just worried this isn't for him. I mean, isn't this sudden? And no offense, but you're not known for long term relationships. I don't want either one of you getting hurt if this goes south."

Nick tensed but held his tongue when Jake squeezed his shoulder. Yeah, this was one of those times he would have to let his Dom be . . . well, his Dom. Jake didn't seem to take offense at Dev's statements as much as Nick did. "Well, it's not as sudden as it seems to everyone else. We actually got together after your wedding, and although I was a little resistant to becoming a couple for the reasons you stated, and a few more you didn't, Nick seemed to have other ideas. Yeah, this is new for him, but we were all new to it at one time or another. And I know I don't have a great track record with relationships, but you and your new bride are exhibits A and B in my defense, Dev. A year ago, this was just a world Kristen wrote about, but then she met you—the Dom who introduced her to the lifestyle. The Dom who never spent more than a weekend with a sub and hadn't been on a real date in over ten years. You're the last person here who should be against this. I expected it from Ian, not you." Devon still seemed to be struggling with the new situation as Jake continued. "The only thing I'm worried about at the moment is Nick being uncomfortable with the fact that he is indeed a sexual submissive, when outside the lifestyle, he's a pure alpha."

He wasn't stupid enough to roll his eyes in front of a bunch of Dominants, but mentally that's what Nick was doing. Jeez, his brothers and Jake were standing at the bar of a sex club, talking about *his* sex life, in front of two women. Could anything be more embarrassing than that?

Lifting her hand to shoulder height, Mistress China wiggled her fingers at the other Dominants. "But I think we found a solution to that for now. Nick can be classified at the club as a switch."

Ian raised an eyebrow. "That's not a bad idea. The subs call him Master anyway. We have several male and female switches here, so no one would think anything of it."

"Are you . . ." Devon paused. His question was about to be directed at Nick, but he caught himself and glanced to Jake for permission—that's the way things were done in this D/s setting. A nod of the head told him to continue. "Are you sure this is what you want, Nick? I'm not trying to be a ball-buster, but this isn't a game we play here. I know you've observed a lot when you've visited, but do you really understand what this is all about?"

The tone of his voice told Nick his brother was sincerely concerned about Jake and him. While he was grateful Dev cared, no one was going to change his mind about this. If he didn't give this a try, he knew he'd regret it for the rest of his life. Straightening his stance, he eyed Devon. "Yeah, I do. I've been doing a lot of research and after talking to the girls yesterday, I'm more convinced than I was before. I don't know what's going to happen down the road, none of us do. But I do know if I walked out that door now and never came back, a part of me would be left behind."

Trained as SEALs, they never left a man behind in combat. It was a loose analogy, but one that his brother got. Dev stared at him for a moment, but Nick refused to back down. This was his life, and he knew his brothers meant well, but the final decision was his to make.

"All right, little brother. I wish you both the best and I hope it works out. We love you both, so don't go fucking this up, okay?"

Ian groaned and rolled his eyes. "Do not . . . I repeat . . . do not call for a group hug, because I'm still bitching that

Angie is gone for the weekend and I refuse to get all touchy-feely with you people. I need a fucking drink."

As their older brother stepped closer to the bar and hailed the bartender, Devon held his hand out and Nick, then Jake, shook it. Taking Kristen by the elbow, her Dom gave her a tug toward the grand staircase. "Come on, Pet. You're the only one I want to get touchy-feely with right now."

22

*A*s Mistress China left the two of them alone, Jake felt Nick's shoulders relax. He didn't blame him for being stressed out over everything, but a Dom knew how to relieve that anxiety. Stepping in front of his sub, Jake blocked his view of the rest of the club and waited until their eyes met. "You okay?"

"Yeah. I mean, I know they care about both of us, but this has nothing to do with them. I didn't expect that from Dev."

"Devil Dog is just worried about you. And rightfully so." He ignored Nick's frown. "Any experienced Dom worries about a new submissive, whether it's a family member, friend, or someone they've never met. This lifestyle isn't for everyone, and we've all seen people become Doms or subs for the wrong reasons. We've also seen subs leave the lifestyle because of a bad encounter with an inexperienced or callous Dom. Questioning a new submissive is very common, Nick. Top it off with the fact they are your brothers, I would be more concerned if they didn't question your decision. All right?"

Nick nodded as the last of the tension eased from his body. "Yeah. I'm good. And you're right."

He couldn't help the smirk which spread across his face. "Of course I am." Nick smiled as he intended. Glancing over his shoulder, Jake spotted the next person he needed to talk to. Turning back to his sub, he instructed, "Go downstairs and see if there's a room available. If there is, tell whoever's on dungeon duty that you're with me, then wait for me in the room. Strip down to your briefs and present before I get there."

Taking a deep breath and letting it out, Nick dipped his head once. "Yes, Sir."

Damn, he loved hearing that from him. As his submissive walked toward the stairs, Jake took a moment to watch him. Nick's jeans hugged his ass like a glove and emphasized his cut waist. A snug T-shirt enhanced the broad shoulders and muscular upper arms. That body should come with an explosives warning. *Boom.*

When Nick disappeared from his sight, Jake headed toward the other end of the bar where Dr. Roxanne London, a pediatrician, and her wife/submissive, Kayla, were having a glass of wine. They were friends of Kristen's and had joined the private club almost a year ago. Roxy was experienced with the bullwhip and was on her way to being approved as a Whip Master at the club, along with two other Doms. Every new Dominant member had to take classes at The Covenant before being cleared to play. The first class covered general play such as spankings, ball-gags, basic restraints, and such, while the rest of the classes included the more dangerous types of play—whips, canes, wax-play, and Shibari rope bondage, among other more skilled activities.

"Good evening, ladies." After they returned his greeting,

he addressed Roxy. "Mistress, I have a favor to ask. Normally I would request a moment alone, but since your subbie already knows about my new submissive, I have no problem with her staying."

Mistress Roxy's eyebrow went up as she eyed Kayla then Jake. "I didn't know you had taken up with a new sub, Jake. Someone we know?"

He grinned at Kayla. "You want to tell her?"

The five-foot-two blonde was a complete contrast to her seven inches taller, red-haired Domme, but they were a perfect complement to each other. Kayla giggled as she fingered her leather and silver collar. "It seems Master Nick is actually a submissive, Mistress. And I'm very happy for you both, Master Jake. I assume he told you about the conversation he had with Kristen, Kat, and I, and I hope we helped him make the right decision. He had a lot of questions and we tried to be neutral with our answers, so we didn't influence him one way or the other. We wanted him to make up his own mind. Did he do the research we suggested?"

"Yes, but he still has a lot to learn," he turned back to Roxy, "which is why I need to ask you a favor."

"Shoot."

Jake crossed his arms. "He's observed the other Whip Masters here before and wants to experience the bullwhip. Carl is away on vacation and China is on the schedule tonight. If Nick wasn't a SEAL and hadn't gone through the SERE training, I wouldn't have agreed to it at this point. But I told him the only way I would do it was if I had another experienced Dom in the room observing his reactions."

Cocking her head, Roxy narrowed her eyes. "I'm not familiar with that training. What is it?"

"SERE? It stands for Survival, Evade, Resistance, and

Escape. Basically, it's the resistance part of the training which helped me make my decision. It's how to survive and resist the enemy in case of capture."

"In other words, torture."

Jake nodded. "In a nutshell, yeah. We talked about it this afternoon as we went over his limit list. I covered the pros and cons with him, and I'm convinced I have his complete trust in this. My concern is that he won't use his safeword due to the training. It was intense and I don't want him falling back into the don't-give-up-your-secrets zone. I want him in subspace, not outer space."

"Okay. I agree it's a good idea to have an observer and I'll be happy to help." Pushing her nearly full glass of white wine toward the bartender, she asked, "Master Dennis, would you mind putting this on ice for me? I'll be back later." When the man waved his acknowledgment while filling someone else's order, she turned back toward her sub. "Kayla, after you finish your wine, please wait for me in the submissives' area."

"Yes, Ma'am. Good luck, Master Jake."

He smiled at her. "Thanks, Kayla. And I'm sorry I interrupted your evening with your Mistress."

Shrugging her shoulders, Kayla grinned back at him. "No worries. It's for a good cause and now I get to catch up on the in-house gossip."

Roxy and Jake chatted on the way downstairs and across the pit. At the near end of the two hallways, which led to twelve private/theme rooms, stood one of the Dungeon Masters who held up a hand with five fingers to Jake. After thanking the man, Jake headed down the hallway to the left, stopping at room #5, and opened the door. *Fuck!* Every time he saw Nick in that flawless present position, his dick hardened in an instant. He didn't think he'd ever tire of him.

Now, if only he could get past his own demons, he might in fact have a shot at something long-term . . . something his friends were all starting to find . . . something good.

ON HIS KNEES, head bent, one hand in the other behind his back, Nick's breath hitched when he heard the door open. The thumping bass of the music from the main room pulsed throughout the air until the door was shut again, muffling the sound. A set of soft footsteps reached his ears and he knew it wasn't Jake. Oh, he was in the room—Nick was certain of it because of the electricity he sensed in the air, causing goosebumps to appear on every inch of his skin—but there was someone else with him . . . most likely Mistress Roxy. He understood Jake's reluctance to do their first whipping scene without an observer. The SERE training had strengthened Nick's ability to take pain, however, the two situations were so different. One was pain for torture, and the way he understood his research and from what the girls had told him, the other was pain for pleasure. If he hadn't become hard as fucking granite two nights ago when Jake had used the flogger to redden his ass, he may not have gotten the difference. But the pain, coupled with the burning of the ginger, had only increased his desire, and he'd had one of the most explosive orgasms ever. And God help him, he wanted to experience it again.

The footsteps approached and soon a pair of black, leather, knee-high boots with spiked heels entered his field of vision. He kept his head down, waiting for permission to look up. The protocol list scrolled through his mind and he prayed he didn't do anything wrong. Tonight, he wanted to be everything Jake wanted in a submissive. He wanted to prove to both Jake and himself that he could do this.

"Look up, subbie."

He'd been right—Mistress Roxy. Lifting his gaze to hers, he tried not show his anxiousness about the upcoming scene. "Yes, Mistress Roxy?"

Standing over him, dressed in a black, skin-tight cat-suit, the willowy redhead crossed her arms and narrowed her eyes at him. *Damn.* When she was in full Domme mode, anyone would be crazy to fuck with her. The woman could be intimidating when she wanted to, which was in direct contrast to her gentle pediatrician demeanor. "You understand why I'm here tonight. While your Master whips you, I will be watching your reactions. If at any time I feel your safety is compromised, I will immediately stop the scene, whether you say your safeword or not. After the scene stops and I'm satisfied with your condition, I will leave you to your Dom's care. Understood?"

"Yes, Ma'am. I understand completely."

She stared at him for almost a full minute, looking for something in his eyes or face. He tried to keep his expression blank. On the other side of the room, something large was moved and then the sound of metal indicated it was locked in place again, but his gaze remained on hers. At last, the Domme nodded and stepped away, as Jake came around and took her place. Reaching down, he cupped his sub's chin. "You ready, Junior?"

Nick didn't hesitate at all. "Yes, Sir. More than ready."

"Strip your shorts off, stand against the cross, and spread your arms and legs. Grab hold of the posts at the top."

Following the orders, he dropped his briefs and then stood naked at the St. Andrew's cross which had been pulled away from the wall. The large apparatus was common in the

BDSM community, and while it was called a cross, in reality it resembled an 'X.' The space behind it provided room for Mistress Roxy to observe without being in the way. Nick had no trouble being nude in front of her for several reasons—she had no interest in men, she was a physician, and he'd lost all modesty about being naked in front of anyone since enlisting in the Navy. As Jake began to shackle his ankles and wrists to the cross, Roxy took a position against the wall and watched intently. After each strap was secured, Jake ran a finger underneath the leather to make sure it wasn't cutting off the circulation.

Once Nick was strapped spread eagle, Jake came around to the back, facing him. He stroked Nick's hair and asked, "What's your safeword, Junior?"

"Red, Sir."

"If you say it, you won't be disappointing me at all. Understand?"

But he'd be disappointing himself if he tapped out. "Yes, Sir."

A slow smirk spread across Jake's face and he began to circle back around. "Then let the games begin. Do your best not to flinch."

Nick swallowed hard. Holy fuck, he was really about to do this. He'd seen Master Carl and Mistress China in action before, so he knew they never broke the skin while whipping a sub. But it was like just before you jumped out of an airplane or when a roller-coaster crested the highest peak and was about to drop—it was that "oh, shit" moment and you knew there was no backing out.

He wasn't prepared for the crack of the whip, and while he tensed, he didn't move an inch in any direction as he waited for the pain that didn't come. *Crack.* Nothing. *Crack.*

Again, nothing. Either Jake was warming up or he was playing a psychological game with him.

"Deep breath, Junior, and let it out slowly."

Nick did as he was told and this time when he heard the snap of the whip, he felt where the tip licked his right ass cheek. *Holy shit! Big fucking difference between the flogger and the bullwhip.* Gritting his teeth, he inhaled through his nose and let it out through his mouth.

"Reach past the pain, Nick, and feel the heat."

He wanted to snort at Jake's words, but instead, tried to find the "zone" like he'd been trained to do.

Crack. This time his left cheek lit up and after the initial sting, he felt the burn that Jake was talking about. The next strike was just above his right scapula, followed quickly by one above the left one.

"Breathe, Nick."

Taking a few breaths, he realized that his cock was getting hard. Jake slowly worked him over, never letting a spot be hit twice, and pausing after a mix of one to three strikes. Nick lost count as the pain morphed into something different . . . something more. He was sweating and breathing hard, but apparently Mistress Roxy didn't see anything of concern which would cause her to stop the scene. All he could focus on was the repeating *crack*, pain, and heat. He started to float . . . how was that possible? How could his feet leave the ground? His head fell forward as his chest heaved.

"Nick, step back."

Huh? How was he supposed to step back when he was strapped to the cross? He lifted his heavy head and realized Jake had stopped and both Dominants had unstrapped him. "No. Don' wanna sssop." *Why's my speech slurred? I sound drunk.*

"We're done. You're in subspace. Enjoy it, but put one foot in front of the other."

Done? How long had it been since they started?

Jake ducked under Nick's arm and supported him as he led him over to the bed. Placing his submissive face down on the cool, clean sheets, the Dom murmured his thanks to Mistress Roxy, and then Nick heard the door open before shutting again. But everything sounded so far away, like in a tunnel. Everything looked blurry. The room seemed to be filled with thousands of bees, buzzing their heads off.

Jake rubbed his ankles and wrists. "You did great, baby. How do you feel?"

"F-ying," he mumbled into the sheets. His head, arms, and legs weighed a ton.

Chuckling, Jake shook his head. "Flying is good. I'm going to put some gel on your welts. You'll feel them for about a day or so, and then they'll be gone."

"Uh-huh."

Nick shivered as Jake spread the arnica ointment over his back, ass, and thighs. While each welt stung when touched, the pain didn't bother him. He tried to concentrate on his lover's caress, but instead, he just floated until his mind went blank.

23

*J*ake couldn't have been prouder. Nick had taken to the whip like he'd done it for years. The Dom had thought for sure Roxy was going to have to pull the plug, but it never happened. When Nick's head dropped and his knees started to buckle, Jake knew he had reached subspace. That floating feeling he had was a result of an endorphin overload. Basically, Nick was "drunk" on the hormone.

After finishing with the medicated gel, Jake dropped the tube on a side table. Since he no longer had to hide his scars, he removed his shirt, boots, and socks, before laying down next to his sub. Gently running his fingers through Nick's pitch black hair, he let the silky strands tickle his skin. A hushed moan escaped the sub's mouth, and the sound went straight to Jake's groin. It would be awhile before Nick recovered, giving Jake time to study him and think. He stared at the closed eyelids with their long, dark lashes . . . women would kill for those eyelashes. Leaning forward, he placed chaste kisses on Nick's right temple and cheek before brushing their lips together. Pulling him into a tender embrace, Jake loved the small puffs of air which caressed his chest every time the sub exhaled.

Could he do this? Could he be the Dom Nick wanted . . . the one he needed? Could he banish his past from his mind and open his heart? *Fuck!* He didn't know the answer to any of those questions, but he was willing to give it a try. For the first time since he'd been with Max, seventeen years ago, he felt he'd found someone he could love . . . but was it enough? The pros and cons of this relationship fought for domination in his mind, and yet there was no clear-cut winner.

Nick stirred in his arms, and Jake realized a half hour had passed. Ice-blue eyes stared up at him. "Hey, what happened?"

"You hit subspace and passed out for a while. How do you feel?"

"Light-headed. Like I had one too many beers."

Jake stood and grabbed a bottle of water that he'd brought in with him. Sitting back down on the bed, he opened and handed it to Nick. "Drink it all." He watched as his sub supported himself on his elbow and guzzled the whole bottle. "How do your back and ass feel?"

"It's weird. The pain doesn't exactly feel like pain . . . more like an intense tingling. Can I see it?"

Helping him up, Jake led him over to where a wardrobe mirror stood in a corner. Nick turned his back to it, then looked over his shoulder. "Holy shit! It looks like I should be screaming in pain, but I'm not."

Jake studied his sub's reflection in the mirror. The red stripes down his back, ass, and thighs were temporary symbols of his submission . . . of his trust. "Not what you expected, huh?"

"I honestly don't know what I expected." He reached

back and fingered the welts on his ass cheeks. "I never understood how people got off on this, but now I do. It's a high . . . not an adrenaline high . . . but kind of like a stoned high. After I started noticing the heat, like you said, it felt like when I had my appendix out a few years ago and they gave me Percocet for a day or two afterward. You start zoning with your head buzzing."

Letting his hand trail down Nick's front torso to his semi-soft cock, Jake let him know it was time to move on the next phase of the evening. Nick's shaft twitched and began to harden again, which gave his own dick the same reaction. "I think you should be rewarded for handling your first whipping so well. What do you think?"

"Hell, yeah . . . I mean, whatever you want, Sir."

Jake smirked at the cocky little bastard. "Do you feel up to fucking me, Junior?"

Eyes widened in shock, Nick's jaw dropped. Jake knew the kid was surprised since he hadn't let Nick take his ass yet. But the kid deserved it after the bullwhip. Stepping forward, he grabbed a handful of hair and crushed his mouth to Nick's. As their tongues sparred, he licked and nipped to let the subbie know he was still in charge. Just because it was Jake's ass that was going to be fucked, didn't mean he was giving up his control. He would still dictate when Nick was allowed to cum.

Sliding his fingers down the muscular arms he loved to touch, Jake took hold of Nick's hands and brought them to the button and zipper of his leather pants. The sub clued in right away and quickly undid them before pushing the material down Jake's legs. He stepped out of them and started walking backward toward the bed again, continuing the sensual assault as they went. Leaving Nick's mouth, he kissed along his chiseled jaw, to the sensitive spot where his neck and shoulder met, and bit down lightly. Their hands were on each other's cock, stroking the other's desire higher and higher. When Jake's legs hit the bed, he pulled away from Nick and sat down before leaning back on his elbows. "Since I'm settling for a hand-job this time, I want you to suck me first."

"My pleasure, Sir."

Nick hit his knees and took Jake's hard shaft into his mouth so quickly, the Dom thought he might lose control and cum right then. He bucked his hips and dropped his head back. "Oh, fuck, Junior. Damn, I love how you give blowjobs."

He thrust his hand into the black strands of his hair again, controlling the pace of Nick's bobbing head. He moaned with everything that wicked mouth did to him. A lick. A suck. A swallow. "Not going to last long if you . . . oh, shit . . . if you keep that up. Fuck!"

Hating to do it, but knowing he had to if he was going to regain control, he pulled Nick off him. The arrogant bastard was grinning like the devil himself, and Jake couldn't help but smile back. He pointed to a dresser against the wall next to the door. "Grab a condom and lubricant from the top drawer. And make sure it's not the ginger lube unless you want your junk in a cock cage for the rest of your vacation."

Nick chuckled as he strode across the room. "Thanks for the warning. I would've been tempted."

Returning to the bed, Nick held up the tube so Jake could see it was the right one. The Dom scooted back on the king-sized bed and bent his knees, placing his feet flat against the mattress. He wanted to watch Nick's face as they fucked. "You may be on top, but you're still the bottom here. No cumming until I say so."

Climbing on the bed, Nick knelt at Jake's feet and

dropped the condom within reach. Even though they'd both had clean physicals, the protection was mandatory within the club. "I think I can handle that. Just remember, I've been tortured tonight, so try not to make me wait too long." At Jake's raised eyebrow, he quickly added, "Please, Sir."

He flipped open the tube and poured some lube on his fingers, then tossed the container aside. With one hand, he coated Jake's asshole with the slick gel and with his other hand, massaged the thick, hard cock inches above it. Jake tucked his hands under his head and enjoyed his lover's touch. Fingers rimmed his hole, while a palm and fingers gripped his cock and stroked it until pre-cum seeped from the slit. As Nick eased one, then two fingers inside him, Jake kept his gaze on the younger man's face. There was more than desire in those blue eyes, more than lust. It was something he'd never seen directed at him before—not even with Max. He knew if he gave it a chance, he could fall in love with this man, but he got the feeling Nick had already fallen in love with *him*.

Nick was up to three fingers now, stretching Jake to take him. It'd been a while since he'd allowed a lover to fuck his ass and he realized he wanted it with Nick more than anything. He moaned and wrapped one hand around Nick's, tightening the grip around his cock. His breathing increased. "Fuck me, baby. Can't wait any longer. Need you."

Pulling his fingers from Jake's ass, Nick grabbed the condom, ripped open the package and covered himself in seconds. He crawled forward and lined his cock up. With barely controlled restraint, he slowly entered his lover, causing both of them to groan in ecstasy. Forcing his eyes to stay open, Jake let his legs fall to the side, giving Nick some more room to work. He hooked his lower legs around his sub's hips, and urged him forward with his feet. "Fuck! You feel fucking awesome. Don't want slow."

"Thank fuck, because I don't think I can hold back."

As Nick thrust his cock in and out, Jake clutched his own, stroking at the same pace. It wasn't long before Nick's jaw clenched and he begged, "Shit, hurry. Oh, fuck! So fucking tight. I'm . . . damn it. Can't stop."

The tingling started in Jake's spine and his balls drew up tight. He wanted to hold back until his sub came first. "Cum, babe. Now!"

Nick thrust in again and went rigid as he threw his head back and roared his release. "FFFuuucckkk! Oh, God-damn."

Two more pumps of Jake's hand and streams of hot cum covered his abs and chest. Obviously not giving a shit about the mess, Nick collapsed on top of him, yet kept most of his weight on his elbows by Jake's shoulders. Both of them were gasping for air.

Petting Nick's head, Jake felt his heart slow down to normal. "Damn, Junior. I'm going to have to let you do that more often."

"Anytime, Sir."

Pulling him down further, Jake took pleasure in cuddling with his sub in the aftermath of their lovemaking. He knew right then, that after all this shit with Alyssa was over, he'd find a way to deal with his past. Nick was fucking worth it.

JORDYN HID in the dark shadows cast by the trees behind her target's house. Dressed entirely in black, she was nearly invisible in the darkness, with her face being the only thing showing. Her jaw clenched. She should have just asked Carter if she could kill the pervert, but knew he wouldn't have agreed to it. Hell, she wouldn't have been able to do it anyway. This wasn't a sanctioned op, so therefore it would be murder—and her morality was something she'd managed to hold on to all these years. *Hmmpf.* A psychiatrist would have a fucking field day with that one—an assassin with a moral code of ethics.

Wagner had been holed up in his Mc-mansion since she'd arrived five hours ago, just after dark. Unyielding patience during her field work was something the she'd learned a long time ago, so waiting around was nothing new. After studying the layout of the house and alarm schematics, she was confident this would be an easy in-and-out job. For a wealthy businessman, he had a pretty poor, and easily by-passed, security system.

Jordyn was now dealing with a time frame, though. She'd received a call from her handler earlier and had less than twenty-four hours to get on a plane to London before heading to Africa for a new covert mission. So, tonight's break-in was a go, no matter what.

When she'd first arrived at her hiding place, there had been several people in the house with Wagner, but they'd left around nine and now he was home alone. It was a little past one in the morning, and the lights had been off for the past three hours. In a text conversation with Trident's geek, she'd been told he could hack into the security system and briefly disable it without anyone knowing he'd been there. That was to her advantage, since cutting it off at the alarm box meant she couldn't turn it on again. This way, Wagner wouldn't discover anything had happened until he found items missing from his safe. Hopefully by then, she'd be long gone and he wouldn't have time to cover his tracks before all hell broke loose and fell on his head.

A quick text to the Brody Evans, letting him know it was time to do his thing, received an immediate response.

Alarm disabled. Good luck and let me know when to turn it back on.

Using the tree line for coverage as much as she could, Jordyn worked her way around the edge of the property until she could make a beeline across the open yard to the side entrance to the garage. While most people had decent locks on their front and back doors, she found most exterior and interior garage doors were lacking in security. In under two minutes she was turning the knob on the interior door and pushing it open with utmost stealth. She had a penlight on her utility belt, but with the clear sky, there was just enough moonlight coming in through the windows for her to see without bumping into anything. All was quiet in the fifteen-room house. Making sure the silence continued, she quickly located the home office right where the floor plans said it would be. Now to find the safe. According to the information she'd gotten with the rest of the email, the girl reported that the safe was behind a hinged painting on the wall. *How fucking original.*

Pausing inside the office door, she listened for anything out of place. Nothing. Tiptoeing across the room, she found the picture of some half-nude woman and rolled her eyes. What better place to hide your child porn than behind erotic art.

Jordyn ran her fingers behind the frame, looking for any trip wires which would set off an alarm. She highly doubted there were any, but she knew better than to skip a step. Her pessimism was what had kept her alive and out of prison in many countries around the world. Finding nothing of concern, she tugged on the bottom right corner of the frame and the painting swung away from the wall, like a cabinet door, revealing the safe. From the back pocket of her black jeans, she pulled out a stethoscope. Yes, Hollywood got that right—the common medical apparatus was also a standard tool for locksmiths and safe-crackers. It was the easiest way to hear the sound the drive cam notch made when it slid under the lever arm in a dial combination lock. The first thing she needed to do was figure out how many numbers were part of the combination. It could be anywhere between two and six. Putting the stethoscope in both her ears, she held the bell end up to the safe and slowly turned the dial, listening carefully for the *clicks*.

Once she had the combination length, she turned her attention to the individual numbers. This is the ideal method for her to get into a safe, because it left no trace of her being there and the safe would remain in perfect working order. While it took most locksmiths close to an hour cracking a safe this way, Jordyn was trained by one of the best jewel thieves of the late 20th century—her uncle. There were only a handful of world-renowned safe manipulators and Ignacio Alvarez had been one of them prior to his death nine years ago in a car accident.

Within minutes, she had the safe door open and was pulling out the contents. Some cash, a bunch of files, accounting journals . . . and, *bingo,* two thumb drives. Reaching to her back waistband, Jordyn grabbed her tablet and booted it up, keeping an ear on the rest of the house. It was still quiet. Plugging in the first memory device, she quickly clicked on the files, finding them all to be text-based documents. She copied every file into her Dropbox folder, then put the drive back into the safe. Inserting the second drive, she scanned the file extensions. *Double bingo*. It was full of photos and videos. After clicking on the first one, her stomach clenched when the sickening photo appeared. *That son of a bitch.* It took everything in her not to sneak upstairs and slit the bastard's throat after slicing off his dick and balls.

Thump.

Jordyn froze at the muffled noise. Something had been dropped or knocked over onto a carpet or rug. Whatever it was, it'd come from upstairs where the bedrooms were. Pocketing the thumb drive, she powered down the tablet, stuck it in her pants and shoved everything else back into the safe, trying to make it look undisturbed. She heard a door squeak in the distance at the same time she quietly shut the safe and returned the painting to its proper position. Hurrying over to the door to the den, she cracked it open. A cough, followed by some muttering, came from the top of the stairs. *Shit.*

Recalling the floor plans she'd been given, Jordyn slipped out the door and across the hallway to the kitchen. From there she kept moving into the laundry room where it was highly unlikely the homeowner would be going to at this time of the night. Hiding behind the open door, she was able to see part of the kitchen as Wagner shuffled in.

The man stood about five-foot-ten and was about two hundred pounds. With her training, he would be no problem if there was a confrontation, but that was to be avoided at all costs. She rolled her eyes as he picked at the wedgie he must've had from his pajama bottoms. *Gross.*

Wagner coughed again as he opened the refrigerator door and light spilled out. Thankfully, it opened in the opposite direction from where Jordyn remained as still as a statue. Twisting the cap off a bottle of water, the man chugged it while shutting the fridge again. After tossing the empty bottle into a bin under the sink, he shuffled out to the hallway again, letting out a loud belch.

Jordyn waited until the man return to his bedroom, and then lingered a few minutes longer just to make sure. When she was certain the coast was clear, she headed toward the door to the garage, and five minutes later was climbing into her rental parked two blocks away in a business lot. After sending a text to Evans to turn the alarm on again, she put the vehicle in drive and disappeared into the night. *Mission accomplished.*

24

*A*lyssa sat on one of the stools for the kitchen island, having cereal for breakfast. She'd been awake half the night after Jake had called and said her mother had been found. While he wouldn't tell her how or where the body was located, he did reassure her that he would help give her mom a proper burial when it was safe to do so. He was still working on finding out if her father had anything to do with her mother's death, but she didn't need any proof—she was certain the bastard had hired someone to kill them both.

The anger toward her father had grown as her shock had worn off. Not only had the son of a bitch ruined her life, but now he'd killed the only person she truly loved in this world. Over the years, Oliver Wagner had ensured that his wife and daughter were kept isolated from relatives, had few friends, and had to rely on him for everything. She wondered what the public would think about the prominent businessman, who had powerful friends in the mayor's office as well as the police department, if they knew what had happened behind closed doors. Before she ran away last year, he'd been talking with people about running for some elected position. She wished she had the courage to report him, but who on the police force would believe her over him? At least Jake, his friends, and the contacts at Friends of Patty had believed her. If she could get her hands on the pictures and videos the pervert had taken, she would have her proof, but then everyone would see what she'd had to do to keep from being beaten. And it hadn't been only her who had been subjected to his rage and abuse—her father had threatened to do worse to her mother if Alyssa didn't cooperate.

She wished the bastard was dead, and even more, she wished she was the one to do it. *Huh. Why not??* Sitting up a little straighter, she let the idea develop in her mind. She was a little older now, stronger too, and could hash out her own justice. No one else would get in trouble and the courts would probably find her innocent because of the past abuse.

"Miss Alyssa?"

Pulling herself from her deadly thoughts, she glanced over her shoulder to see Tiny heading for the door. She hadn't heard him come down the stairs—for such a huge man, he moved so quietly. "Yeah?"

"I have to go fix one of the cameras in the woods. I noticed it was moved and rewound the video to see what happened. A bird hit it, so nothing to worry about. I'll be back in about fifteen minutes. Henderson is outside . . . I'll tell him what's going on."

"Okay." She liked the big guy a lot. He reminded her of a big teddy bear, and was mindful that his size could intimidate her, so he always approached slowly, doing nothing which would startle her. Doug was just as nice, but was even shorter than Jake, so he wasn't as threatening looking—his adorable dimples also helped with that. But she'd learned long ago, size didn't matter when it came to monsters. They came in all shapes and proportions, and were sometimes sleeping in the room next door.

The door opened again and Henderson walked in, covered in mud. Alyssa did a double take, her eyes growing wide. The man had leaves and other bits of debris falling from his clothes. "Doug, what the hell happened to you?"

He'd left his sneakers outside on the porch, and was pulling his wallet, keys, and phone out of his pockets, placing them on a small table by the door. His gun was removed from his hip and he released the magazine before ejecting the bullet in the chamber. All three were added to the growing pile. The last thing he took off was his shoulder holster. "It was either this or get sprayed by a mother skunk. That rain we had last night loosened up the dirt and when I tried to get away from momma, I ended up sliding down the hill on my butt."

She couldn't hold back her laughter and roared to the point her stomach hurt. "That's too frigging funny! It looks like you slid down on more than your butt. You're covered, but at least you don't stink."

"There is that," he admitted dryly. "I'm going to run upstairs and shower really quick. I'll clean up any mud tracks when I'm done." He started for the stairs. "If something doesn't feel right, or anyone pulls up, hit the alarm, then head to the panic room. No exceptions, okay?"

There were several alarm buttons located throughout the house. If one was pushed, it set off a very loud siren, which could be heard up to three miles into the woods. Jake had showed her how to work everything, as well as how to secure herself in the downstairs panic room. He'd said it was better to alert everyone and have it turn out to be nothing, than to worry about looking silly and place herself in danger—the opposite of the story of the boy who cried wolf.

"Yup. I'll be fine as long as momma skunk doesn't come looking for you."

"Cute, smart mouth."

His smile told her he was okay with her teasing, even though his tone was sarcastic. While he headed upstairs, Alyssa brought her cereal bowl to the sink, washing and then drying it. She wandered over to the door and stared out at the lake. It was beautiful up here, despite the quiet and isolation. How she would love to have a place like this someday.

After a few moments, her eyes were drawn to the table next to the door. Henderson's big, black gun looked exactly like the one she'd shot before. When her mom and she had been moving from contact to contact, escaping her father's clutches, one of the men, a retired police officer, had shown her how to shoot one night. He'd instructed her on how to load and unload a gun, how to take off the safety, aim, and squeeze the trigger. While he wasn't giving them a weapon of their own, he made sure she knew how to use one if she had to. Afterward, she'd had the best sleep in years. For some reason, the knowledge had eased her fears a little.

She glanced over her shoulder at the stairs. Seeing she was still alone, she picked up the gun and inserted the magazine, pulling back on the slide to load the next bullet. Biting her lip, she looked around again. Tiny would be a few more minutes and if she moved fast, she could be gone before Doug came back down. She hated to do this to them, but the only way she was going to be completely free from her father was to kill him. Before she could chicken out, she grabbed the bodyguard's wallet and car keys, then hurried out to the car and started the engine. Hopefully she wouldn't get stopped by the police because her license was in the purse she'd accidentally left in the park's bathroom when Pete Archer had arrived to get her. At the time, she'd been so freaked out, she didn't realize it until they were on the plane, and by then it was too late.

Throwing the car in drive, she was about to accelerate when she remembered Tiny telling her that the phone he'd given her could be tracked if she got separated from them. Pulling the cell out of her pocket, she dropped it out the window, then drove away.

"Hey, Nicky. Wake up." Jake slapped him on the ass through the bedsheet.

"Shit!" Nick flipped over on his back and glared at him. "What the fuck?"

After pulling a T-shirt over his head, Jake tucked it into his jeans and threw on a pair of sneakers. "Craig Allman wants to meet in a half hour, and it's a twenty-minute drive from here." *Here* being Jake's apartment where the two of them spent the rest of the night after leaving The Covenant. "You coming or sleeping all morning?"

Sitting up, Nick rubbed his sleep-filled eyes. "Jeez, what fucking time is it? And thanks. Now my ass is burning again."

"You're welcome, and it's oh-seven-hundred. Shake a leg, Junior."

Leaving the guy to get up and dressed, Jake headed out to the kitchen and threw a K-cup into his Keurig. Grabbing a couple of travel mugs, he made one for Nick and another for himself. He'd woken to the sound of his cell phone ringing and wasn't too surprised to find it was the fed calling him.

Once he knew the extent of the ATF investigation into Wagner's affairs, he would offer to help them in any way to get the son-of-a-bitch put away for a long time.

The second mug finished brewing as Nick shuffled out of the bedroom, wearing his jeans from last night and one of Jake's clean T-shirts. "Please tell me one of those is for me."

Jake handed him one. "Feel okay this morning?"

"Yeah." He paused. "But one question. Is it normal to get hard because my clothes are rubbing against the welts?"

Chuckling, Jake grabbed his mug and car keys from the counter. "Yeah. It's not uncommon. I'm told it's an unconscious recall thing. Kind of like a certain scent triggering a memory. Your body is associating the sensations it's feeling with sex."

Nick followed him out the door and to the truck. "Does that mean after a while, just the mention of a whipping is going to make me hard as a fucking rock?"

"Pavlov's dog? Yeah, it happens."

"Fucking great." After they climbed into the SUV and closed the doors, Nick turned to him. "Listen. Remind me later to tell Ian and Dev not to mention anything about me coming out to my folks. They deserve to hear it from me and I want to do it in person when we see them for Thanksgiving in a few weeks. Is that all right with you?"

"Sounds good to me."

Even with the morning traffic, they arrived at the truck stop, where Allman had suggested they meet, a few minutes early. Jake was sure the fed had taken extra precautions to make sure he wasn't followed or tracked by a GPS, just as the two of them had. And the interstate gas station and diner was so busy with out-of-state truckers, no one would be paying any attention to three more men in their midst.

Leading the way into the bustling diner, Jake scanned the faces of the patrons and spotted Allman at a table for four all the way in the back. The man's appearance was different from yesterday, but his unshaven face, baseball cap, old T-shirt, and ripped jeans made him fit in among the truckers.

Jake approached the booth and held out his hand, which the other man shook. He then gestured between the fed and Nick. "Craig Allman, this is Ian and Dev's brother, Nick. Uncle Sam's Navy gave him a few weeks leave, so he's been working with me."

The fed shook Nick's outstretched hand. "Nice to meet you. Your brothers have some pretty big shoes for you to fill."

As they all sat, the younger man rolled his eyes. "And they never let me forget it."

A harried waitress plopped several menus and an insulated pitcher of coffee on the table with a murmured, "I'll be right back," before hurrying off again. Taking the initiative, Nick poured cups of the strong sludge for each of them.

Nodding his thanks, Allman slid his cup closer before adding a dollop of cream and a few sugars. "Before we get started, how's the team doing? I heard a rumor that Devil Dog got married and Ian isn't far behind."

Even though he was anxious for the information on Wagner, Jake knew how these games with the feds were played. A little small talk, followed by a bunch of questions about what he knew about their mutual target, would precede any forthcoming intel. And even then, he'd be lucky if Allman told him everything. The U.S. alphabet agencies —the FBI, CIA, ATF, and DEA, to name a few—hated sharing information with each other, but they were even stingier when it came to local police departments or private security companies.

"Yup. The rumors are true. And you can add Boomer to that list. He got engaged over the summer."

"Damn. They're dropping like flies around here. What the hell is in the water you guys drink?" Not waiting for an answer to the rhetorical question, Allman continued. "So, fill me in on why you were at the press conference yesterday, looking like you wanted to murder my target."

Pushing his untouched coffee to the middle of the table, Jake leaned back in the booth. "What do you know about his wife and daughter?"

The fed shrugged. "Went missing last year, about two weeks apart. No one reported seeing them since, until the wife's body was tossed off a bridge a few days ago in Colorado." When Jake's eyes narrowed, Allman held up his hand to stop him from saying anything. "And before you get your panties all twisted, I had no knowledge Wagner had located them and ordered the hit. I was down in Colombia finalizing a few things for his deal with the Diaz cartel. He hired those goons on his own and I found out about it after I returned to Tampa the morning the wife was killed. Wagner told me to contact them to find out what was taking them so long. Unfortunately, by that point it was too late." While Jake had been pretty certain the man was unaware of the hit being placed on Carrie and Alyssa, he was glad to hear him confirm it. But it wouldn't have been the first time government agents had turned their backs on a few individuals if it meant the end result would benefit a greater cause. "Now, since I'm not stupid and can put two and two together, why did you help them disappear? Apparently, Wagner kept his family and business lives separate as much as possible. My discreet inquiries these past few months got plenty of speculation, but nothing else."

Jake's gut churned as it always did when he thought about what Alyssa had gone through. "The prick was sexually abusing the daughter since she was twelve. Physically abusing both of them, too."

"Fuck!" The loud curse burst from the fed's mouth and they all glanced around, making sure it hadn't attracted any attention. He lowered his voice again. "I only heard he was a wife-beater. But a fucking child molester with his own daughter? Now I have to figure out how to finish this assignment without putting a bullet in his dick and another in his head."

When the waitress finally made it back to them with an apology for taking so long, all three men quickly ordered the "Hungry Man's Special" from the breakfast menu, making the woman's morning a little easier. After she left them alone again, Allman asked, "So, do you know where the girl is?"

Neither Nick nor Jake gave any indication they were aware of Alyssa's location, but it was the latter who answered the other man. "Nope."

"See, I'll call bullshit on that, since I traced the last call she made from her cell to you."

"Fuck. Does Wagner know? Wait a minute. Did you set that tail on me?"

Allman grimaced as he swallowed a gulp of his acrid coffee. "Yeah. I knew Wagner would have me investigate who she contacted and didn't want him questioning me if he talked to the two fuck-ups he sent on the hit. I told your tail to observe and nothing more. Figured you could handle yourself." He chuckled. "Want to tell me what you did to them? All they said was they had a run-in with you and refused to follow you anymore."

While Nick grinned widely and chuckled, Jake just smirked. "Let's just say Egghead and Polo were able to sharpen their interrogation skills." He paused as a female trucker walked past their table on the way to the rest rooms. "All right . . . give us the lowdown on why you're sitting on Wagner."

"You're not going to tell me where the girl is?" When Jake gave him a what-do-you-think look, Allman sighed and relented. "Fine. At least I know she's in good hands and probably far away from here. The last thing I need is a teenage girl mixed up in all this."

Taking a sip of his coffee, Nick frowned at the bitter taste. "Shit. I thought truck stops were supposed to have good coffee." He pushed his cup to the side, then glared at Allman. "So, are you going to tell us what *this* is? Or do we have to play twenty fucking questions? Because I, for one, hate that fucking game."

Snorting, the fed shook his head. "Yeah, you'll fit right in with the rest of Trident." He rested his forearms on the table. "Wagner came up on our radar about a year ago. Before that he was hometown-oriented—didn't have many dealings that originated outside the Tampa area. Mostly white-collar stuff like money laundering." The waitress returned with their orders and the fed waited until she was out of earshot before continuing. "Apparently one connection lead to another, and next thing we know, his name is being mentioned with illegal guns. I think it was just a matter of opportunity knocking and his greedy little hands getting itchy. Word was he became a middle-man for the Diaz cartel's arms business, so my bosses sent me under. The guns get shipped as phony business orders, then distributed via his companies to clients in the Southeast. We've just been waiting for the opportunity to get Diaz up here."

Suddenly losing his appetite, Jake knew where this was going and he wasn't happy about it. "Let me guess—you guys don't give a fucking crap about Wagner. You want Emmanuel before the DEA or FBI can get him and you plan on having Wagner cut a deal and testify. That prick is going to walk when this is all over, because you know damn well he's the type to rat instead of going to prison."

"Fuck," Nick muttered under his breath and Jake was surprised the kid didn't go on a rant. There were only two ways Alyssa was ever going to be safe and one of them just went down the shitter.

Allman held up his hand with a look of regret on his face. "I know. I'm not happy about it either after dealing with this asshole and it pisses me off even more after what you just told me about the daughter, but it's not my call."

Even though anger coursed through him, Jake knew not to take it out on the undercover guy—he was just following orders from higher up on the chain of command. "All right. So, when is this all going down? And where?"

"The shipment is coming in day after tomorrow. Diaz, himself, will be there along with a few cartel members who are spread out up and down the east coast. He's coming to the states to start branching out again—wants to show his U.S. contacts he's the real deal and can supply them with whatever they need. When I was down in Colombia, I overheard two of his lieutenants talking about the white-slavery trade. Looks like he's getting things back to where they were before his brother died."

Jake knew all too well what the Diaz cartel had been like under the eldest brother, Ernesto. Members of the original

Trident team had been on SEAL Team Four at the time the drug czar was being investigated by the U.S. government. It was during one of their missions that the man was ultimately killed in a shootout.

"Where?" he asked again.

Allman shook his head. "Sorry, Jake. I know you guys are good at what you do, but I'm not risking this op for anyone —not even a teenage girl. I've worked on this too long to have it fucked up."

When Nick growled and opened his mouth to say something, Jake subtly kicked his ankle under the table. "Look, I understand where you're coming from. But is there any way you can make sure the deal is for the weapons charges only. If he's got a blanket immunity, there's no way we'll be able to go after him for the rape, child abuse, and murder conspiracy charges."

Mulling it over a moment, Allman chewed and swallowed a mouthful of food. "Not sure about the murder charge, since I'm privy to the act—even though it was after the fact. His lawyers will make sure that's in any deal. As long as we don't come across evidence of the other charges, I think we can keep them out of it. I can talk to my superiors and the federal prosecutor, but I'm not guaranteeing anything. Most likely, they'll jump at a chance to have their cake and eat it, too, but you know as well as I do, things can become cluster-fucks. Do you think you'll be able to nail him?"

Jake's cell phone rang and when he saw the number, he answered it. "Donovan."

"I've got what you need," the female voice told him. "Can you meet me at the airport? I have to take off on an assignment as soon as possible."

"Yeah. Where?"

"Cell phone lot where you wait for arrivals, in a half hour."

Jordan gave him her rental car description before hanging up. His gaze met Allman's curious one. "In answer to your question, yeah, I think we can nail him." Pulling out some cash, he threw it on the table to cover the bill and tip, then gestured for Nick to slide out of the booth. "We've got to go. Call me if anything else comes up, Craig."

"Same goes for you."

Minutes later, Jake and Nick were back on the highway, this time heading to the airport. Traffic was still a little heavy, but they were only ten minutes away from Tampa International. Just as Jake changed lanes, his phone rang again. This time he activated the Blue Tooth feature and Tiny's voice came over the speakers. "Reverend, I've got bad news and you can kick our asses later. Alyssa's gone—took off on her own."

His hands gripped the steering wheel. "Fuck! What the hell is she doing?"

The big man's baritone voice was filled with worry and regret. "Honestly, I think she's on her way to kill her father." Jake and Nick looked at each other in shock. "Long story short, we got distracted with stuff and she took Henderson's gun and money. She dumped her cell phone in the driveway before taking off in our SUV. At most, she had a ten-minute head start before we realized she was gone. I called Sheriff Montgomery and asked him to check the roads heading out of town, but most of his deputies are out on a bad, multi-car accident. His brother volunteered to come get us. If we don't find her, we'll head to the airport. I'll call Ian and have him send CC up with the jet. Sorry, man."

"Shit." Jake was pissed, but it would be a waste of breath to bawl the guy out. It was obvious Tiny and Henderson knew they'd screwed up, but Alyssa had taken advantage of the situation and probably would have ran off anyway at some point. Was she really on her way to kill her father? *Fuck a fucking duck.* "All right. Listen. We're on our way to meet Carter's contact. She apparently has what we need. There's other shit going on that Alyssa has no knowledge of and she's walking into a minefield down here. If you find her, lock her down tight. And call me the second you have her."

"Got it."

As Jake disconnected the call, Nick gaped at him. "Is she out of her fucking mind?"

"Apparently. Damn it." He slammed his hand on the steering wheel then, realizing he was about to miss their exit, glanced in his blind spot before quickly changing lanes. "I don't know what the fuck she thinks she's doing, but we've got no way to track her. As far as I know, the vehicles up north are older models, so they don't have locators in them. But shoot Egghead a text and ask him if they do, just in case." Nick pulled out his phone and began typing. "If not, we're just going to have to wait for her to show up, which means tailing Wagner and that's going to piss off the feds, but I don't fucking care at this point."

When they pulled into the designated cell phone lot, Jake spotted Jordyn's vehicle and pulled in next to her, facing the opposite direction, so they could talk without getting out. Both rolled down their driver's windows and he got his first look at the woman who seemed to have the man-whore, Carter, twisted in a knot. She was about thirty years old and Foster had been pretty close in his imagined assessment—slender, yet fit, long black hair pulled up into a ponytail, and exotic brown eyes. Jake's guess of South American heritage was neither confirmed nor denied when she spoke without an accent of any kind as she handed him a thumb drive. "This is the original from the safe. All his kiddie-porn is on it—and there's more than one victim." She ignored the men's simultaneous curses and held up another drive. "I copied data from another drive that I left behind. This is the diary he kept on his other crimes—money laundering, arms and drug dealing, and some other stuff. Know anyone who'd be interested in getting this anonymously? We can't just hand it over without explaining how we got it and screwing up the chain of evidence."

"Send it to Keon at the FBI. He'll make sure it gets to the right people." Larry Keon was the Deputy Director, the number-two man in the agency, and Trident's contact. He'd helped them on numerous occasions and the team returned the favors every chance they got.

"Fine." Jordyn pulled down her sunglasses from where they'd been perched on her head and covered her eyes, but not before he saw them fill with loathing. "Tell that asshole, Carter, not to contact me again. I'm tossing my phone in the airport, so the number you have is no longer valid." She put her vehicle in drive, her frown dropping further. "And nail this fucking pervert to the wall for me—otherwise, I'll be tempted to come back and do it myself. And I guarantee it won't be pretty."

As she drove away, Jake turned to face Nick with his eyebrows almost reaching his hairline. "Damn. Carter's going to have his hands full if he goes after her the way I suspect he will–sooner or later. And I can't wait to watch the sparks fly when he lights up that firecracker."

25

*P*utting on her turn signal, Alyssa exited the highway at a rest stop just outside of Tampa and pulled up to the gas pumps. She was exhausted after driving straight through to Florida. Thank God she found a GPS unit in the vehicle's glove compartment, since she would have been hopelessly lost without it. The trip should have taken her a little over nine hours to get to Tampa, according to the calculations. But with the traffic, pit stops for gas and food, and a three-hour nap at another rest stop in Georgia, it was now close to ten o'clock at night.

Along the way, she'd thought about how, where, and when to approach her father. It would be hard to sneak up on him at the house, since she was sure he'd changed the alarm code again. He had a habit of doing that every few months, without telling anyone, and it'd driven her mother crazy when she came home and couldn't shut it off. And her father always had other men around—men she didn't like. While her father had never forced her to have sex with anyone else, she never liked the way some of his associates and friends had eyed her like she was a piece of meat and they were starving.

The best idea she came up with—and it wasn't a great idea, either—was to lure him somewhere private, with no one else around, and ambush him. Once she killed him, she would toss the gun in one of the many lakes or swamps in the area so no one could connect it to her. After that was where she became unsure of what to do next. Would Jake help her? She was sure he would eventually figure out what she did. Would he turn her in to the police? From her experience, anything would be better than letting Oliver Wagner live and continue to molest her or any other girl. Yes, she was aware she hadn't been the only one, but she never knew who the other girls were or how many of them had been abused. Her bastard father liked to compare her to the others while he was doing vile things to her.

She shivered and forced the memories from her mind. For now, she would gas up the empty tank and then find a place to sleep until the morning. She had to be on her toes when she faced down her abuser because when it was over, there would only be one of them left alive and Alyssa didn't have a death wish. Even though for the past year she'd been scared her father would find them, she'd also learned that her future was what she made of it. And she wanted the future she'd dreamed of long before her perverted father changed her life forever.

"Anything?"

A hushed round of "negative" answers flooded back through Jake's headset. Marco, Brody, Nick, Devon, and he were scattered throughout Wagner's neighborhood and the surrounding areas in discreet locations, keeping an eye out for Alyssa. It was a little before oh-one-hundred hours . . . plenty of time for her to have made it back to Tampa, even if she made some pit stops. They'd been in the area since six p.m. and nothing unusual had caught their attention. Boomer, Foster, McCabe, Tiny, Henderson, and one more operative on loan from Blackhawk Security would be taking over the watch soon, so the first shift could get some sleep. Ian had flown up to Washington D.C. for another one of the meetings he'd been having with the Pentagon and he was still being closed-mouth about what was going on.

Jake was more than worried for the teenager, he was terrified. Nothing good would come from her going after her father. She would either wind end up getting herself killed or arrested for pre-meditated murder—and at seventeen, she'd be tried as an adult. *Damn it!* Why the hell didn't she just leave this up to him? He would move heaven and earth to help her and put her father where he could never hurt her again.

"Reverend, we're here to relieve you." Boomer's voice was loud and clear through the earpiece. "Where's everyone located?"

Tapping the mic, Jake gave his teammate his location and then the others followed suit. Minutes passed before the human hoot of an owl alerted him to Boomer's approach several yards behind him. He'd been in the woods behind Wagner's house, keeping an eye on the backdoor and yard.

The youngest member of Trident's Alpha Team, dressed in black and camo like the rest of them, sidled up to him in complete silence before he spoke. "All quiet?"

"Yeah." Jake stood from his prone position and handed over his night vision goggles. "Brody caught her SUV on a traffic cam on I-75 when she crossed over from Georgia about five hours ago, but the Florida system is down with a glitch and he hasn't been able to locate her since. I let Allman know we were out here. He's not thrilled, but knows if Alyssa tries to kill Wagner, it could screw up his op."

"Do you honestly think she's going to try and kill him?"

He sighed and tilted his head from side to side, working out the kinks which had settled there. "Yeah, I do—but I don't blame her for wanting to. I just hope we find her first."

Boomer nodded his agreement, then dropped to the ground to take over the watch. Stealthily finding his way back to where he would meet Nick a few blocks away, Jake tried to think of where Alyssa might be if she'd arrived in Tampa by now. The possibilities were endless, but he knew of several crappy motels which didn't require credit cards upon check-in. Places like that usually charged by the hour though, and he hated to think of the teenager in one of them. But the alternative wasn't much better—sleeping in the vehicle somewhere.

As he approached his truck, he noticed Nick sitting in the driver's seat, so he hopped in the passenger side and tossed his headset in the middle console. "A chauffeured ride? What more can I ask for?"

Putting the SUV in drive, Nick smirked at him. "How about some sex in the shower when we get home?"

Even though Jake's cock twitched happily at the thought, he shook his bigger head. "Later. For now, I want to hit a few motel parking lots and other places where she might be holed up until morning. I've got a bad feeling about this and we need to find her before it's too late."

"Damn. I hate when the right thing to do overrides my sex life."

"Me, too, Junior. Me, too."

"It's me, you bastard."

Oliver Wagner froze for a moment at the young, female voice coming through the cell phone earpiece. "You little cunt. Where the hell are you?"

"Tampa."

What the fuck is the bitch doing here? Tampa was the last place he expected her to show up. Well, at least he didn't have to have those fuck-ups look for her anymore.

"If you don't come meet me with those pictures and videos you took of me, you sick son of a bitch, then I'm going to the press."

He growled as rage filled him. "You wouldn't fucking dare."

"I've got nothing to lose anymore. You killed my mother. You made sure I was isolated from anyone else that would help me. I'll leave you and your perverted lifestyle alone. All I want is the pictures and videos, so I can destroy them. If I find out you made copies, I'll go to the press."

Shocked at how strong and determined she sounded, Wagner mulled over his options. There was no way he was turning anything over to the little bitch, but making her think he would was the perfect way to draw her into a trap. He'd kill her, then have two of his minions take the body out into the Gulf of Mexico and sink it. "Fine," he spat out. "But then I never want to hear from you again. If you go to the press or police, I'll fucking kill you myself." He rattled off the address of the building where his landscaping business equipment and vehicles were stored—since today was Sunday, it would be closed. The area was also isolated, so he didn't have to worry about anyone reporting anything unusual or any witnesses. Opening his desk drawer, he pulled out the .38 caliber handgun he kept there. "Be there in one hour or the deal is off. If that happens, I'll hunt you down and make you regret it."

"Just bring everything, you bastard, and I'll be there."

The line went dead and Wagner took several deep breaths to keep from throwing the cell phone against the wall, shattering it into hundreds of pieces. The little cunt would rue the day she defied and threatened him.

———

"Reverend, target's on the move."

Jake put his SUV in drive. "Copy that, Devil Dog. We're ready to tail him. Everyone else stay in position and keep an eye out for our girl."

It was ten minutes to nine in the morning and the two surveillance teams had switched places, once again, in the area surrounding Oliver Wagner's property. Nick and Jake's hour-long tour of the no-tell motels in the middle of the night had been fruitless. And Tampa was too big of a city, with plenty of places for Alyssa to be hiding at, for them to even hope of finding her if she didn't want to be found. The interstate traffic cameras were up and running again, but it was too late for them to be of any assistance. The city-wide traffic cams might be useful, but Jake wasn't too optimistic that Brody would find her after he'd hacked into the system. The geek was currently in his war-room at Trident doing his best to find her. However, the black SUV she'd taken was as non-descript as they come, so chances of spotting it among the thousands of other vehicles in Tampa was slim.

Knowing Wagner would most likely be leaving the

house at some point during the day, Jake and Nick had been parked nearby, ready to follow him when he did. While on the first shift the night before, Marco had snuck up the driveway and tagged the man's BMW with a tracking device, right next to the one the ATF had attached to the undercarriage months earlier. Now, sitting in the passenger seat, Nick turned on the tracker's receiver and it beeped sharply as the screen lit up. "Got him. He's going to pass right by us."

Sure enough, a few seconds later, the steel-grey vehicle drove past where they were idling in the lot of a baseball field, down the street from the residence. Jake waited until Wagner made a left turn at the intersection, before pulling out to shadow him. If they drove to a busier part of town, he'd get closer, but for now they were relying on the tracker.

"Take the second right—he's heading east."

Following Nick's directions, Jake tailed Wagner to a seedier side of town for another twenty minutes. Bypassing blocks of apartment buildings and businesses, they were lead toward a mainly commercial yet sparse area. Here, the individual properties took up at least three to five acres each, so everything was spread out a bit.

"Slow down. He turned left up ahead, but not onto a street. Must've pulled into one of these buildings."

The SUV slowed and passed several commercial sites. Jake kept one eye on the road and the other on the property lots, until he spotted the BMW parked next to a white pick-up truck. Wagner was disappearing into a weather-beaten warehouse with two other men on his heels. "There he is, walking into that grey building." Seconds after he passed the entrance to the property, he slammed on the brakes. "Fuck!"

Nick's gaze whipped around and he tried to figure out what Jake had seen. "What is it?"

"The SUV Alyssa was driving is parked on the side of the warehouse." Jerking the steering wheel to the left, he spun the truck around and stopped at the entrance to an adjacent parking lot—pulling in front of the other one would alert the occupants to their presence.

Devon's voice came over his headset along with some interference. "Reverend, you cut out. Did you say you spotted our girl?"

Rattling off the address on a dilapidated sign stuck in the ground near the entrance, Jake shoved the gear shift into park. "Haven't spotted her yet, but the SUV is here. Start hauling ass, but we can't wait for you. There's a least two tangos with Wagner."

Damn. Fuck. Shit. And damn, again. The teenager must have contacted her father and arranged to meet him here. God help her if shit went down before they got inside. They leapt from the vehicle, drawing their weapons. Nick fell into step next to Jake, their eyes on the lookout for Alyssa and/or trouble.

"Cops?" Devon asked over the airwaves.

"No," Jake responded in a low voice, hoping he didn't regret that decision. "We're going to try and do this without creating a hostage situation and screwing up a federal undercover op. We'll stay wired so you can hear everything go down."

"Copy that. Be safe, brothers."

The asphalt was cracked and crumbling in spots with green and brown weeds popping up here and there. Scattered litter forced them to take extra care not to kick anything or trip. The few windows in the building were covered in dust, dirt, and grime, making them impossible to see through and a large garage door was down in place. The smaller metal door the men had entered was still ajar by about eight inches. As they silently approached the structure, Jake hand-gestured for Nick to go around back. They were outnumbered and it would be better if they went in from two different directions, doubling their vantage points. He also hoped Nick would spot Alyssa before the other men did.

As the kid veered off, Jake crept closer to the open door, where he paused and listened. He was unable to see inside due to the bright sunlight outside and the darkness within. But his gut clenched when he heard Wagner's voice echo throughout the structure, demanding the teenage show herself. Fuck that duck again, this was about to get ugly.

"I'M HERE, you little bitch. Where are you?"

Alyssa peeked around the tractor she was hiding behind, then jerked back again. *Shit.* Her father wasn't alone—she should have expected this. She didn't recognize the two men, one blond guy, the other bald, but that didn't mean anything. Her father employed a bunch of creepy, intimidating men. Shivers of fear and foolish remorse surged through her body. This had been a stupid idea. *Stupid. Stupid. Stupid.* Why hadn't she thought this through better? The hand holding the gun quivered and she swallowed the lump in her throat.

"Come on, Alyssa. Let's fucking get this over with. I don't have all day."

Glancing around, she realized she was screwed. She'd left the backdoor open as an escape route, but she couldn't get to it from where she was hidden without being seen.

Maybe they hadn't spotted her vehicle around the side of the building. If they didn't, they might think she had changed her mind about coming here.

"Alyssa," her father growled. "There's no point hiding. I saw the truck outside, so I know you're here."

So much for that little prayer. Sounds of feet shuffling reached her ears, but she couldn't pinpoint where they were coming from—the acoustics in the building amplified and distorted everything. She shifted her squatting stance and searched for a way out. Maybe if she stayed low, she could get behind the trailer about ten feet away. From there she might be able to work her way around to the backdoor.

Holding her breath, Alyssa was ready to make the quick dash, but a hand came around her mouth and another around the gun, twisting it out of her grasp. "Gotcha."

Her scream was muffled as she tried to squirm out of the man's grip, but her fight was useless as he dragged her out into the open and shoved her down at her father's feet. When his bald henchman handed him her gun, Oliver Wagner sneered at his daughter. "What's this? Thought you would shoot me? You wouldn't have the guts."

Pushing herself to her feet, she held out her hand. "Give it back to me and I'll prove you wrong." She wished she sounded stronger. Even she didn't believe her words, but she couldn't keep the tremors from her voice.

In the blink of an eye, her father backhanded her across the face and she fell to the ground again. Pain exploded through her cheek as she tasted blood in her mouth. The bastard glared at her. "You little cunt. Too bad you're too grown up for my liking anymore, but I'm sure the boys here will glad to teach you a lesson in respect."

Oh God, no. The fear she felt before was nothing compared to what ran through her veins at this very moment. While the bald guy licked his lips in anticipation of a little fun, the blond guy just stared at her with an expression she could only call cold and calculating. He scared her more than the other two men put together—and knowing her father, that said a lot. Crab walking backward, she tried to scramble away, but Baldy reached down and grabbed her ankle, dragging her forward again.

"No!" she screamed, kicking her other foot at him, trying to dislodge his tight grip.

"Let her go!" Jake's voice filled the building and everyone froze. Well, everyone except Alyssa—she thrust her free foot upward, catching Baldy in the crotch. The man bellowed in pain and released her leg, but when she got her feet under her and stood, her father grabbed her around the neck and held the gun to her head. The other two men had pulled out their weapons and were pointing them at a trailer near the front entrance. She couldn't see Jake, but apparently the men had zeroed in on his location.

Holding her in front of him, her father yelled, "Get out here or I'll kill her right now."

Terrified for Jake, she struggled against the hard grip, but it was useless. She prayed he hadn't come alone. If anything happened to him, she would never forgive herself.

"Why don't you let her go, jackass, and we'll forget the whole thing."

"Fuck you!" Oliver bellowed then lowered his voice and growled at his men. "Get the fucking bastard and kill him."

NICK ROUNDED the back of the building and was relieved to see the rear door was ajar, making it easy for him to sneak in without the rusty hinges announcing his presence. He stopped a few inches away from the doorjamb and took a quick peek in, only exposing his head for the briefest moment. He was in luck. There was plenty of landscaping equipment and trailers for him to use as cover. Unfortunately, that same stuff was preventing him from seeing who was in there and where they were located.

Under the cloak of silence, with his gun held close to his chest and the muzzle pointing forward, he cleared the corner. Extending his arms in front of him, he let his weapon lead the way.

"No!"

He halted at the sound of Alyssa yelling, followed by Jake's voice. "Let her go!"

Heading in the direction of the teenager's cry, Nick's presence stayed masked by a tractor. As Wagner and Jake continued to shout orders and insults at each other, he peered around the side of the big piece of machinery. Three men with guns and one terrified female hostage—*great, just fucking great.*

Since everyone's attention was focused on the trailer Jake was hiding behind, Nick inched further around the green John Deere, just in time to hear Wagner tell his men, "Get the fucking bastard and kill him."

Not on my watch!

The two goons stepped toward the trailer and Nick aimed his gun at the bald guy. "Take one more step and . . ." He never had time to inform him that he'd be a dead man because the asshole spun around in the direction of Nick's voice, the gun coming around to fire. But Nick beat him to it, firing twice in rapid succession. Both bullets hit their mark, dead center in the man's chest. Before the body hit the ground, Nick was already pivoting and searching out his next target.

The other goon had disappeared behind a pickup truck and was exchanging gunfire with Jake. Confident he wasn't needed there at the moment, Nick tried to locate Wagner and Alyssa, who had disappeared from view. Through the echoing reports of bullets being discharged, he was able to hear the teenage cry out in pain from behind some other equipment. Making sure he wasn't in the other asshole's line of fire, he hurried over and cocked his head around a huge, diesel engine.

Wagner still had his daughter by the neck, choking and dragging her toward the rear entrance Nick had used. Alyssa was struggling, but she was no match for the larger man. "Let go of me!"

Aiming his gun at the bastard's head, Nick stepped out into the open. "Freeze, asshole!"

Wagner whirled around, placing Alyssa between them and held the muzzle of the gun at her head. "Who the fuck are you?"

"Your worst nightmare. Let her go."

The man seemed to be weighing his options as Nick took a few more steps forward, trying to ignore the look of terror on the teenager's face. "You hurt one hair on her head and it'll be the last thing you do."

"I don't think so."

The man's eyes flashed to something behind Nick at the same time Alyssa screamed, "Look out!"

Wagner shoved the girl toward Nick, blocking any shot, but he was already spinning around to find the other threat. Two shots were fired almost simultaneously and neither had been from Nick's gun. Excruciating, hot pain tore through his chest, and a vaguely familiar voice stopped him from firing his weapon at the man who'd appeared behind him. "ATF! Don't shoot!"

Allman.

Nick's legs began to give out as he looked back at Wagner to see the man was dead on the floor with a bullet hole to his forehead. Alyssa was also on the ground, crying but alive. His knees hit the cement flooring, and he heard her scream his name as a black shroud descended over him and he collapsed into the darkness.

26

*T*rying to keep his mind on the guy shooting at him, and not the sounds of Nick engaging the other two men and Alyssa's cries and screams, Jake crouched down behind a trailer. From what he could tell, Nick had taken care of one of the goons, but Wagner was still out there.

Something behind him clattered, but a shuffled foot seconds before had come from the other direction. The guy was trying to make him chase a red herring. *Not happening, asshole.* Turning the tables, Jake picked a rock out of the tread of a huge tire he was squatting next to and threw it to his left. Just as he'd hoped, a shadow appeared to his right. The guy rounded the trailer looking toward where the rock had landed and by the time he noticed Jake to his left, it was too late—he was in the former SEAL's gun sites. But the asshole wasn't going down easy. He swung his gun hand around, however, Jake was ready for it and fired his weapon, hitting the goon in the face. In a reflexive reaction, the man's finger squeezed the trigger, but the shot went off harmlessly several feet to Jake's left. The body was dead before it hit the floor.

Just to be safe, Jake stood and stepped forward, before kicking the man's gun to the side. Pivoting, he tried to zero in on where Nick and Wagner were, but Alyssa screaming "look out", followed by two gunshots, had his blood running cold.

"ATF! Don't shoot!"

A split second of relief was shattered at the teenager's next words. "Nick! Nooooo!"

Shit!

Circumventing the trailer, Jake spotted Allman disappearing around the far side of a platform holding two large, diesel engines. Running like his life depended on it, he wasn't prepared for what he found. Wagner was dead. Alyssa was on her knees crying and Nick . . . *oh, God, Nick . . .*

Jake's heart and gut felt shredded in that moment, and a fear, unlike anything he'd ever known, gripped him in its talons.

Shit! Shit! Shit!

Allman was on his knees, ripping open the kid's shirt and glanced up when he heard Jake approach. "He's alive, but it got him in the chest. Call 911."

Unable to look away from the blood seeping out of Nick's upper torso, Jake fumbled in his pocket for his phone. He quickly pushed the digits.

"9-1-1. What's your emergency?"

———

SITTING ON A CHAIR, bent at the waist, Jake held his head in his hands. Thick, heavy tension hung in the air of the surgical waiting room. In his mind, he replayed everything that'd happened for what felt like the thousandth time since the ambulance carrying Nick pulled away from the scene. After watching it speed down the road with lights flashing and sirens blaring, Allman had filled Jake, Devon, and the rest of them, in on what'd happened.

The fed had gotten a text from Wagner telling him to meet the others at the storage garage without further explanation. Traffic had been heavy and he'd pulled up just as the gunfire started. Upon entering the building, Alyssa's screams had him dashing in her direction. Unfortunately, his arrival had inadvertently set things in motion for Nick to be shot. Allman had been able to make the shot that killed Wagner a split second after the man had fired at Nick.

The rest of the team had shown up about three minutes later. Devon had been as white as a ghost when he ran into the building, his gaze searching for his injured brother. Jake had almost forgotten they'd all heard everything go down. Apparently, they'd muted their mics, so as not to distract Jake and Nick with unnecessary chatter.

When the second rig of paramedics was ready to transport Alyssa to the hospital, Jake had hopped in with them. Even though she was basically unharmed, sans a few scratches and bruises, they still wanted her to be looked at by a physician and the teenager had refused to go without him. Allman had handled the local police and feds who'd shown up, but Jake was going to have to give his formal statements to the ATF, FBI, and local P.D. as soon as Nick got out of surgery.

Fuck! What could he have done differently? There had to have been an alternate scenario which didn't result in Nick fighting for his life. If he died . . . no! Jake refused to let that thought be completed. The kid couldn't die. *God, please. I know it's been a long time since I've asked you for anything, but please let him live.*

He glanced around the room. Three quarters of the occupants were here awaiting word on Nick. Rick and Eileen Michaelson, Boomer's parents, and Jenn were sitting with Alyssa, trying to reassure her that everything would be all right and it wasn't her fault. The ER doctors had checked her over and released her into his care after he explained the recent deaths of both her parents and claimed she was his niece. Devon and Kristen, Angie, Marco, Brody, Boomer and Kat, Mitch, Kayla, Tiny, and Henderson were scattered around the room, some standing, others sitting. Mitch's parents were on vacation and he was holding off on calling them, while his brother was waiting in Atlanta for word on whether or not he needed to make the trip for their cousin. Kayla's wife, Dr. Roxanne London, had been with the solemn group earlier, but was now checking on one of her pediatric patients who'd been brought into the emergency room. Trident's secretary, Colleen, was holding down the fort at the compound with the help of Foster and McCabe.

Jake's brother, Mike, had driven their mom to the hospital after she insisted on seeing for herself that Jake was okay. They didn't want to be in the way, so they hadn't stayed long, but promised to check in with him later. The two were still in the dark about his relationship with Nick and it hadn't seemed like the appropriate time for him to tell them.

Sitting next to him, Angie reached over and rubbed his shoulder in silent support. She'd been on an early morning flight returning from New York when everything had gone down and Tiny had driven to the airport to pick her up and bring her to the hospital. Although he'd grown to love all the women of Trident like the sisters he'd never had, Angie was the one he was closest to. While he'd been helping Ian protect her months ago, the two of them had just clicked.

He looked up when Angie gasped, stood, and ran into Ian's arms as he walked into the room two seconds before his parents did. When Devon had called his oldest brother, Ian had abruptly ended his meeting at the Pentagon and rushed back to Tampa. CC had flown him up to D.C. and had been waiting for him at the airport for an evening flight anyway. The extremely wealthy Chuck and Marie Sawyer had taken their own private jet as well. Thankfully, they'd been at home in Charlotte when Devon called them, instead of halfway around the world on one of their charity trips. The Sawyer matriarch was a plastic surgeon who spent a good portion of her time helping the organization Operation Smile perform facial reconstructive surgery on children in third world countries.

Jake, Devon, and the others all stood to greet the newcomers. Chuck hugged his second-born son. "Any word?"

Devon shook his head. "Not yet, Dad. He's been in there for over two hours. The good news is the bullet went straight through. Less damage that way . . . we hope."

Making her way through the group of family and friends, Marie kissed and hugged everyone. When she reached Jake, he let her pull him into an embrace, but couldn't look her in the eye. It was his fault the Sawyers might have to bury another son.

Jake shook hands with Chuck, again avoiding eye contact, and then sat back in his seat to wait for the surgeon to come let them know Nick's condition. It was another forty minutes before a tired-looking man in his fifties, wearing scrubs, entered the room. "Nick Sawyer's family."

The doctor's eyes widened when the group of eighteen all stood and hurried toward him. He held up his hands in reassurance. "It looks like he's going to be fine. Sore, but fine. Once we got the bleeding stopped and gave him a transfusion for the volume he lost, it was just a matter of repairing the damage to his muscles and the subclavian vein that the bullet nicked. He's a lucky guy. The angle of the bullet's entry helped it stay away from the spine. And if he hadn't been in such good shape, things may have been different. Now, only two people can go see him in recovery and a nurse will let you know when they can go in. I'm sending him to the surgical intensive care unit until I reevaluate him tomorrow, just as a precaution."

While everyone else sighed with relief and hugged each other, Marie identified herself as a physician to the surgeon and stepped outside the room with him to get a more technical report on Nick's condition. The relief which coursed through Jake wouldn't replace the guilt he felt. Even though the circumstances were completely different, he blamed himself now as much as he had when Max had ended up in the hospital with devastating injuries so many years ago.

Feeling himself closing in on an emotional breakdown, he knew he had to get out of there. Turning to Ian and Devon, he said, "I've got to go give my statement to the feds. Alyssa's been cleared to give hers tomorrow. I'm not allowed to be in with her when she gives it, so I contacted Reggie to be her lawyer. He'll get her through it." His gaze met Devon's. "Thanks for letting her stay with you tonight. I think she'll do better with the rest of the girls around. I'll check in with you later."

The brothers exchanged a look he couldn't decipher, then Ian eyed him with concern. "Okay. You all right?"

Taking two steps closer to the door, he swallowed hard then nodded. "Yeah. Glad the kid is okay. I'll talk to you later."

Feeling like a coward, unworthy of his team's brotherhood, Jake fled with tears in his eyes.

27

*A*fter snatching a beer from his fridge, Jake shut the door with his hip. His other hand was holding his phone to his ear. "I'm glad you're getting settled in, Alyssa. Boomer's parents are great people, and I'm only a phone call away if you need me."

"I know you are, Jake. And they're very nice. I still can't believe they offered to help me. It's a little weird, because they keep saying this is my home now and I'm not a guest, but I still feel like I have to ask before I do anything or eat something."

"That'll pass after you all get used to each other." He threw the bottle cap in the garbage pail and ambled out to the living room, plopping down in the recliner he'd been moping in all day. The teenager's call was the only positive thing that'd happened in the past two days.

"That's what Eileen said. She's taking me to register for my G.E.D. classes on Monday, then shopping for books and whatever else I need. Tomorrow is my first appointment with my new therapist, and Rick is going to teach me some self-defense. He says every girl should know how to kick some effing ass." She giggled. "His words, not mine."

Letting out a snort, Jake leaned back until the footrest popped up. "Yeah, he's got a military mouth on him. Just don't start repeating it."

"I won't. Oh, the pizza is here. I gotta go. Thanks again for everything, Jake."

"You're welcome, sweetheart. I'll talk to you soon."

"'Kay. Bye."

"Bye." Jake disconnected the call and tossed the phone on the side table next to him. He was glad she sounded happy. Rick and Eileen had apparently discussed the orphaned teenager between them after they'd found out she had no other family, and then offered to let her come live with them in Sarasota, an hour south of Tampa. If all went well during the next few weeks, they intended to file for legal guardianship.

When they'd picked her up at the compound yesterday, he'd been there to give Eileen five hundred dollars toward Alyssa's clothes shopping. Pete Archer had swung by her former home in Canon City, Colorado to retrieve her things. But when he'd gotten there, he found the landlords were in the middle of throwing everything out, since the crime scene had been released. Pete had only been able to salvage some pictures of Alyssa and her mom, and a few other items he thought she might want. He was packaging them up and mailing them to her in Sarasota. Knowing she needed a whole new wardrobe, Jake insisted on paying for it.

The Michaelsons would take good care of her and give her the guidance she needed to finish her education. With her sweet personality, he doubted it would take her long to make a bunch of friends. In the meantime, Jake had one of the lawyers Trident used working to make sure she received her father's estate—well, what hadn't been seized by the government. Thankfully, some of his businesses had been legit with no ties to his illegal activities. Reggie Helm had been in contact with Oliver Wagner's lawyer and would be filing the necessary paperwork with the courts to ensure the girl's financial future was secure. Reggie was also arranging to have Carrie Wagner's remains sent to Florida and Jake would then help Alyssa find the right resting place for her mother.

With Craig Allman's help, the Canon City, Colorado detectives were able to get enough evidence to issue a warrant for the arrest of the two men who'd murdered Carrie Wagner. Their vehicle had been spotted in Mississippi by the state police. A high-speed chase developed, resulting in the suspects plowing their vehicle into the back of a tractor trailer, killing both men instantly. Jake was glad to hear that—two fewer mouths to feed on death row in Colorado.

Unfortunately, not everything went as well as a result of Oliver's death. This morning, Allman had called to tell him that Emmanuel Diaz had heard about the death and that he'd been duped by the ATF, so the shipment of weapons disappeared. Months of undercover work had gone down the drain thanks to a newspaper photographer who'd seen the police activity at the warehouse and taken pictures of the scene. The police and feds had tried to keep the identities of the dead a secret until after the sting, but the photographer had gotten shots of the vehicles in the lot. From there, it hadn't been hard for the press to run the license plates and Wagner's name had been made public in connection with the incident.

As he brought the beer bottle to his lips, the doorbell rang and Jake glanced at the time on his cable box.

Eighteen-thirty hours. *Who the hell could that be?* Placing his beer next to his phone, he stood and hurried to the door. He wasn't prepared for the person he found on the other side.

"Is there a reason you're here, while my son is in the hospital, driving everyone nuts with his surly attitude? I expected better from you, Jake."

He sighed and stepped back to allow Dr. Marie Sawyer to enter, knowing he was about to get an ass kicking. Nick's petite mom was a force to be reckoned with when she got her Irish up about something. She was one of the most caring people he knew, but when someone was doing her loved ones wrong, then look out. Jake shut the door with a click and followed her back into his living room. Gesturing for her to take a seat on the couch, he waited until she was sitting before easing back into his recliner again, leaving the footrest down this time. "He told you about us."

It wasn't a question, but she still answered him. "Yes, but not intentionally. Apparently, Nick talks in his sleep when he's under the influence of narcotic painkillers. But before that, I knew something was wrong, because there was hope in his eyes every time the door opened. Followed by disappointment when it wasn't the one person he wanted to see."

He ran a hand down his face in frustration, the coarse whiskers he hadn't shaven in days scratching his palm. "I don't know why the hell he wants to see me. It's my fault he's in there. He could've been killed. It should be me laying in the hospital."

"Bullshit."

Jake's gaze whipped up to meet hers. He didn't think he'd ever heard her curse before, despite her husband and sons' foul language. The baby-blue eyes her sons had inherited narrowed as she glared at him.

"Yes, he could have been killed, but you know as well as I do, Jake, there are no guarantees in life. What I don't believe is your claim that it's your fault. Would Ian or Devon have done anything differently than Nick or you did? I know all my boys, and that includes everyone at Trident, because I love all of you . . . *all* of my boys would have done exactly the same thing to protect that girl and their teammate. I wouldn't expect less from any one of you. No mother wants to bury their child—I've done it once before and hope to God I don't have to go through it again. But if I do, and if it's because he was saving an innocent young woman's life in the process, I'll be damn proud, despite my grief."

During her speech, Jake's gaze dropped to the floor. She didn't understand, she couldn't.

"Do you love him?"

He shook his head and his response was hoarse as something inside his soul began to break. "I can't."

"That wasn't what I asked you, Jake Donovan." Her glower pierced him like a dagger. "Do you love him? Do you honestly want to walk away from him and be alone for the rest of your life? Or do you want to overcome whatever has been haunting you all these years and be completely happy? Finally have someone who loves you as much as you love him? And don't bother denying it, because if you didn't love him, you wouldn't be hiding in your apartment *looking* like you lost the love of your life." She rose from her seat and Jake followed suit, towering almost a foot above her, but she waved him off. "I've said my piece and now I'll stay out of it. The decision is yours to make. I hope for both of your sakes, you make the right one. I'll see myself out."

Jake stood there with the weight of the world on his shoulders long after she was gone.

SITTING IN HIS IDLING TRUCK, Jake stared at the building in front of him, trying to find the courage to go into the lobby of the Brentwood Arms. He'd never been inside the condo complex in Clearwater, but had heard the units were upscale and spacious. This was the last place he expected to find himself, but before he went to talk to Nick, there was someone else he had to apologize to first.

Shutting the engine off, he climbed out and hit the remote lock on his keychain. He forced himself to put one foot in front of the other until he reached the door. His hand shook as he reached for the handle. Turning around, he took a deep breath while running a hand through his hair. *You can do this, Donovan. You're a Navy SEAL, for God's sake! Get a fucking grip!*

Doing an about face once again, he opened the door before he chickened out. The desk guard eyed him suspiciously. "Can I help you?"

"Um, yeah . . ." He cleared his throat while the man waited. "Sorry. I'm here to see Max Sterling. Unit 610."

The guard picked up the phone. "What's your name? I have to check with him before I can send you up."

"Jake Donovan."

Part of him wanted the guard to say there was no answer, but Jake didn't think he could find the courage to come back another time. He had to do this. Marie Sawyer and Trudy Dunbar were right. It was time to overcome his demons.

"Go on up. It'll be on your right when you exit the elevator."

"Thanks."

While waiting for the elevator car, Jake scanned the lobby. It was a nice place. Opulent. Classic. Not his style, but still quite nice. Above his head, a ding sounded seconds before the doors opened. Stepping in, he punched the button for the sixth floor and less than a minute later found himself knocking on the door of unit 610. The man who opened the door didn't seem happy to see him. He was about five eleven and a hundred and seventy-five pounds, but his expression said he wanted to take on the man who had six inches and thirty-five pounds more than him, most of which was solid muscle. Jake had no idea who the guy was, but he evidently knew who Jake was.

"Let him in, Ray."

The deep, rumbling voice came from beyond Jake's view, but he'd recognize it anywhere. Frowning, Ray did as he was ordered and took a step back, allowing him to enter. Max was in the process of standing when Jake walked into the large, finely-furnished living room. His heart clenched at the sight of the man. He was two-inches shorter than Jake, but still had the commanding presence of a Dom, which would be noticed immediately by anyone in the lifestyle. His short, dark blond hair was receding a little, but he was still a very handsome man. "Come here, Jake. I won't bite."

Swallowing hard, Jake took several more steps forward until he was about a foot away from the other man. Whatever he'd expected, wasn't what happened. Max held out his hand and when Jake took it, the man pulled him close and hugged him tight. "I'm so glad you finally came to see me. I didn't think you'd ever get past it."

Stunned, his eyes filled with tears as his former Dom pulled away and brought his hands up to Jake's newly shaven face. The touch was gentle as his fingertips created an image of the features his hazel eyes would never see again. "I don't know why it surprises me, but you've changed. You're about an inch or two taller than you were at seventeen. And it seems the military took good care of you. I'm just sorry I can't say the same."

"What?" Jake's voice was hoarse again, his emotions getting stuck in his throat. He tried clearing it, but the coarseness was still there. "What are you talking about? I was the one who should've been there for you. I should've . . . I should've gone back to the hospital and taken care of you. I couldn't right away, but when I was able to . . ."

Max sighed and cut off whatever his former lover was about to say with a slash of his hand in the air. "Enough, Jake. Sit down." Yup, there was the commanding Dom Jake remembered. "Ray, stop glaring and get him something to drink. Water? Soda? Sorry, we have nothing stronger. Neither of us drink."

Glancing at Ray, he saw the man's expression had softened a little, but he was still trying to figure out what Jake was doing here. "Water is fine. Thanks."

Ray nodded and disappeared into the kitchen as Jake sat on the couch across from the winged-back chair Max took. A teasing grin came over Max's handsome, yet scared face. "We've been together for eight years and he still can't figure out how I know when he's frowning. I won't tell him because it's too much fun to mess with him."

Returning, Ray handed Jake a bottle of water before taking a chair next to Max. He remained silent as the Dom spoke. "Jake, you were seventeen, even though you looked much older. Hell, thinking back now, I should never have approached you. But there you were, a hot, jock quarterback, looking like you should be in Hollywood, willingly volunteering at the food pantry, and I didn't care that you were too young. I was a new Dom—still learning. I should have known better. But this . . ." He gestured to his eyes. "This was not your fault. This is the result of a homophobic jackass. Unfortunately, the jackass was your father."

Jake thought back to that horrible weekend. Max had taken him to an underground BDSM club they'd been to a few times. They had been in a relationship for two months, and Max had told him early on that he was a Dom and wanted Jake to submit to him. At first, he'd thought it meant the twenty-one-year-old man wanted to abuse him, but he soon found out the lifestyle was not about abuse—far from it. It was about trust, honesty, and pleasure. It was about control, and while Max was the Master, Jake had been the one who was in charge. His limits and his safeword gave him the ultimate power in the exchange. While they'd been playing in private, Max had wanted to show his beautiful young sub off in a public scene.

Nervous, but wanting to please his Master, the man he was falling in love with, Jake had consented. The scene had been planned out in advance, so the only thing that'd had his knees shaking was the fact that dozens of people would be watching them.

"Don't worry, babe. They'll love you. No one will ridicule you here for enjoying kink. I'll have you in subspace in no time."

Jake calmed as Master Max ran a hand up and down his back. He could do this . . . it wasn't something they hadn't previously done. "Yes, Sir."

"That's my boy." Max grabbed the front of his shirt and brought their lips together in a sweet, yet commanding kiss. "You don't know how much your consent pleases me."

Smiling, Max led his submissive into the club. While it looked like a triple X video and fetish store in a seedier section of Tampa, the basement had been transformed into a dungeon where gays and straights could indulge in their individual kinks. As they entered a door marked private at the back of the store and descended the stairs, Jake's heart-beat sped up. The smells and sounds from below made him hard instantly, and he groaned inwardly, knowing he wasn't allowed to touch his cock now that they were playing—not even to adjust himself. Max owned it during play, and any contact Jake's hand made with it would result in punishment. And there was no way he wanted that tonight, because Max's punishments usually resulted in a serious case of blue balls.

When they reached the bottom of the stairs, Jake took a deep breath and lowered his gaze to the floor, respecting the submissive rules of the club. From somewhere across the room, a loud crack of a flogger sounded and a woman cried out, then begged for more. Flesh slapped against flesh in another area, while the roar of a man cumming filled the air.

"Take off all your clothes, boy, but for now you can keep your briefs on. I'm not quite ready to share that particular beauty with the others yet. Let them dream of what it looks like for a bit. Tease them."

Jake did as he was ordered and was soon standing with only one scrap of navy blue cotton preventing him from being completely nude. He knew the only reason he'd been allowed to keep them on was Max was aware of his nervousness and inexperience with the lifestyle. He was easing his sub into the scene. A Domme dressed all in black sidled up to Jake, but purred at Max. "Are you sure he doesn't like pussy, Master Max? Because that huge package is something I would love to impale myself on . . . over and over again."

While the Mistress was standing within inches of him, she didn't touch Jake at all. Not without Max's permission. And since his Master didn't share, it wasn't going to happen. "He is damn fine, isn't he?"

It had been weird at first, how some the Doms and Dommes talked about their subs as if they were pets and couldn't answer *for themselves, but Jake had learned to accept it. He followed Max around the room as his Master spoke to several other Doms, remembering to keep his eyes averted. Max had told him that every club and Dom had their own protocols, but it was best if a sub avoided eye-contact with a Dom unless being spoken to.*

It wasn't long before Jake's accelerated breathing and heart-rate weren't from nervousness, but instead, anticipation. And his Master recognized the fact. He led his submissive to an area he'd reserved for their scene. A St. Andrew's cross stood in the corner and it was what Jake was going to be shackled to. They had done a similar scene the weekend before, but it had been in the privacy of Max's apartment.

Stepping up to the cross, Jake waited for his Master's command.

"Strip, my sub. Let me show everyone here how beautiful you are."

He swallowed hard then dropped his briefs, not daring to look at anyone's reactions. He wasn't ashamed of his body ... quite the opposite. Playing sports all year round had made him lean and sinewy. The girls at school were always coming on to him—of course, they didn't know he was gay. None of his friends or family did. Hell, he hadn't even admitted it to himself until he'd lost his virginity to Vanessa Thatcher when he was fifteen. While he'd cum, since she'd been warm, wet, and willing, in the aftermath he'd felt unfulfilled and the whole act had been forced on his part. It was then that he started examining his attraction to guys instead of girls.

Master Max caressed his back and shoulders. "Are you ready, boy?"

"Yes, Sir."

Two hours later, just after midnight, Jake walked into his house after noticing his father's truck was gone, which wasn't too unusual. The man owned a bar/restaurant and probably had to run out to help his staff with something. Still feeling buzzed about the earlier scene with Max, Jake grabbed a snack and then turned on the TV in the living room to catch the sports highlights like he normally did.

Unfortunately, what happened after that had been far from normal.

28

"Code Blue, ICU. Code Blue, ICU."

The overhead alert for a person not breathing interrupted Jake's account of what occurred all those years ago as Nick listened from his private hospital room's bed. After Jake had left Max and Ray's apartment, he'd come straight here, even though it was long after visiting hours were over. The expression on Nick's face when he'd awakened, earlier, and saw him sitting next to the bed had been a combination of hurt and relief. Jake was hoping to expel the former by opening his heart at long last and spilling his guts about the past that'd haunted him for years.

"So, what happened next?" Nick's voice was dry and raspy, so Jake poured a cup of water from the pitcher on the bedside table and handed it to him.

After making sure Nick was okay, he leaned back in his chair. "I got a call from Max's neighbor who I'd met a few times. He said Max had gotten mugged outside his apartment complex and beaten within an inch of his life. I rushed to the hospital, but wasn't allowed in to see him because I wasn't family. The cops were still there, and I couldn't risk answering questions about who I was, so I went home." His voice caught in his throat and his eyes watered. Damn, he never cried like this.

Gingerly reaching over, Nick took his hand, squeezing it in support and understanding. "That's the night you got the scars, isn't it? Your dad found out and beat the crap out of Max, then turned his anger and homophobia on you."

Nodding, Jake used his other hand to wipe a single tear which had spilled over onto his cheek. "Yeah. He was waiting for me when I got home. Beat me with his belt, telling me no son of his was going to be a faggot . . . and a lot of other shit I don't need to repeat. I couldn't go to school, much less move, for about two weeks after that. Mom called me in sick and nursed me back to health. The bastard wouldn't even let her take me to the doctor."

Nick's thumb rubbed over the back of Jake's hand. "What about Max? I take it he didn't tell the police it was your father, or didn't he know who it was?"

Shaking his head, Jake let out a deep breath. "No, he knew. My father made sure Max knew why he was getting beaten. He never told anyone, though, because he knew it meant outing me and he refused to do that. Even when he was told he would never see again."

"Shit. He lost his sight completely?"

"Yeah. And all this time I thought he blamed me. I mean, I blamed me, why shouldn't he?"

Tugging on his hand, Nick waited until their gazes met and he had Jake's full attention. "He didn't blame you because it wasn't your fucking fault, Jake. You had no control over what your father did or believed. Just like you had no control over me getting shot. You're not God. So, fucking get over it, or you're never going to be happy."

Jake snorted in wry amusement. "Yeah, that's pretty

much what Max said to me tonight. Anyway, that's my story . . . by the time I recovered, Max had been transferred to a hospital closer to his family. He moved back here about nine years ago. And I told my bastard of a father he could take his homophobia and shove it, along with my football scholarship to Rutgers. Two hours after I graduated high school, I enlisted in the Navy, and the only reason I ever came back to Tampa was because of my mom and brother."

Silence filled the room for a few minutes, but it was a comfortable one. Jake had cleansed not only his heart and mind, but his soul as well. For the first time since before that fateful night, he felt he might have a bright, happy future ahead of him. A sappy grin spread across his face.

"What's that look for?"

He chuckled. "I think this is what your future sister-in-law was talking about when she drew that picture of me." At Nick's confused expression, he explained, "Angie said I always had this sad look to me when I thought no one was watching or something like that. And she wanted to draw me again someday when I met the love of my life and was truly happy."

"The love of your life?"

Jake stood and placed a hand on either side of Nick's head, bending over so they were only inches apart, staring into each other's eyes. "Yeah, Nick. The love of my life. You. That is, if I haven't screwed up and pushed you away one too many times. Please, forgive me."

Reaching up, Nick cupped Jake's cheek and the Dom leaned into the gentle touch, his gut clenching, waiting for the words that he hadn't lost this wonderful man. "I'll forgive you on one condition."

"What's that?"

"If you kiss me . . . Sir."

Hell, yeah. Jake closed the distance and brushed Nick's lips with his own. Gentle at first, then more insistent. His tongue probed and without hesitation Nick's lips parted, allowing him entry. Sighing with pleasure, he tasted and teased until there was the sound of a throat clearing behind him. Jake pulled slowly away. If whoever it was had a problem with what they just saw, well then, it was just that . . . their problem. Turning, he smiled at a tall, auburn-haired, female nurse who was grinning as well.

"Sorry to interrupt. But I need to take Nick's vitals." She pointed at her patient. "And stop blushing. My brother and his husband have been together for years. This doesn't bother me at all. In fact, I think it's awesome your boyfriend got off his duff and came back to apologize for whatever he did. I was tired of you moping." She turned her finger toward Jake. "And you. I take my patient's recovery seriously, so no more being a shmuck."

Both men laughed as she wrapped the blood pressure cuff around Nick's upper arm. "Don't worry, Brenda. I'll make sure Jake doesn't act like a shmuck anymore."

A few minutes later, after Brenda left, Jake settled back into his chair. Nick turned on his uninjured side and studied his lover's face. "So, how the hell did you go from getting beaten with a belt, to the point it left those scars, to becoming a Whip Master and even getting whipped yourself?

Sighing, he ran a hand through his hair, wincing when a finger got caught in a knot. "Need a frigging haircut," he mumbled.

"I like it long. Now, answer my question."

"After I finished basic training, I got stationed in Pearl Harbor for a year and a half. It wasn't long before I found a club where I could channel my anger for my father into something that wouldn't destroy me. I wasn't ready for anything beyond a D/s relationship and I was still feeling my way into the lifestyle, so, believe it or not, I ended up with a Domme. And she introduced me to all the things I hadn't discovered yet."

Nick raised an eyebrow. "A Domme? Seriously?"

"Yeah, ass-hat. But that's all it was—a D/s relationship with no intercourse, although she did get me off in other ways when I needed it. Mistress Lani was bi and in a longtime relationship with her female submissive, but she willingly took me on to teach me how to be a Dom. However, I first had to finish learning how to be a submissive. Lani was a bit of a sadist and she's the one who trained me on the bullwhip. In the beginning, she used it as a tool to help me get past the beating my father had given me. With my safeword and trust in her, I knew I had control over the scene and could stop anytime."

"Something you didn't have the night he beat you."

Jake nodded his agreement. "Exactly. And that's why, every once in a while, I have China or Carl scene with me. To remind me, no matter what, I'm the one in control."

"Another fuck-you to your father, huh?" Nick shifted to his back again, trying to get comfortable.

"Yeah. You know, the funny thing is, I never knew how he found out back then. Not that it matters, but I was always curious."

"He found out because of me."

Surprised, Jake's gaze flashed toward the open doorway at the sound of his brother's voice. "Mike? What are you doing here? What do you mean because of you?"

Mike Donovan shut the door behind him and leaned against it. The sadness in his expression spoke volumes. "I'm here because Max called me."

"What? He called you? Why?" Jake's head was spinning. "How the hell do you even know him?"

"I didn't before tonight. Apparently, he knew who I was and where to find me. He called the bar after you left. Said you were on your way here and he was concerned about you." Gesturing to the other chair in the room, he asked Nick, "Mind if I sit down?"

Nick's eye's narrowed. "Go ahead. But first, how long were you outside listening?"

"Since the nurse left." Taking the seat, the older man's face was etched with a combination of regret and pain as he prepared to unburden his soul. "Guess I should start at the beginning. I saw you that night, Jake, with Max, outside that video store. And I saw him kiss you. I'd dropped off a date and was cutting through that area to get home. Sitting at a red light, I was just looking around and happened to spot you. Pure coincidence." He ran a hand down his face. "I was shocked at first. And then . . . I did the stupidest and most selfish thing of my life. I told Dad what I saw . . . where you were."

Jake's voice fractured in disbelief. "You what? Why? Why would you do that, knowing what a bigot the man was?"

"I was jealous. Of you." Unable to meet his brother's stare, Mike kept his gaze on the foot of the hospital bed. "Here I was, the older brother, trying to do everything I could to gain our father's approval, and I couldn't do it. I couldn't measure up to the golden boy of the family. I was like Dad—mediocre in sports and school—and there you were, captain of the football team, straight-A student, and going to Rutgers with a full football scholarship. And where was I going . . . to the local community college. Dad had a fucking shrine to you at the bar, with all your damn trophies and framed articles from the newspapers. And for one fucking night, I knew something that would knock you down a few pegs in his eyes. I didn't think he'd . . . well, I didn't fucking think, period. The moment the words were out of my mouth, I knew I'd made a mistake. But it was too late. First, he called me a liar, and then the next thing I knew, he was grabbing his car keys. He must have waited for you guys to come back out and then followed Max home." He paused and then the big man's eyes filled with tears he didn't bother wiping away. "I'm so fucking sorry, Jake. And to top it all off, I hid in my room like a fucking coward while he beat you. I turned that bastard on you like a rabid dog, and I couldn't even find the courage to fix what I had done. I'm so fucking sorry."

Jake was stunned and waited for the anger to come, for the urge to beat the hell out of his own brother . . . but instead of anger, there was just sadness. "The bastard beat you emotionally as bad as he did me physically. Why didn't I ever see that before? The son of a bitch. He better be rotting in hell." Standing, he pulled his brother up into his arms and held him tight. "It's all right, Mike."

"No, it's not. I ruined your life."

Pulling back, Jake grabbed Mike's face and forced him to look into his eyes. "No, you didn't. The bastard did. And if you think about it, it would have happened sooner or later. Whether he found out then or later on, the results still would have been similar. But in a way, things worked out better for me. I went into the Navy, became a SEAL, have a bunch of guys who are my brothers as much as you are, and I fell in love with this idiot laying in the bed behind me. I should be thanking you, Mike, because despite what happened back then, I'm pretty damn happy with my life. Only, I'm just starting to realize it now."

The tension saturating the air eased, and the three of

them talked for close to an hour before Nick's eyelids drooped and he fell asleep. Feeling better than he had in years, Jake walked out of the hospital with Mike. A nearly full moon hung in the sky, providing more illumination than the parking lot lights. Mike's vehicle was parked two spaces down from Jake's, and before he veered off, Jake pulled his brother into a hug. "I love you, bro. Never, ever think I don't. One thing I've ultimately learned is to leave the past where it belongs. I'm burying my ghosts and you need to do the same."

"I know. And I love you, too. See you tomorrow? Stop by the bar and I'll give you some lunch to bring to Nick. Hospital food sucks."

He slapped Mike on the back. "Definitely. He'll love you for it."

Climbing into his truck, Jake started the engine, his heart, mind, and soul in unison for the first time in his adult life. *Well, it's about fucking time.*

EPILOGUE

*J*ake smiled as he walked through *Ian's Oasis*, the man-made, garden of Eden that Angie had given Boss-man for his birthday a few months ago. The pavement had been pulled out from between the residential and training buildings, and grass, trees, shrubs, and outdoor furniture had been put in, among other features. He'd just left Nick's apartment, heading around to the other entrance of the building, with his lover/submissive by his side. They were on their way to the oldest Sawyer brother's place for Thanksgiving dinner. Angie and Ian had invited everyone—and they did mean everyone—for the holiday. The entire Alpha team was going to be there, with their significant others if they had one, and a few members of the Omega team, who hadn't had anywhere special to be, had been urged to join them. Jake's mother and brother, Chuck and Marie Sawyer, Rick and Eileen Michaelson, Jenn, Jake's snitch, Todd, and, last but not least, Alyssa completed the guest list. Hell, even Carter had been invited. Ian had left a message on his voicemail, but it was unknown if the guy had gotten it or was anywhere near Tampa to accept the offer. And by now, everyone knew Jake and Nick were a couple and they'd all been happy for them.

Beside him, Nick fiddled with the new chain and pendant Jake had given him last night. Members of the BDSM community would recognize the white gold and black onyx collar and charm as a symbol of being in a committed D/s relationship, but to the rest of the world, it looked similar to a yin-yang. However, instead of two curved pieces fitting together, there were three. The meaning behind them varied with whomever you spoke to. Each section could stand for the parts of the lifestyle—Bondage, Domination and Sadism/Masochism—or safe, sane, consensual. But to Jake, the three pieces stood for him, Nick, and their love for each other.

Nick had been stunned when Jake had presented it to him, but quickly knelt and allowed his Dom to place it around his neck. It had been their own private commitment ceremony. Someday, Jake planned on having one in the club, but for now he was content with just having the simple collar around his submissive's throat. Nick was to wear it whenever possible, taking it off only when the military or a mission required it.

While his shoulder and chest muscles were still pretty sore, Nick's recovery had been going well. The stitches would be coming out Monday and then he would start physical therapy when he returned to California a week from today. NCIS had interviewed Nick, Jake, and Alyssa after the feds did and agreed Nick had been shot while protecting the teenager. It helped that the two Navy officers doing the investigation were the ones who had helped the Trident team figure out why they were targeted by an assassin last year. So, if all went well, Nick would be able to join his team when their next rotation came up for

OCONUS missions again in February. Until then, the team would be training on the west coast.

Pulling Nick's hand away from the pendant, Jake linked their fingers together. "I love how that looks on you."

The kid grinned. "So do I. You know, I really wasn't expecting it, but I'm happy and proud to wear it."

"You won't have a problem with anyone in the lifestyle in San Diego recognizing that you're a submissive?"

Halting in his tracks, Nick turned toward him. He brought Jake's hand to his lips and kissed his knuckles. "I can handle it. I still have a lot to learn, but I do know that you are my Master and I am your submissive. Outside of the bedroom, for the most part, you treat me as your equal, unless I'm screwing up somehow. I love you and I love our relationship the way it is. And if anyone has a problem with it, then that's just it . . . it's their problem. Besides, they'd have to be pretty stupid to mess with a SEAL, right?"

Jake's heart filled with the love that was shining in the blue eyes gazing back at him. Cupping Nick's chin, he leaned forward and brought their lips together. The kiss was as sweet and meaningful as his sub's words had been, minus his little snark at the end. Feeling the stirring in his groin which always seemed to be present when they were this close, Jake reluctantly pulled back. "If we don't stop now, I'm going to be sporting a hard-on walking in there, and I would rather your parents don't see it. But I love you too, babe. Very much."

By the time they let themselves into Ian's apartment, Jake had field-stripped his sniper rifle in his mind and willed his cock to behave. He was a little surprised to see just Nick's folks and brothers sitting in the living room, chatting and nibbling on the hors d'oeuvres which had been spread out on the coffee table. A football game was on the huge flat-screen TV hanging on the wall with the volume on low. With a quick glance into the kitchen, he waved to Angie, Kristen, and Jenn, who were busy preparing the feast. The foursome sitting in the living room stood and greeted them, along with Beau, who'd been curled up at Marie's feet. After shaking hands with the men, Nick, then Jake, hugged and kissed Doc Sawyer hello. Out of everyone, she'd been the most thrilled with Jake and Nick's repaired relationship.

Turning to Ian, Jake raised an eyebrow. "Where is everyone? I figured at least Egghead and Boomer would be here pigging out by now."

Gesturing for them to take seats next to each other on one of the couches, Ian sat back down in his recliner. "They'll be here in a bit. I told you guys to come a little earlier than the others because we wanted to talk to the two of you."

Jake took a seat, but Nick hesitated a moment before sitting down next to him. There was caution in his voice when he replied to his brother, "Okay. What about?"

While Jake was as wary as Nick, he kept it to himself. Eyeing the Sawyer family one-by-one, he noticed the men all seemed to be in on the upcoming conversation, but the matriarch had a look of confusion on her face, matching her youngest son's. If Jake hadn't known the family so well, he might've been very afraid of what was coming next. But Ian and Dev were as much his brothers as they were Nick's. And Chuck and Marie had "adopted" their sons' teammates a long time ago.

Ian leaned forward, his elbows on his knees. His serious stare was directed at Jake. "We wanted to know what your intentions are concerning Nick."

Beside him, Nick groaned and rolled his eyes. "Really, Ian? Are you frigging kidding me?"

From the other couch, Marie gasped. "Ian!"

Stopping any further outbursts by holding up his hand, Ian never took his eyes off Jake. "Mom, it's okay. There is a point to this, but first I want to hear Jake's answer."

Leaning back, Jake made himself comfortable and set his right ankle on the opposite knee. It was obvious his bosses and their father had something in mind and he didn't take offense at the question. "Well, obviously, our relationship is still new, but I think I found the person I was meant to be with. We've been talking, and with Nick returning to California next week and me working here, we're going to do the long-distance thing for now. When he's INCONUS, I'll be taking time off, whenever you can spare me, to fly out there. He's got two years left on his tour and I'll support his decision to either re-up at that time, or get out and come work here. Or whatever he wants to do. We have plenty of time to figure that out."

"So, this is a long-term commitment for both of you?"

Taking Nick's hand in his, he rested both on his thigh. "Yeah, it is. Between Doc Dunbar's help, Mike's confession, Max's blessing, and Nick, I'm ready to be happy in my life. Completely happy, and not just going through the motions."

Nick was getting restless. "What's this all about, Ian?"

Instead of the eldest brother answering the question, Devon handed Jake a large manila envelope he hadn't noticed before. Taking it, his brow furrowed in question. "What's this?"

"You know all those conference calls and visits Ian's had with the Pentagon lately?" When Jake nodded, Dev continued. "Well, he's been working on a new contract with Uncle Sam. We're going to need a west coast team, and we want you to be in charge of it, at least until it's up and running, which will take a while. It'll be stationed out of San Diego."

Jake didn't know who was more stunned, Nick or him. At the moment, someone could knock him over with a feather if he was standing. He glanced back and forth between Ian and Devon, his mouth opening and closing a few times before he found his voice once more. "I . . . wow . . . um. But what about the team here? Our team?"

"Your position here will always be available to you. Even if things don't work out between you two, but I don't think that will happen. You're good for each other. By the way, you two cost me a hundred bucks. Boomer, Ian, and I had a pool for who was going down next. I had Egghead."

After taking a swig of his beer, Ian chuckled. "And I won. But I had no clue it was going to be with Nick. And I agree. You will always be part of this team, Jake, no matter what. Whenever Nick opts out, you can either stay with the new team out there, running things, or come back here to us. For now, if we need a sniper, we have three choices—we can have you fly to wherever we need you, or we can borrow from the Omega team, or grab one of Chase's guys. You'll need to occasionally meet me in D.C. for consultations at the Pentagon, or fly out with us for a mission, but we can work out the details of that later." He jerked his chin toward Jake's hand. "That folder has the few candidates who didn't make it onto the Omega team, but are still eligible. And I've added some more possibles to the list. You'll be in charge of screening them, but the final decision will be a consensus between you, Dev, and me. We'll get you set up with a training facility and anything else you need out there. You can rent out your condo to one of the new guys, if you want, and then stay in Nick's place here when you're in town." He paused. "So, what do you say, Reverend?"

This was so unexpected. Swallowing hard, Jake's gaze bounced from one Sawyer to the next. Ian and Dev were waiting patiently for his answer, but Marie grinned and nodded her head, while her husband winked his approval at Jake. The last eyes he met were those of his lover. "What do you think?"

Nick smiled. "I think I'll be very ticked off if you don't say yes, but it's still your decision. I didn't think we'd be moving in together so soon, but I have no objections."

Squeezing Nick's hand, he leaned over and kissed him just as tenderly as he'd done before they had gotten here. He was thrilled when Nick didn't hesitate to kiss him back despite being in the company of his family. "I have no objections either. It looks like I have some packing to do."

"And I'd be more than happy to help, Sir."

WANT TO READ MORE ABOUT JAKE AND NICK? READ THEIR SHORT STORY EXCLUSIVELY ON MY WEBSITE.

CONTINUE READING FOR A PRE-VIEW OF MARCO'S STORY

EXCERPT FROM WATCHING FROM THE SHADOWS: TRIDENT SECURITY BOOK 5

*A*cross the backyard, Marco "Polo" DeAngelis watched his buddy roughhouse with four fatherless children in the newly fallen January snow. Curt Bannerman and he had flown into Fort Dodge Regional Airport the night before, then driven an hour to Stormville, Iowa, to the home of Dana Prichard—widow of their former teammate, Eric Prichard. The retired Navy SEAL had been murdered in a hit and run incident a little over a year ago. The man who'd killed him had been a hired assassin targeting specific former members of SEAL Team Four.

The SEAL community was tight-knit, and when one of them was killed or incapacitated, the others would step up and help out all they could. Shortly after Prichard's funeral, a rotating bi-weekly schedule had been set up. Once every four months, Marco's name had come up and he traveled from his home in Tampa, Florida, to meet another team member in Iowa for the weekend. They would stay at a local motel and help Dana with anything that needed to be done around the house and yard. Landscaping, a new roof, and a bathroom renovation had been on the to-do list, among other things, over the past fifteen months. This morning the two men had painted six-year-old Amanda's bedroom pink and purple, since she'd declared she was too grown up for the old Winnie-the Pooh décor.

If there was nothing pressing that needed to be done at the residence, they sometimes gave Dana a weekend to herself without the kids or took the entire family on an excursion. They'd gone on a camping trip one of the weekends Marco had been there, and on a trip to the Six Flags Park in Iowa City another time. Personally, he preferred to work when his weekends came up—kids made him a little antsy. It wasn't that he disliked them, he just didn't have the greatest childhood and didn't know how to relate to them like Bannerman did. And he also had no desire to have children of his own—a decision he'd made a long time ago.

While Marco finished stacking the firewood they'd split earlier, Bannerman and Amanda, the only girl, threw snowballs at her brothers—nine-year-old Justin, ten-year-old Taylor, and twelve-year-old Ryan. It wasn't long before Dana stuck her head out the back door. "Dinner's ready! Come and get it!"

Thank God, because he was so cold, his cock and balls were trying to crawl up into his pelvis. The temperatures had barely reached thirty degrees all day, and for a five-year resident of Florida, that felt like ten below. He had no idea how Curt was putting up with it, since the man lived a few hours away from him in Daytona Beach. Next trip, he would invest in some thermal underwear, because the heavy jacket, gloves, and hat weren't warm enough.

As the kids rushed inside, Curt ambled over, brushing the snow from his blond hair. "Hand me the axes. I'll put them in the shed. You're looking a little hypothermic there, Polo."

"Ya think?" he snorted, his Staten Island accent coming through. "It's colder than a witch's tit out here. I knew there was a reason I moved to the Sunshine State."

Curt bent over and pulled one of the axes out of the old tree stump they'd used, then took the one Marco handed him. "I could get used to it again. You forget—I'm from Montana. This is nothing—a tropical heat wave."

"Yeah, well . . . why don't you stop ogling the merry widow, tell her how you feel, and then you can live in the Tropics of Iowa all year round."

Even though his cheeks were red from the cold, the six-foot-four, two-hundred and twenty-pound man blushed. "What are you fucking talking about? I'm not interested in Dana."

Crossing his arms, Marco rolled his eyes. "Please. Don't give me that. You get a goofy fucking grin on your face every time she walks into the room. Probably a fucking hard-on, too, but I have no desire to confirm that by taking a look at your junk. Every time someone can't make it up here for their weekend, you've been filling in. And don't tell me it's because Eric was your best friend."

"He is . . . was . . . damn it." Scowling, Curt turned and strode toward the shed, but Marco followed on his heels. He knew the survivor guilt the guy was dealing with because he had his own ghost of Prichard. The deceased SEAL had taken Marco's place on a fact-finding mission many years ago and it'd resulted in him being added to the assassin's hit list.

"I know he was. But you know better than I do that he'd want you to have a good life without him. Same goes for Dana. I've seen the way she looks at you sometimes. And the kids and you get along great—so what's the problem? It's been almost a year and a half since he was killed. Get off your fucking ass, before someone steps in and snatches her up."

Curt whirled around so fast, Marco almost got hit in his cold cock with an ax. "Who's going to snatch her up? Someone else been eyeing her?"

He smirked. "Thought you weren't interested."

"Don't fuck with me, Polo. Who the fuck else is interested in her?"

Finding amusement in the other man's fast change in attitude, Marco shrugged. "I don't know for sure, but Egghead mentioned the Sheriff seemed to be sniffing around a lot when he was up here two weeks ago." Brody "Egghead" Evans was his best friend and teammate at Trident Security, and was the biggest computer geek in the world—or close to it.

"Fuck that shit."

The big man's gaze went to the rear entrance of the house and Marco slapped him on the shoulder before taking the axes from him. "So, you gonna man-up and tell her how you feel?"

Curt nodded, his eyes never leaving the backdoor. "Damn fucking straight."

"About fucking time." He watched his friend make a beeline for the house. Even though a wife and kids wasn't in Marco's future, he had no problem with his buddies having them. But settling down was something he was never going to do. He'd rather cut off his left nut than walk down the aisle and have a bunch of rug-rats. No way . . . no fucking how.

TAKING A SIP OF HIS BEER, Marco relaxed in a sitting area near the bar of the BDSM club, The Covenant, which was located on the same property as Trident Security. One couldn't ask for more than having his work and play areas within forty yards of each other, especially when he enjoyed both. He listened to his bosses, Ian and Devon Sawyer, discuss the meeting Ian had taken part in on Friday at the Pentagon in Washington D.C. about their new government contract. Their other teammate, Jake Donovan, had met Boss-man there and then had flown back to San Diego to his temporary home. Jake was currently in charge of establishing Trident Security's west coast facility there and was living with his boyfriend/submissive, Nick Sawyer, who happened to be the bosses' younger brother. Nick had just under two years left in his own Navy SEAL career, stationed in California, so the set-up had worked out perfectly for everyone.

At the feet of the Dominant Sawyers, their submissive women sat on pillows, chatting quietly in their club lingerie. Kristen was Devon's wife, while Angie Beckett and Ian were in the process of planning their spring wedding. Between Ian, Devon, Jake, and their other teammate, Ben 'Boomer Michaelson, the men of Trident were dropping like flies as they had all met the loves of their lives over the past sixteen months. The only two men left on Trident's Alpha Team who were single were Brody and Marco, and the others were betting on who was going down next. Marco felt sorry for anyone who'd bet on him, because it was a losing wager.

He'd gotten home a few hours ago from Iowa and instead of just crashing on the couch like he wanted to, he'd ended up here for Devon's birthday. It wasn't exactly a party with presents and all, just another excuse for them all to get together for a few drinks and maybe some play down in the pit. While the main second floor of the club housed the bar, offices, and a fetish store, the pit, as it was dubbed by the members, was the huge recreational room downstairs. It was filled with a wide assortment of BDSM equipment in both public areas and private rooms.

Even though it was still early in the evening—a little after eight-thirty—the club was bustling with activity. On Sunday nights, the place usually emptied out by eleven, so people could get some sleep before starting their work week the next day. From their pillows, Kristen and Angie began giggling uncontrollably at something near the bar and the three men turned their attention in the same direction.

"Ho-ly shit!" Devon shook his head in stunned amusement, while Marco almost fell out of his chair as laughter spilled forth and tears filled his gunmetal blue eyes. Speaking of a losing wager.

Ian's head dropped back as he groaned loudly. "Is he fucking kidding me?" He glanced at Marco. "Let me guess, the Giants beat the Cowboys in today's football game."

"Yup." That was the only word he could get out as he held his six-pack abs and gasped for air.

They all stared as Brody strode toward them, good-naturedly chuckling at members' comments along the way. Dressed in his usual snug, faded jeans, T-shirt, and cowboy boots, the only thing that was out of place was the fact he had his button fly undone. And instead of his junk hanging out, it was covered by an elephant trunk and ears—the thong the loser had to wear in the bet Marco and he had made. Every few steps, the well-built geek would stop and wiggle his hips at some of the female submissives, causing the impressively filled trunk to flap around. By the time he reached his teammates the entire bar area had erupted into fits of hysterical laughter.

Stopping a few feet from Marco, his best friend pointed a finger at him, unable to hide his grin. The man had no shame. "Just fucking wait, asshole. I can't wait until the next time you lose a bet."

Although he wasn't too worried, Marco knew the guy was already planning his revenge and he might not put it off until the next wager. "Um, if I remember correctly, you were the one who swore the Cowboys would win and the junk trunk was your idea." He wiped away a tear which threatened to escape and turned his head toward Kristen and Angie. "I don't know, ladies. I think I would've filled it out better than Egghead. What do you think?"

Before either of the women had a chance to respond, one of the submissive waitresses, Cassandra, hurried over, wearing an expression of alarm. She did a double take at Brody's crotch, but then directed her words to Marco. "Sir, Master Ben is in the lobby on a phone call and he told me to come get you. He said it's an emergency."

The mirth died quickly as the he leapt to his feet followed by Ian and Devon. Brody tucked the elephant in his pants and was a step behind Marco's heels as he ran toward the lobby. Cell phones were not allowed out on the club floor, and all calls and texts had to be taken outside—a rule which was strictly enforced. His initial thought was something had happened to Boomer's girlfriend, Kat Maier, but she was standing by her Dom's side, worry on her pretty face as the group hurried up to them.

"Hang on a sec." Boomer pulled the cell phone away from his face and held it out for Marco. "You remember Jake's ex on Clearwater P.D.? Drew Murdock? He's at a crime scene and your business card was there. When he couldn't get a hold of you, he called Trident's main number and I'm on-call, so it got bounced to me."

While he'd never met the cop Jake had dated for a few weeks over a year ago, he knew the name. Marco took the phone and brought it to his ear. "DeAngelis."

The officer had obviously heard Boomer tell him who was on the phone. "Hey. Sorry to call like this, but I'm at house over here in Clearwater with a home invasion and I've got an unconscious assault victim. We haven't been able to find her cell phone or a list of emergency contacts. She just moved into the neighborhood and the house is trashed, but I found your business card on her refrigerator. Does the name Millicent Williams ring a bell?"

While his teammates and their women waited for details, Marco shook his head at the unfamiliar name. "Millicent? I have no idea who that is." But something niggled his brain.

Over the phone, he could hear the squawks of police radios and the voices of other officers working the scene. "Hang on a sec. There's a diploma on the wall here in the home office. Her full name is Millicent Harper Williams."

The blood drained from Marco's face and his gut clenched as he finally made the connection to his deceased sister's best friend—the woman who invaded his dreams since their one night together thirteen months ago. "Harper? Harper Williams was assaulted?" Around him, the men and Kristen's eyes flashed wide as they recognized the name as well, but Marco held up his hand to stop anyone from asking questions he didn't have any answers to yet. "Fuck. Is she all right?"

"She got beat up pretty bad. The paramedics are on their way with her to Largo Medical Center. She's still unconscious. And DeAngelis . . . the main reason I'm calling is . . . her baby is missing."

A roar equivalent to jet engine surged through his head

and a wave of shock and confusion struck him hard. "Baby? What fucking baby?"

Get *Watching From the Shadows* today!

Baby? What baby?

Retired Navy SEAL, Marco DeAngelis, is determined to stay single and childless forever. But sometimes life gives you what you never knew you wanted.

After finding out she's pregnant, Harper Williams comes to the realization she'll be raising the child alone, since Marco won't return her calls.

When Harper is violently attacked, the two are, reluctantly, thrown together again and become embroiled in a web of lies and deceit of someone else's making. Will they lose their baby . . . and their lives?

ACKNOWLEDGMENTS

Thanks to my Beta-readers—Abby, Charla, Jessica, and Julie. As always, without you, this book would never have been ready for publication.

Thanks to Judi Perkins, my graphic designer, for the amazing new cover!

Thanks to my editor, Eve Arroyo, for helping to make this book the best that it could be.

Thanks to the Trident Security Series readers and fans, for loving the Sexy Six-Pack as much as I do.

AUTHOR'S NOTE

The story within these pages is completely fictional but the concepts of BDSM are real. If you do choose to participate in the BDSM lifestyle, please research it carefully and take all precautions to protect yourself. Fiction is based on real life but real life is *not* based on fiction. Remember—Safe, Sane and Consensual!

Any information regarding persons or places has been used with creative literary license so there may be discrepancies between fiction and reality. The Navy SEALs missions and personal qualities within have been created to enhance the story and, again, may be exaggerated and not coincide with reality.

The author has full respect for the members of the United States military and the varied members of law enforcement and thanks them for their continuing service to making this country as safe and free as possible.

ABOUT THE AUTHOR

A proud member of Romance Writers of America (RWA), Samantha A. Cole is a retired policewoman and former paramedic who is thrilled to add award-winning author to her list of exciting careers. She has lived her entire life in the suburbs of New York City and is looking forward to becoming a snow-bird between New York and Florida someday. Her two fur-babies, Jinx and Bella, keep her company and remind their mom to take a break from writing every once in a while to go for a walk, which is the best way to deal with a stubborn case of writer's block.

An avid reader since childhood, Samantha was often found with a book in hand and sometimes one in each. After being gifted with a stack of romance novels from her grandmother, her love affair with the genre began in her teens. Many years later, she discovered her love for writing stories was just as strong. Taking her life experiences and training, she strives to find the perfect mix of suspense and romance for her readers to enjoy.

Her standalone novel, The Friar, won the silver medal in the 2017 Readers' Favorite Awards in the Contemporary Romance genre out of more than 1000 entries.

While the original planned stories for the Trident Security series have been completed, they have brought many opportunities for Samantha to spread her wings and bring her readers more characters and stories to love. Look for her new Trident Security Omega Team series, Doms of The Covenant Novella series, Blackhawk Security series, and more from the Malone Brothers series, in addition to several standalone projects.

CONNECT WITH SAMANTHA A. COLE

www.facebook.com/SamanthaColeAuthor
www.smarturl.it/SACbookbub
www.facebook.com/groups/1631022810469872
www.samanthacoleauthor.com
www.smarturl.it/SSPNL
www.twitter.com/SamanthaCole222
www.samanthacole.allauthor.com
www.smarturl.it/SamanthaColeYoutube
www.instagram.com/samanthacoleauthor
www.pinterest.com/samanthacoleaut
www.goodreads.com/author/show/5580362.Samantha_A_Cole